PRAISE FOR
TARA MOSS AND *FETISH*!

D0869323

PATIENCE

As he waited for his girl to come through the double doors, he hid as best he could his growing excitement. Like a big cat hunting, his movements were considered, slow and unremarkable until the very moment of attack. He imagined her heavily made-up face, her sleek curves and those slender feet, wearing stilettos for his private pleasure. She would make her way home alone and he could take her when the ideal moment presented itself. And there *would* be an ideal moment. He knew that. The photo in Catherine's wallet was fate. Now his prize had paraded down the runway in sexy dresses and whore's shoes, *just for him,* and soon he would have her. The waiting would be over....

TARA MOSS

FETISH

LEISURE BOOKS NEW YORK CITY

For Janni Moss

A LEISURE BOOK®

December 2005

Published by

Dorchester Publishing Co., Inc.
200 Madison Avenue
New York, NY 10016

ISBN 0-8439-5633-X

The name "Leisure Books" and the stylized "L" with design are trademarks of Dorchester Publishing Co., Inc.

Printed in the United States of America.

Visit us on the web at www.dorchesterpub.com.

ACKNOWLEDGMENTS

Among the many people I want to thank for their help in bringing my first novel to life, I would like to make a special mention of Selwa Anthony, my guiding hand and unbeatable literary agent; my tutor and friend Marg McAlister; Dr. Kathryn Guy for her friendship and medical consulting; my buddy Senior Constable Glenn Hayward for his police consulting; Dr. Robert Hare Ph.D. for his consulting on psychopathy; and the entire team at HarperCollins, particularly Angelo Loukakis and my editor Rod Morrison, for believing in me. Special thanks to Chadwicks and Sisters in Crime for their great support. Much love to my pals Linda, Anthea, Pete, Alex, Phil, Michelle and little Bo for helping me through; Nicholas for the wisdom; Christopher for the Conundrum; and everyone who has been so supportive on this journey. Most of all, my father, Bob, my sister Jackie and all of my wonderful family for their ongoing love and support. I appreciate you all.

FETISH

PROLOGUE

She wore stilettos—burnished, black and stylish, with thin straps that bit into her pale, slender ankles. Her heels clicked on the winter pavement as she made her way up the street alone. He strained to capture the sound they made, the beguiling music pulling him in like the Pied Piper's song.

Click, click, click . . .

Slowly he drove past, observing the girl through the hungry eyes of a predator. She was young, raven-haired and seductive, wearing a short black skirt to reveal willowy bare legs. A winter jacket fell to her thighs but wasn't enough to keep her slim legs warm; he could see goose bumps, and the bluish hue of cold, bare skin.

Click, click . . .

He passed her again minutes later. The street was nearly empty, but still she did not acknowledge his presence. She continued instead on her misguided course, her pretty face set with determination.

Walking alone.

Lost.

1

The clouds above her were leaden-heavy with the threat of rain. He could see no umbrella. How far would she be willing to walk once the skies began to cry? Surely she didn't want to get wet. Surely her feet were tired. It was inevitable that she would need him.

Patiently, he watched her remove a map from her heavy shoulder bag. Jet, silken hair fell over her face as she unfolded it and struggled to make sense of the intricate web of streets, roads and lanes. She squinted with concentration, and when the clouds finally opened, showering her with cold droplets, she shot an irritated look at the lowering sky, before scanning the street for shelter. There were no taxis, no telephone booths, no open cafés or corner stores. Nothing for blocks.

The rain began to fall more heavily.

Click . . .

The girl set off again, walking faster, aimlessly. Her black bag weighed upon her shoulder, the map scrunched in frustration in her hand. Raindrops made slick, shimmering lines down her soft, hairless legs.

He pulled up beside her.

Now is the time.

He unwound his window. "Are you OK?" he asked. "You look lost."

"I'm fine," the girl replied, and glanced nervously up the street. Her accent was foreign, American, or perhaps Canadian.

"Are you sure? This isn't a safe area for you to be walking alone." He made a show of checking his watch. "My wife is expecting me home for dinner, but I could spare a few moments to drive you where you need to be." A gold band shone on his left ring finger. He'd polished it specially for occasions like these.

Her eyes rested on it for an instant. "Oh, no . . . I'm all

right, I think . . ." Her face was beautiful; youthful and achingly flawless, and her pale complexion was rosy with exertion, radiating warm light like a soft porcelain lamp. "Do you know where Cleveland Street is?" she asked.

"Oh dear. You're nowhere near Cleveland Street. We're on Philip now. Here, let me show you on your map." He beckoned her closer, and she slowly walked over to lean against the passenger side door. He could smell the odour of sweet, young sweat. Her face was glistening, now only a foot from his.

"Here, hop in for a sec. You're getting all wet." He pushed the passenger door open for her.

She stepped back and watched the van door open, uncertainty etched on her face. For a moment she didn't move, and he wondered if she would accept his help. He smiled harmlessly, not allowing his impatience to betray him. Then, with raindrops rolling down her forehead, the girl shrugged and slid onto his dry passenger seat.

Sheltered from the rain, she looked relieved. She passed him the map, offering a wide, friendly smile that revealed a set of perfect white teeth. She left the passenger door open, with one slender leg stretched down to touch the wet pavement.

He forced his eyes away. "We're here." He pointed to the map. "You need Cleveland Street, which is here. You've got to walk up this way, then . . ."

Her scent overwhelmed him; honeyed, wet smells, musky and damp between her legs. He sensed that her heartbeat was slowing. She was relaxing for him, trusting him. He kept talking, explaining in soothing, paternal tones. It looked impossibly far on her map, indeed the distance sounded inconceivable as he spoke.

In reality it would have been a short walk.

* * *

3

Night coated the city with an impenetrable, inky blanket. The clouds had shed their rain and had rolled away, and the sleepy streets glistened with moisture as the van passed quietly over them. With eyes well adjusted to the dark, he drove to a large isolated parking lot, turned off his headlights, and coasted towards his chosen spot under some tall, overhanging fig trees.

His beautiful girl whimpered softly behind him as she had from time to time during their drive together. He fetched a pair of gloves and put them on. After checking that the driver and passenger doors were both locked, he made his way to her, carefully closing the heavy curtains that separated the cab from the rear of the van. He switched on a battery-powered lamp, blinking for a moment while his eyes adjusted. The thick black blanket had fallen down to the girl's stomach during the drive. Her arms were still held straight up above her head, wrists secured to shackles on the wall, her body lying flat against the van's floor. Her thin, pale blue, knitted top was decorated with haphazard splatters of blood; the same treacly blood that glistened around her hairline. A dark mole the size of a lady beetle stood out against her pale neck. With eyes half open and full of salty tears that streaked mascara down her cheeks, she was moaning again, shifting weakly.

Impervious to her weeping and plaintive struggles, he reached for his supplies. He would have to gag her now. She had remained placid since he hit her, but she might become noisy, and even in their isolated spot, he couldn't risk that. Her eyes followed his movements as he brought the gag close to her face, and widened at the sight of the red rubber ball and its long leather straps. She was becoming lucid. The timing was good. He had long ago lost interest in unconscious victims.

4

"It's all right. I won't hurt you," he lied. There was no sense in getting her excited until she was fully secured.

He yanked her jaw open with both hands and shoved the rubber ball inside. The girl's watery eyes became huge saucers of shocked blue and she choked out a stifled protest. He pulled the straps around her head and fastened the buckles at the back, his fingers running through the gummy blood oozing from her crown.

One day he would have his own soundproof room. Oh, how the reactions, the screams excited him. But for now he had to do without that particular luxury.

Gagged and bound, the girl began struggling with surprising strength; swiftly he straddled her and punched her square in the jaw with one gloved fist. Her eyes snapped shut and she let out a muffled cry, the tears coming harder. Her body convulsed with sobs, and he felt himself become more fully aroused. He ripped the blanket off her—diminutive breasts jiggled under her thin top, her miniskirt was riding up around her hips, but the black stilettos were in place on the girl's dainty feet.

He moved down her body and removed her right shoe. *Lovely. Perfect.* Her toes were smooth and delicately formed; he was very pleased. He slipped the stiletto back on, enjoying the look of it more knowing what perfect digits it housed. He reached for his blade and moved back up his latest possession. She was bleeding but conscious, blue eyes open again and rolling wildly with panic. With one long, graceful movement he sliced through her flimsy top, splitting it open from waist to neck. She wore a plain, cream-coloured bra. He cut through the centre clasp and it snapped open, leaving her pale chest exposed. He cut through her skirt and cotton panties, and placed them in a neat pile with her other clothing.

She was naked for him.

Immune to her stifled pleading and now desperate flood of tears, he continued.

At daybreak, the man decided it was time to leave the parking lot. Although he hadn't slept a single wink, he wasn't tired. Sitting beside the girl's silent body, he felt calm and powerful. Curious, he looked through the girl's things before disposing of them. He opened the large black bag she had been carrying and found a heavy, ten-by-twelve-inch book—a model's portfolio. He flipped through it. The photos inside showed the girl in several benign poses; smiling, walking, or standing. Boring. He also found a wallet with a Canadian passport, an address book and a crinkled letter addressed to a "Catherine Gerber". He unfolded the letter and read:

> Dear Cat,
> I really look forward to seeing you. Six months is too long apart! Thanks for coming back for my mom's funeral. She would have wanted you there. She always said you were daughter number three. I doubt I could have survived it without you, and Dad appreciated you being there, too.
> Enough depressing stuff! As I told you on the phone, I will arrive Thursday morning at 7.45 on Japan Airlines flight JL771 from Tokyo. If you aren't in when I arrive, don't forget to leave a key for me somewhere. The agency has already booked me for a shoot at La Perouse on Friday. Talk about no time for jet lag! Thanks for letting me stay with you. We have so much to talk about. See you soon . . .
> Your best friend always,
> Mak

A skerrick of a smile infected his lips. It would make a good souvenir. He checked through the wallet, which held

6

little interest for him, until he found a compartment with photos. Girl with family. Girl with man. Girl with blonde.

He stared transfixed at the photo.

Girl with blonde.

She was intriguing. Tall, with beautiful, thick platinum hair that cascaded down past her shoulders. Who was she? The photo looked like it had been taken in a foreign city. He turned it over and read the smudged writing: *Me 'n' Mak making it big in Munich!* He stared captivated for a while and then lovingly placed the photo in his wallet, beside one of his mother.

He read the letter again.

La Perouse.

That wasn't far away.

He took the letter and address book and stowed them in his briefcase. He gathered up the girl's clothes, put them in a big garbage bag, and when he was ready, climbed into the driver's seat and drove away unseen into the crisp, dewy morning.

1

"Sorry, I'm tied up at the moment," the giggling voice on the answering machine announced. "But leave a message, and if you're lucky I'll call you back."

Makedde Vanderwall shook her head and waited for the tone. "Hey Cat, I just got in. I'm about to jump in a taxi. I know you're there." She gave Cat a few seconds to pick up the phone. "Hmm. If you're *really* not there, I trust you've left a key in a self-explanatory location . . ."

Mak looked forward to seeing her friend. Almost as much, she looked forward to getting out of her slept-in clothes and into a hot shower. Her black turtleneck top felt a bit too travelled-in and her favourite Levi's had been stained by weak coffee. The coffee's target had been the cup of a business man seated in 34J, but the apologetic steward missed due to a sudden change in altitude. Or perhaps attitude, Mak was unsure.

She strode across the airport terminal, bags in tow, and inadvertently turned a few heads. As a six-foot blonde, Makedde attracted attention wherever she went, though she barely noticed these days. Old jeans and morning hair

9

made little difference to the rubber-neck effect.

The flight from Canada was excruciatingly long, and she again wondered whether the five hundred dollars saved by taking the roundabout route had been really worth it. The lengthy wait at customs would have been unbearable if she had known that Catherine wasn't going to be at the airport. Nonetheless, after more than a day of travel she was a mere thirty minutes away from a happy reunion. She dragged herself to the taxi stand outside and joined the long queue of tired and bedraggled international travellers.

Winter rain had made the roads and footpaths shine. Perhaps July was not the best time to visit Australia, but it was between psychology courses for Mak, so she had to take the opportunity when it came. Her modelling days were numbered and she could still count the figures of her bank balance on six fingers, *including* the decimal point. She hoped it would be a working holiday with lots of working, and a much needed cash injection. A taxi pulled up and popped its boot, and in no time Mak was hurtling through the rain towards Bondi Beach.

Twenty minutes later the taxi crested the rise on Bondi Road, passing Waverley Oval as the clouds parted. Golden rays of sunlight reflected on the twinkling, green grass of the cricket oval, and by the time they reached the top of Campbell Parade the clouds had completely disappeared, as if Bondi had a special arrangement with the gods of weather. It lifted her spirits to take in the spectacular stretch of shimmering sand and surf. Two whole months to enjoy the beautiful coastline and catch up with her best friend. Perhaps a bit of travel and a revived modelling career was just what she needed to invigorate her lagging spirits.

Makedde stood outside a weatherworn, three-storey, red-brick block of flats on Campbell Parade and checked the address again as the taxi pulled away. She buzzed the intercom for number six and waited. And waited. She tried the door. *Must've had a late night*, she thought with slight irritation. The lock was broken, and the outside door opened to reveal a shabby, rickety timber staircase. It appeared she'd have to drag the bags in herself, and knock until Catherine woke up.

Makedde lugged the suitcases up the stairs, cursing the books and winter clothes that weighed them down. She reached flat number six, which was barely distinguishable by a small metal "6" hanging upside down on a loose nail, appearing at a glance as number nine. She knocked on the door.

No answer.

"Urrrrr . . ." she growled with growing frustration.

She left her bags at the top of the stairs and ventured to the mailbox outside to search for a note or a key. When she found box number six empty, save for a Thai delivery menu, she felt the first twinge of a headache. She groped around inside the box, hoping her eyes were deceiving her. No luck. Empty.

It was after 9 a.m. on a Thursday morning and surely most of the building's inhabitants would be working or surfing, so she walked back up to number six and laid into the door with a fierce and futile burst of pounding.

The flat was unresponsive.

She slumped against the door and rested her aching head in her hands. *Chill*, she thought. *Chill, and find a phone*.

Hoping no one would bother to drag her cumbersome baggage away, she stepped onto the street and spotted an orange hooded public phone booth a block away. She walked briskly over to it, pulling a crumpled piece of paper from her pocket. The phone ingested her coins in a hurried, metallic gurgle, and rang several times before someone answered.

"Book Model Agency." The greeting was monotonous and disinterested.

"Hi, this is Makedde Vanderwall. Could I speak with Charles Swinton, please?"

"He's busy right now."

"How long will he be?"

"Can I take a message?"

Mak closed her eyes. "Look, I just flew in from Canada and I'm standing outside one of your model's flats with my suitcases, and there's no one here to let me in or give me a key. I really need to speak with Charles."

"Just a moment."

After a couple of clicks, a man's voice came on the line.

"Hello Charles, this is Makedde Vanderwall . . ." She explained her situation as politely but firmly as she could manage.

"We have an extra key for the Bondi flat here if you want to come in," he replied.

"I'm standing out here with two very heavy suitcases. Could you have someone put it in a taxi and send it over?"

Twenty-eight minutes later a taxi pulled up and Makedde let herself in with the extra key. The accommodation was modest—typical for travelling models—a studio flat with twin beds and a tiny kichen and bathroom. Although the bed looked short enough for her feet to hang off the edge, she savoured the thought of getting horizontal on it. Catherine had only been living in the furnished flat for a month, but Mak noticed that she had already added her special touch to the place. The sparse decor had been livened up with an assortment of chic fashion magazine cut-outs—ads for Gucci, Chanel, Calvin Klein and Aussie designers Morrissey and Lisa Ho coated the walls in a collage of dizzying couture. She could just imagine the landlord's expression at seeing the miles of sticky tape holding the pictures in place.

Followed by one hundred mascara-enhanced vacant

stares, Makedde took in the small flat—the cramped bathroom, the half kitchen with its minibar-sized fridge, and the large window which opened onto a stunning view of southern Bondi Beach. Across from the window, the two single beds were made with mismatched covers, each with its own uncomfortably thin-looking pillow. A pint-sized, seventies-style chest of drawers separated the beds, and Makedde saw a notepad resting on it, beside the phone. She picked it up and read the hastily scrawled message.

JT Terrigal
Beach res
16
14

Makedde couldn't make much of the note. She had been expecting some hurried excuse for Catherine's absence, but the message did not appear addressed to her, or anyone else for that matter. Catherine mentioned that she might have a date for the weekend, but she refused to say with whom. Was the note related to that? The writing looked rushed. Perhaps Catherine had to leave at the last minute?

Puzzled and disappointed, Makedde embarked on a more thorough inspection of the flat. The fridge door, which would have been a natural choice, was littered with takeaway food menus, but no notes. The answering machine was flashing its red "messages" light. Makedde pressed the play button. The first two messages were dial tones, then, "Catherine, it's Skye from Book. Call me." There were a few clicks and pauses, but the next message was her own voice, "Hey, Cat, I just got in. I'm about to jump in a taxi . . ."

She suspected that sometime during the day she would receive an excited and apologetic phone call from Cat, describing how her secret Romeo had swept her off her feet and whisked her away for a scandalous sojourn.

So much for the welcome wagon.

Makedde decided to make herself at home, and the first thing on her list was that long-awaited hot shower. Unfortunately, the bathroom proved to be even more cramped than it looked. It was either an ill-conceived design in minimal space, or an illegal conversion from a closet; something she had seen before in other models' flats. She had to stand on the toilet seat to get to the shower/bathtub, because the sink hung over the seat, and there was no space to move in between. After kneeling on the toilet seat to brush her teeth, she shuffled across and climbed into the tub.

Mak showered under a refreshing stream of hot water, gratefully soaping away the stickiness of travel. She towelled off and, still warm, crawled into bed wearing a T-shirt and pair of boxers which had retained her affections long after their original owner. She had not slept well in many months, and hadn't managed to sleep at all on the flight. She was too tired to even think about staying awake to adjust her circadian rhythms. Instead, she set the alarm for 5.30 in the afternoon so she could call Book agency for the following day's photo session details, and check for any messages Catherine might have left. Sleep came swiftly, but her rest was haunted by disturbing dreams.

Catherine is reaching out . . .

Catherine is stretching through layers of dreamscape, terror shattering her beautiful features. She is pulled further and further into a cryptic, black expanse. Her face, ghostly and pale, is stretched into a silent scream. Her eyes are growing larger and larger, rounder and more frightened as she is pulled further. A thick, lifeless mass of dark swallows her slowly. She is begging, pleading, as she is swallowed.

Nothing will bring her back.

The phone rang.

Makedde sat bolt upright, beads of sweat covering her face. The clock said 5.22 p.m.

"Hello?"

It was Charles Swinton, her booker, confirming the details for the following day's photo shoot at La Perouse. The job was scheduled for an early start and it would be a long day. In spite of the recent rain they didn't require an early morning weather check; they were confident it would clear up.

"Uh, Charles . . . has there been any word from Catherine?"

"No. I suspect she's run off early for the weekend. By the way, you're up for the Becky Ross fashion launch too. We should have it confirmed tomorrow."

"Becky Ross?"

"The soapie star. She's big at the moment. She's promoting her own line of clothes. Should be excellent exposure for you."

"Great. Let me know." Makedde thanked him for the key to the flat and said good-bye. She lay in bed, waiting for the phone to ring and hoping Charles was right. Catherine could get carried away, in love with love itself, and convinced that her latest man was none other than Prince Charming in a Porsche. It had happened before.

It was only 5.30 p.m., but it was past midnight in Canada. She struggled to stay awake but by 10 p.m. her energy quietly packed up and abandoned her, and her eyelids locked shut. She drifted off with a dog-eared copy of *Mindhunter* in her hand.

2

The following morning was mercilessly cold, with a biting southerly that whipped along the coastline, causing the caravan to shudder and groan like a feverish old man. Makedde stood inside its open door, savouring her last moments of warmth.

It was odd that Catherine had not called or left any messages. Even if she was taking advantage of a couple of extra days off to enjoy a romantic weekend away, she could have at least phoned. Who was this guy, anyway? Mak hoped it wasn't the same unnamed man Cat had been seeing for nearly a year, but in all likelihood it was. Cat had dropped a few hints—he was very rich, plenty powerful and he lived in Australia. No doubt he was what made her choose the Southern Hemisphere to continue her career. Makedde strongly suspected he was married, but when she pressed the issue Cat just grinned guiltily. Apparently this man made her swear, under "penalty of death" as she put it, to complete secrecy over his name and the details of their affair.

Makedde never could get the guy's real name out of her

friend, so she came up with her own. Whenever Cat had showed up with a new piece of flashy gold jewellery, Makedde had simply asked, "So how's *Dick*?" She might have been brash enough to ask, "So, how's *your* Dick?", except that any man wanting to keep a stunner like Catherine a secret was obviously not "hers" in any sense.

Makedde shivered, watching the photographer and his entourage, rugged up in parkas and long pants, make their way down to the water's edge. Her thoughts drifted away as the assistant waved. It was her turn to join them.

The moment she stepped from the warm caravan her skin broke out in indignant gooseflesh. Harsh wind whipped through the red-chequered picnic blanket she had wrapped around her. She could see the crew setting up on the sand below, and from their strained postures it was obvious there would be no shelter.

"I'm too old for this," Makedde mumbled to no one in particular. *I'm twenty-five. Shouldn't I be finishing my psychology degree? Shouldn't I be having babies like my sister?* She dismissed her thoughts as quickly as they came, pushing down the pain that had risen quickly within her. Adjusting the hot-water bottle strategically shoved down the back of her suit, Mak hurried down to the shoot.

Minutes later she was posing elegantly, with the wintry ocean lapping at her feet and her blonde hair flying back from her face. For a moment her mind focused completely on her body—aware of how her size-ten feet were positioned to minimise their length; the turn of her hips; the angle of her shoulders and the graceful placement of her hands—all in relation to the camera lens. Once she was satisfied that her pose was right, she allowed her thoughts to wander.

Makedde was grateful for her lack of appetite the night before, because her stomach seemed a little flatter than usual. Some girls were known to swear off liquid for several days before a "body shoot" as it was called, but Mak rarely went to those lengths. She heard rumours of laxative abuse, too, but what was the point? Self-induced diarrhoea? She was generally chosen for her healthy look, with the bonus of some curves, so she tended to worry more about all-night chocolate binges than mere sips of water. Besides, she told herself, if they had wanted a waif, they would have chosen one of the many teenage models subsisting on coffee and cigarettes.

As the photographic team silently examined her appearance, Makedde stretched up and tightened her stomach, assuming a well-practised pose that made the best of her feminine physique and presented the aqua-blue bikini at its most "saleable". The two representatives of the swimwear brand, who scrutinised every inch of her, seemed happy with the fit of their tiny garment.

Once the Polaroid was snapped Mak leapt for the blanket, now lying a couple of feet away, and wrapped it around her shivering body, jumping up and down in her battle against the cold. The others took no notice.

Tony Thomas, the photographer, was unhappy with the quality of the light. He barked orders at his assistant, his instructions flying past Makedde's ears in muffled gusts of wind. She looked on with restrained amusement as the assistant brought out a large, gold reflector board and gamely struggled to keep control of it. The client and the art director watched the clumsy spectacle with stony frowns.

"It's got to look *summery*," one of them insisted. "Can't you do something with her hair, Joseph?"

Joseph was a delicate-looking man who applied make-up to a face the way many artists tend to their cherished canvases; adding a touch, stepping back, squinting, and then adding another. Today though, his own face was pinched in frozen displeasure. He stepped towards her, careful not to disturb the sand where the shot would be taken, and tried pinning her mane of hair back. The wind promptly rebelled, sending a couple of pins flying into the water and others dangling from the very ends of her hair.

She had known it would be winter in this corner of the globe, but had temporarily forgotten that this was irrelevant as far as the clients were concerned. Summer designs were always shot the winter before their release; including swimwear. When no one was paying much attention, she held the hot-water bottle against her chest. Perfect for minimising nipple-itis.

The chilly day dragged on. Lunch consisted of some rather sad, wilted salad greens that the photographer's assistant was sent away to fetch. Makedde could have sworn she saw the photographer scoff down a cheesy focaccia and a beer when no one else was looking. By five o'clock she was relieved at the prospect of shooting the last outfit. It was a daringly high-cut, bright yellow zipper front swimsuit that was an ode to a decade when "Christy" referred to Brinkley, not Turlington. As usual, things became rushed as the client pushed to end the shoot before twenty minutes past the hour. That was the magic minute when models had to be paid for the extra hour's work. It was amazing how many photo shoots ended at nineteen minutes past.

As time was at a premium, Makedde was forced to change on the beach with a towel held in front of her by the embarrassed photographer's assistant who did his best to look the other way. A decade of modelling had cured Makedde of any romantic views of modesty, and she stripped fast and changed like a pro. She wrapped herself in the thick blanket again, holding her trusty hot-water bottle tightly against her, while the others searched for an appealing backdrop for the final shot. Sensing the tension over time, she had held off since the lunch break, but her full bladder could no longer be denied.

"I'll just be a sec!" she called out to them, pinching her knees together and hopping in the international signal for "I have to pee". Joseph was the only one to laugh.

She turned and started up into the tall, yellow grass, relieved at the prospect of relief. Dry blades scratched her shins as she moved farther away from the group, looking around for a patch of high grass that might offer some semblance of privacy. She noticed a curious smell, then something half hidden in the tall grass caught her attention.

A shoe?

She checked to see that the others were still searching for the next spot to shoot and, satisfied, she pushed further into the grass. As she drew closer, her eyes widened at the sight before her. Involuntarily her mouth stretched into what must have been a scream, although her ears could not hear it.

A rush of blood swelled inside her head, pounding mercilessly. She was barely aware of shouting, and the sound of feet running up from the beach. Images spun in front of her eyes—bold slashes of dark stain on pale skin; dark hair matted with gore; disturbing shapes of flesh—body parts missing. Long red wounds gaped open along a naked torso, revealing organs and flesh, and worse, the dark hair, matted with blood, partially covered a face that seemed far too familiar.

There were arms around her now, dragging her through the grass, dragging her away from that horrible mess, away from the smell that lingered like a sickness. She tried to speak. At first nothing came. There was confusion all around her. Finally she heard with horror the words that came from her own lips.

"Oh God, *Catherine*. Oh God . . ."

* * *

Mak was dimly aware of a young woman perched beside her with a steaming cup in her hand. On the far horizon the last glimpse of a violent, red sunset lit up the skies like hellfire. All around them was activity, voices and the static and garbled sounds of police radios. Her uniformed companion silently observed her. They were removed from the action, several feet away from an area cordoned off with police tape. Artificial light flooded the grassy dune, transforming the faces huddled around it into pale, fixated masks. Latex-gloved hands scribbled in small police-issue notebooks, and Makedde was reminded of her father's notebook, with its official-looking cover. She wondered what vicious brutality it had witnessed, and what sickening incidents had been recorded in it.

The strong breeze was bitterly cold on her face, and she was shivering, even though she had been wrapped warmly in several plain, heavy blankets. Looking around, she saw flashlight beams piercing the descending darkness like fireflies. She recognised the make-up artist, Joseph, disappearing towards the parking lot with a uniformed officer, and further down the beach she saw Tony Thomas having a heated discussion with a tall man in a suit. The man was standing calmly with what looked like Tony's camera in his hands, his stance speaking clearly of authority while Tony, looking even shorter than his five-foot-five, was gesturing angrily at him.

Tony's camera? What would they want with that?

When the discussion appeared to die down, Mak watched Tony being led past her, head down, towards the vehicles in the bustling parking area. Police surgeon, pathologist, crime-scene officers, detectives; they were all there, recording and measuring, calculating in their attention to detail. She could see the police photographer sending out sudden bursts of light in the growing darkness. Each of them went about their job with a familiar single-mindedness.

Different faces, same morbid business.

She remembered her father's colleagues. Their jobs took on a new meaning under these new, horrible circumstances. Beat cops, detectives, medical officers; they had seemed like part of the family for as long as she could remember. Some had even visited the hospital where her mother had been staying when she was sick. Her dad had refused to leave the hospital room. Three months, and he stayed there every night in an uncomfortable cot beside her.

"How are you feeling now?" A soft voice broke into her thoughts. "I'm Constable Karen Mahoney. Are you warm now? Would you like to see a doctor?" The voice was calm and reassuring, the round face sympathetic. Makedde thought of how this woman would, day after day, see unspeakable pain and remain calm and detached.

"No, I'm fine. I don't need a doctor, I guess I . . ." Mak's voice trailed off. "Have you seen her? The girl?"

"Yes. Here, why don't you have some coffee?" She handed Makedde the steaming cup. "You may know the victim? Is that correct?"

Catherine.

A chill ran up her spine. A body; bloodied and mangled, so very dead. Could it be her?

"I . . . I think I might know her. I'm not sure. I thought it was her—Catherine Gerber. I'm staying with her, but she's not there . . ." The words came out as a senseless ramble.

"It's OK. I understand this must be difficult. You were the first to find the body, is that right?"

Makedde nodded slowly.

"We'll need to ask you a few questions and we may have to get you to identify the victim at a later time. Is that all right with you?"

Makedde nodded again slowly. Nothing had prepared her for this. Sometimes she had a sixth sense about things, a kind of intuition that forewarned her. But not this time.

Perhaps I was mistaken? Maybe it was just the dream . . . *The dream.*

Now awake, the details were lost, the nightmare fragmented; just pieces of terror floating free, interchangeable and meaningless. There was a sense of horror and loss over Catherine, but it was all too abstract to comprehend. The line between nightmare and reality had grown incredibly thin.

Mak concluded with desperate optimism that she'd been mistaken. She just thought it was Cat because of the bad dream. And the dark hair. Lots of people have dark hair. Cat would call. She looked up to see a tall man in a suit towering over her. It was the man she had seen with Tony Thomas. With the crime-scene lights behind him he was an impressive, faceless silhouette.

"Miss Vanderwall, I'm Detective Senior Sergeant Andrew Flynn. This must have been quite a shock for you." His voice was deep, with a pleasant Australian accent. He sounded strangely calm, and when she didn't respond he continued, "I understand you were the first to discover the body, and you may be able to make an ID? Is that correct?"

"Yes. Well . . . I saw her first but I don't know if it's really Catherine."

"Catherine?" He was writing in his notebook. "Can you tell me her full name?"

"Catherine Gerber. She's a close friend. A model from Canada. That is, if it's her. I don't know." She felt her throat tighten, like her heart, into a painful, bitter knot.

His voice continued, calm and professional. "It would be helpful if you could be certain. Would you be available to ID the body sometime tomorrow morning?"

"Sure . . ."

"I'd like to ask you a few questions now, if you don't mind. Then Constable Mahoney will see you home."

She answered each of his questions and he patiently took notes. Her mind wandered through a surreal landscape of fear and confusion, annoyed she was having such trouble making sense of things. Her answers came out muddled sometimes, but the detective just went on, gently probing.

"I'm Canadian. I arrived yesterday on a three-month work visa. I'm staying in a model's flat in Bondi with Catherine. It's my second time in Australia."

"So you saw Catherine when you arrived?"

"Well, no. I went straight to the flat but she wasn't there. I was hoping to hear from her yesterday or today."

"And did that seem odd to you?"

"Very," she replied with somewhat more clarity.

He nodded to himself. "When was the last time you saw her?"

Her mind drifted back to the day of her mother's funeral. She was bidding her own mother farewell; how could she have known it would be the last time she would see her best friend alive?

"Last time I saw her was nearly six months ago in Canada. She came to my mother's funeral service."

"I'm very sorry." He paused thoughtfully. "How well do you know Tony Thomas, the photographer from your photo shoot today?"

"I've only worked with him once before."

"Did you notice anything unusual about the job today before you found the body? Any odd behaviour? Suggestions?"

"No, I didn't notice anything odd."

"Do you know who suggested the location for the photos?"

Mak thought for a moment. Some of his questions seemed strange to her.

"I think Tony would have suggested the location."

"Did he know about your connection to Catherine? Aside from being in the same agency?"

"I don't see how he could, unless someone else told him."

"Thank you, Miss Vanderwall. You've been very helpful. Constable Mahoney will take a statement from you, and drive you home. I'll be in touch tomorrow morning. Here's my card. If you have any questions, or if anything comes to mind, even if it seems insignificant to you, please don't hesitate to call."

She held his card in her numb fingers and watched him walk back towards the lights, blending in with the white, expressionless faces of the men and women whose job it was to face violence every day.

The young policewoman drove Makedde to her Bondi Beach accommodation, and after giving the expected, "How are you feeling now? Is there anything else I can do?" she left Mak alone. It was odd to walk in, feeling Catherine's presence everywhere, with the image of the mangled corpse flashing feverishly behind her eyes.

Makedde shivered.

She leant against the window, palms against the glass, and peered at the outside world; couples laughing, strolling down the beach, carefree and oblivious. It suddenly seemed so foreign. Exhausted, Makedde pulled the shade down, plunging the flat into darkness. She was emotionally drained and incapable of undressing or taking off the thick make-up Joseph had applied. When she collapsed on the bed, she felt the sensation of falling long after her body hit the mattress. The dark room spun in a haze above her.

It's all a terrible dream.

I'll talk to you tomorrow, my friend.

* * *

It seemed like minutes later when the phone attacked her ears with a determined peal. By the third ring the receiver was at her ear, her mind still in deep sleep.

Finally . . . Catherine.

The voice on the other end was speaking to her. "What? Sorry . . ." she croaked, the words coming out like she was clearing her throat.

"This is Detective Flynn. Is this Makedde Vanderwall?"

"Yes."

"We would appreciate if you could make an ID at the Glebe morgue this morning."

The world came crashing into focus with horrifying clarity.

It was 9 a.m. already.

"Yes. I'll come down."

When she hung up the receiver, she found herself fully dressed, sitting up in bed, confronted by a harrowing image in the wall mirror across from her. During the night her dark make-up had streaked in dramatic lines down her cheeks. She tried to wipe it away with one kohl-smudged hand and succeeded in making it worse.

It just wouldn't go away.

3

A taxi dropped Makedde off at a series of drab, brown doors marked "NSW INSTITUTE OF FORENSIC MEDICINE". She wondered how many people regularly walked past the unassuming façade without realising it was the morgue.

Mak had fainted the day before, and had no intention of doing so again. It wasn't that she had never seen a dead person before. She had accompanied her father to the morgue on many occasions when she was younger. As Vancouver Island's most respected detective inspector he had free rein to take Makedde wherever she wanted to go; and even at an early age she'd shown an unusual appetite for the macabre. She begged for trips to the station and city morgue the way other kids begged for a Barbie doll or extra pocket money. But he had purposely steered her away from the more horrific scenes; instead she had witnessed fleshless skeletons found in the forest years after death, or the smooth, peaceful corpses of the naturally departed.

Makedde had never seen a dead person looking, *smelling*, so violently, horribly dead as the girl she had discovered the day before. A beautiful girl, who had perhaps been Catherine, lay cold and lifeless in a freezer beyond the imposing brown doors in front of her. She had lost two of the most important people in her life in just six months. It hadn't been trips to the morgue that acquainted Makedde with the impact of death. Unwittingly, her mother taught her that hard lesson, and now so had Catherine.

With sour dread in the pit of her stomach, Makedde mustered up her courage and stepped through the front doors. *I can do this.* A white-faced clock high on one wall told her it was 10.30 a.m. Detective Flynn had seen her enter and was walking towards her. "Miss Vanderwall, thank you for coming. This shouldn't take too long. Please, come this way," he said quietly.

She followed him through a single door marked "Relatives Waiting", barely paying him any attention. She was entirely focused on the horrible sight waiting for her in the viewing room. Detective Flynn closed the door behind them and they sat down on the grey, cushioned seats. The waiting room was self-consciously pleasant, with warm, off-white walls, bland paintings, and a few plants. It reminded her of the counselling room in the Vancouver General Hospital, where some social worker had done his best to help Makedde and her family cope with Jane Vanderwall's long and painful battle with cancer.

Another closed door stood before them, and she could hear movement behind it. Makedde's heart leapt into her throat at the sound of a metallic wheel squeaking beyond the door.

She's lying on some cold, metal trolley; helpless.

Minutes later a small, ginger-haired man identified as Ed Brown by his name tag ambled in and told them that she was "ready". He opened the viewing room door, and Makedde walked inside like a woman in a trance.

It was unlike anything she had expected. She was prepared for a glass window and a curtain and some guy in a gown who would pull back the sheet, but there was none of that, only a small wooden divider between Makedde and her dead friend.

The attendant spoke to her softly in a soothing, emasculated voice. "I've left one arm out for you, if you wish to touch it. A lock of hair is also available if you would like. Don't be afraid to ask for it. You would be surprised how many people really do appreciate it."

Touch it.

Makedde was silent, staring.

"I'll leave you now. Take as much time as you need."

With that, the uniformed attendant left, leaving Makedde and Detective Flynn alone in the room with a silent, cold china doll.

Makedde would be naïve not to admit that it was Catherine, with that once-vibrant face, inches away. Catherine's face was colourless, her body cloaked in a series of green and white patterned blankets, with a hood covering her skull like a chador. The stench of death that had lingered in the grass the evening before was slightly less powerful now, but the sharp tang of tea-tree oil could not mask it completely.

A hand hung limply off the metal tray, asking to be touched. There were deep red marks around the wrist.

Touch it.

Makedde looked away.

Detective Flynn placed his hand lightly on her shoulder. "Are you all right?" Makedde didn't answer. "Is this the body of Catherine Gerber?"

"Can I see her hair? She had beautiful, long, dark hair. She looks different with the shroud."

"Her head has been shaved, I'm afraid. All murder victims have their heads shaved. Her head wounds are quite extensive." He sounded apologetic.

"Oh."

"Can you positively confirm that this is the body of Catherine Gerber?"

Makedde paused, staring silently at the human-like form that lay before her. "Yes." The tears began. She tried to contain them, but they welled up and rolled soundlessly down her cheeks.

"Thank you, Miss Vanderwall. You can stay for a while, if you wish. There's no rush. I'll be waiting for you just outside the door when you're ready."

Makedde heard the door close behind her. She stood as far away from the corpse as she could. She backed right into a chair, and sat down. With blurry eyes she noticed a television screen in the upper right-hand corner of the viewing room. It seemed to be a strange place for a television. For a moment she imagined Catherine opening her eyes to watch a show, like a person waking from sedation in a hospital room. Makedde suspected the television was for viewings where the body was so badly decomposed or infected that it had to be in a separate room. With half her insides spread about in the grass, the insects and animals would have had Catherine fast. She could have been nearly gone by the time she was discovered.

Is that what her killer wanted? If he had, he would have chosen somewhere much more private. No, he wanted to shock. He wanted her found quickly.

She rose and moved towards the body of Catherine Gerber.

Towards *that hand*.

Grief-stricken, Makedde steeled herself, reached out, and touched the hand, holding it tenderly.

It was cold.

"Good-bye my dear friend," she said quietly. Before letting go she whispered one last thing. "I promise you justice, Catherine. I *promise*."

She left the room knowing that her friend was gone. She wasn't on a tray in the viewing room in the morgue. She wasn't about to be zipped into a body bag and wheeled into a cold freezer.

She was somewhere else . . . somewhere better.

Makedde switched her brain to professional mode, distancing herself, as best she could, from the horrors of the present reality. The morgue had a sterile chill that seeped into her bones the longer she stood within its walls. She was dying to leave, but she had the P443 identification statement to fill out first, and she had questions to ask of Detective Andrew Flynn.

Her throat felt tight when she spoke. "When will her foster parents see her? She's a long way from Canada."

He replied with impersonal, well-practised sensitivity. "Her body will be released to them at the earliest possible date."

Mak knew Catherine's foster parents. No one would be hurrying out to make sure that things were handled properly. Eventually Catherine's body would fly across the continents in a cold, generic container for a funeral that would be small and economic.

Makedde read the form.

This statement made by me accurately sets out the evidence which I would be prepared, if necessary, to give in court as a witness.

"Will I have to stay for the trial?" she asked.

"You'll have to be here for the trial, but you won't have to be here *until* the trial. It may take some time to finish the investigation. We would arrange for your flight from Canada if necessary."

"I'm not leaving just yet," Makedde said firmly.

"Good."

She continued through the form.

My relationship with the deceased is . . .

Friend. Best friend.

Her mind drifted back to that limp, cold hand. "I noticed she had ligature marks on her wrist."

"Yes."

Makedde gave him a look that clearly asked for more information. When he didn't respond, she said, "He tied her up, didn't he?"

"We suspect she was bound."

Bound.

"With what? Didn't look like rope or cord," she probed.

The detective looked at her strangely, and she realised she could be sounding very odd, or even guilty to anyone who didn't know that she was a student of forensic psychology raised in a household where crime was dinnertime conversation.

She changed the subject. "Will you need someone else to make an ID as well? I'm afraid I may be the nearest thing you'll find to a relative. Her foster parents weren't very—" *loving.* She searched for a polite way to word it. "*Close.* They weren't very close to her."

"At this point, you're all we have. We appreciate your cooperation."

"This doesn't seem like a run-of-the-mill murder to me," she said, trying to get a reaction. "I'm guessing you don't see that sort of . . . *damage* in your average Sydney murder."

Detective Flynn turned to her, and with a grave face said, "There is nothing average about any murder, Miss Vanderwall. This investigation is my number one priority."

Catherine's life demanded it.

* * *

Hours later Makedde was back at the Bondi Beach flat, but she wasn't alone.

"Again, I'm sorry to have to do this," Detective Flynn said, as a small forensic team descended on Makedde's accommodations. "I appreciate you giving us consent. It really is important to do this as soon as possible."

"I understand the circumstances are unusual."

And they were unusual. Not only was Mak the victim's closest link and witness to the discovery of the body, but she was also staying in the deceased's flat.

"Are you dusting?"

"Yes."

The flat would soon be a mess. Black carbon fingerprinting powder was difficult to remove. Lanconide was used on the darker surfaces and was equally stubborn but less obvious because it was white. Mak had seen it at crime scenes, but never thought she would have to lay her head in a room invaded by its stain. She watched uneasily as a uniformed forensic cop stopped in front of the collage of magazine photos and began videotaping. His head tilted back as he captured Catherine's stolen ambitions on video.

Makedde felt her eyes glaze over, and suddenly Detective Flynn's hand was at her elbow, keeping her steady. "Here, sit down." He led her to the couch. She hadn't realised how weak she felt.

"I'm fine, really," she said unconvincingly as she sat down. "Do I have to be here for the search? I'm not sure I want to be."

"Generally we prefer it, so that there are no . . . *misunderstandings*."

"Well I'm not planning on suing anyone for looking through my underwear, and there is nothing of value here." She didn't want to witness a search from such an intimate standpoint, and was relieved when Flynn suggested she sit at a café next door until they were done.

"It shouldn't take too long. The flat is small," he said. "Would you like someone to sit with you?"

"No," she snapped back a little too quickly. "I, uh . . . really need to be alone."

Makedde walked straight to the door without glancing back at the searching detectives as they went about their work. She negotiated the stairs with care, recognising that she was numb with shock and her senses were unstable. When she hit the street door and stepped outside, the winter wind greeted her with a strong slap of cold reality.

4

The Sunday paper offered Makedde no condolences. There was no comforting escape into a pleasantly challenging crossword, or interesting but passionless read about the life of a celebrity or politician. Instead she was immediately confronted by a shocking front page headline: *MODEL SLAIN*. This sensitive title was accompanied by a photo of Catherine, with the morbid caption, *Catherine Gerber, third victim of brutal murder in Sydney this month*. In the picture, Catherine's fine features oozed glamorous detachment. She appeared blissfully unaware of her fate.

Mak wondered if Book agency had offered the photograph to the press, and if Catherine would have liked it. She looked beautiful, and no doubt every reader's eye was drawn to her haunting image on this bleak Sunday morning. She folded the paper in half and put it on top of the bedside chest of drawers with Catherine's picture facing down. Mak no longer felt up to reading the paper. She no longer felt up to doing anything.

The persistent odour of death lingered in her nostrils.

She sniffed in little breaths of air, and there it was, the pure, morbid reek of decomposing flesh. Makedde raised a bare forearm and inhaled the smell of her own skin.

Death.

Death in her pores.

Uninvited tears threatened to flow as she leapt from the bed and ran to the bathroom, her breath hard and fast. She was letting things get to her, losing control. She had to fight it.

Calmly now.

Calmly.

She squeezed mint toothpaste onto her index finger and forced it up one nostril and then the other; a trick she'd learnt from a pathologist years ago. The smell of a cadaver can cling to nose hairs, making everything smell of the deceased. She washed it out, and the fresh, toothpaste fragrance remained. Breathing in a mint-scented world, she left the bathroom and walked straight to the small fridge in the kitchen. She removed a large slab of marzipan chocolate, the wrapper crinkling as she pulled back a corner. She paused guiltily, salivating and stressed, and put it back in the fridge, slamming the door. *Don't do it*. Mak turned and started to walk away from the kitchen and then turned back and dove for the fridge again. In an instant the wrapper was off, her blood soaring in a sugar ecstasy.

Mak turned her attention to the old television set sitting across from her. The small box begged for her to flick it on, so she did, and her ears were immediately accosted by the loud volume. The ancient remote control was the size of a brick, and was running out of batteries. It took several tries to reduce the volume. A smiling newscaster loudly reminded her that on this day in 1969, before she was even conceived, the first man walked on the moon. They cut from the smiling newscaster to old footage of a spacesuit-bloated Neil Armstrong triumphantly touching down on the moon's dusty surface.

"One small step for man, one giant leap for mankind."

Man-kind.

The two words seemed perversely mismatched.

As she lowered the volume further she noticed that beneath the blaring noise the phone had been ringing. She answered it with a deceptively chirpy, "Hello?"

Click.

The dial tone resumed.

Mak stared into the earpiece for a moment and then hung it up. How rude. She turned her eyes to the quiet television again and was horrified to see Catherine's face staring back at her. Panic rose in her, a cold sweat breaking out over her body. In an instant the remote was in her hands and she was pressing the off button. It wouldn't work. The television image panned across the front doors of Book Model Agency, and then lingered on the crime-scene tape around the tall and trampled grass. Makedde pressed the off button repeatedly.

Dammit! Turn off!

Finally the set obeyed and the image flickered away.

Heart pounding and eyes rimmed with stubborn tears, she lay down on the bed and stared at the cracked paint on the ceiling, breathing deeply, trying to relax.

Think of something else, anything but Catherine.

As a child she had stared for hours at the stucco ceiling in her room, wondering what it would be like if the world was upside down, and people walked on ceilings, stepping over chandeliers and smoke detectors, and reaching up to turn on kitchen taps that would send water flowing straight into their mouths. She tried to return to that life, to let pleasant fantasy captivate her, but she could not.

I need a friend. I need someone to live through this year with me.

Makedde opened her wallet and pulled out a few crinkled photographs. She examined each one lovingly, and when she found the one she wanted, she slowly smoothed it out, carefully bending the corners back into shape. Cat had the duplicate photo, and she had inscribed this one with the optimistic inscription, *Me 'n' Mak making it big in Munich!* She studied the smiling faces of Catherine and herself posing in Marienplatz. Cat looked so young. With watery eyes Mak studied her own face in the mirror across from her bed. The woman in her reflection looked much older than in the photograph.

There was a time when Mak and Catherine would sit before a mirror and play with make-up for hours. Makedde had a model's kit overflowing with shimmering colours and powders. She taught Cat how to apply it; a sweep of charcoal here, a slick of lip gloss there. She would play with dramatic eyeliner and deep red lips. Brigitte Bardot eyes, or Madonna's frosted lips. Everything looked great on Cat's thirteen-year-old complexion. Everything. She had such a beautiful, even-featured face. The same face that would six years later stare back at Makedde from a morgue tray; tortured and wasted.

Tomorrow she would pack up Catherine's things and rip down the collage of magazine photos. But she would keep a picture of her friend in a special part of the room; the photo of them together in Munich, perhaps. That was the normal, rational thing to do. Wasn't it? A sane photo of happier times, to honour her friend. She would have to make the flat her own, because she would stay in Sydney for a while; as long as it took for the police to find Catherine's killer.

She remembered a couple of recent postcards and letters from Cat that she had stashed in her suitcase. One of them had been written from the Bondi address. Perhaps she wrote it while seated in exactly the same spot. Indulging her sense of loss, Mak walked to the smaller of her two suitcases and removed the correspondence from a zippered pocket on the outside. Her heart ached at the sight of the familiar, cheerful handwriting.

Dear Mak,
Greetings from down unda! It's almost July. Soon you'll be hanging out with me with the kookaburras and the Aussie babes. Even their winter is sunny, like a Canadian spring, I swear. Fabulous! I can't wait till you are here.
I'm happy to be nearer to the love of my life. He is busy, and for the moment our love is still a secret, but he isn't continents away now. He's such a great guy, and classy too. You'll adore him. It won't be a secret for much longer. You'll meet him soon. We'll laugh about all this mysteriousness!

Her heart skipped a beat at the thought of the clandestine lover. Why did this man need to be a secret? She had assumed he was married and that Catherine would eventually get smart and break off the relationship. But she never did. For the past year she had foolishly pined for the elusive Romeo.

With rage slowly building within her, Makedde imagined the words he must have used to keep her hanging on—*"I'll divorce my wife and marry you, I promise. But she couldn't go through a divorce right now. Not yet. I love you, and soon we'll be together always. Just wait a bit longer."* How many times had those words been spoken throughout the history of illicit relationships?

Urgent curiosity and a sense of purpose pushed Makedde's sadness aside. She pulled Detective Flynn's card out of her wallet and dialled his mobile number. She had forgotten to tell the police about Catherine's affair. What if it was important? She would tell Flynn what little she knew about the unnamed paramour. No . . . she would come to see him in person and let him see the letters. That would convince him to follow the lead.

After a few rings, he answered.

"Detective Flynn, this is Makedde Vanderwall."

"Hello, Miss Vanderwall. How can I help you?"

"You said I should call if I had any further information. I know it's Sunday, but I was wondering if I could come down. I have something that might interest you."

"It's all right, I'm coming in later anyway. Is 4 p.m. at Homicide all right?"

"Four is fine."

"See you then."

Knowing that he was working on Catherine's case on a Sunday reassured her a little. She was glad she would have a chance to talk with him about it in person. Looking out the window, she noticed for the first time the blue, cloudless day. She decided to go for a walk along the beach and compare her little life and its tragedies against the immensity of nature. It always made her problems seem insignificant.

Makedde dressed in faded jeans, her favourite Betty Page T-shirt, a warm navy jumper and comfortable walking shoes. With her mind racing to recall every detail of the relationship that Catherine had ever alluded to, she set off on her walk.

5

Faint sunlight filtered through closed red curtains, turning the room to midnight crimson. Exposed by rumpled bed-sheets, his sweat-soaked skin glistened in the unearthly blood-glow. A weak, incomprehensible noise escaped his throat as his fingertip made contact with shiny, black leather. Eyes shut, he lovingly fondled the shoe, stroking the long, thin heel, with its sharp, well-worn point. He traced his fingers gently down the length of the leather sole, his breath quickening.

Her toes.

With agonising deliberation he fingered the thin ankle strap, pausing at its small, metal buckle to press his finger onto the sharp edge.

Her ankles.

He watched with grotesque pleasure as it pierced the skin, a tiny droplet of blood trickling down his finger.

Whore.

Rolling onto his bare belly he ground the stiffness of his groin hard into the bed and pulled the shoe to his face, deeply inhaling its sharp odour. His exposed buttocks writhed and jerked with spasmodic gesticulations.

Hunger built within him. Frustration, anger, violence and pleasure coursed through his veins.

Bound flesh.

Blood.

Scenes replayed; every stroke, every cut remembered. But each time less powerful, less fulfilling. He needed more, much more. He thrust the shoe down towards the source of his release and his climax filled the stiletto with a spew of milky vexation.

More.

6

Hours later, Makedde waited patiently outside the office at Central Homicide, distantly aware of suggestive stares from several young, bored detectives. She was not in the mood. Knowing that the uni-student look rarely helped her to be taken seriously, she had changed out of her jeans into something slightly less casual. She wore her tailor-made, slim black pants; a well-travelled favourite that she had specially made to fit her. She paired them with a crisp white man's shirt she'd bought on King's Road in London, and a cashmere jacket from New York, a comfortable and versatile classic.

Time ticked by. She checked her watch. It was 4.15 p.m. Fifteen minutes later she was still waiting. Flynn was obviously busy.

An argument taking place in the next room diverted her attention. Raised voices spat through the walls, growing louder and louder, too loud to ignore. The words were hard to make out, but the tone was unmistakably emotional. It had the whiff of a nasty lover's quarrel, and Mak felt embarrassed at her unintended eavesdropping.

Then a woman's voice broke clearly through the walls. "I guess the living are second-rate in your book! I'm over it!" This outburst was punctuated by a thunderous crash inside the room. Several detectives looked up, alarmed. Another crash. It sounded like something big was being smashed repeatedly against a wall. A young man leapt from his chair and ran towards the door, and was nearly hit in the face when it opened unexpectedly. A beautiful, petite, dark-haired woman emerged, her face flushed. She turned back towards the room and bitterly exclaimed, "You're pathetic!" before striding proudly past the desks. Her head was held high as she ignored the silent looks from the detectives. Wearing a smart-looking suit and a very nasty frown, she made straight for the elevator, arms folded across her chest. As she was swallowed up by the closing doors, she gave the men a sneering, superior look. She seemed quite intact, so clearly it wasn't her who had been hurled against the wall.

The instant she disappeared the room erupted in nervous laughter. Detective Flynn emerged with his fists tightly clenched and his face set in a vicious scowl. He looked like he was ready to kill.

A detective playfully called out, "Ya know what Cassandra means in Greek?"

"No, Jimmy, I don't know," Detective Flynn shot back angrily.

"It means 'confuser of men'."

"Oh, fabulous. Thank you. Where were you four years ago when I needed you? Fuckin' women."

A fresh burst of laughter filled the room, and Detective Flynn cracked a grim smile.

"You sure can pick 'em," said another, younger detective, still laughing.

But Flynn was no longer in the mood for it. "Don't push

it, Hoosier," he snarled, fixing the detective with a black look. What had the woman done to elicit such a strong reaction? And what was that noise?

Flynn turned to see Makedde waiting and a red flush instantly coloured his cheeks. "Uh, Miss . . . Miss Vanderwall . . ." he spluttered awkwardly. Makedde smiled, embarrassed for him.

"I'm sorry to have kept you waiting," he continued, quickly composing himself. His voice again took on the polite, detached lilt that it had the day before. "Could you wait just another moment?"

She nodded, and he disappeared into the mysterious room again. A minute later Flynn emerged, calmer. "You have some information for me?"

With an extended arm he escorted her to the private room that she knew would be used for interviews. The stark room had a well-used Formica table as its centrepiece. She noted that the table legs were screwed into the floor and wondered how many cops had been assaulted with it before they'd taken the extra measures. Some of the other detectives were still snickering as Flynn shut the door behind them. She decided that she wouldn't make any reference to his argument. It was none of her business.

Andy motioned for her to sit, but when she pulled a chair out he said, "Sorry, not that one." She noticed one of the metal legs was badly bent. She tried another, unmangled chair, and he sat opposite.

Makedde recalled the few interviews she had been permitted to watch in secrecy from a two-way mirror not unlike the one she sat opposite now. Her father was an expert interrogator. He built rapport with his suspects, put them at ease, and then trapped them with their own words. A somewhat different approach to throwing chairs. But then, to be fair, that woman was clearly not a suspect.

Mak wondered whether Detective Flynn was a good inquisitor. She hoped he was. She was certain that a few detectives had made their way over to the interview room as soon as the door closed behind them. If they had stared at her in the waiting room, they would certainly be staring at her now. It was Sunday afternoon, and no doubt they were tired and bored. She could feel their eyes. Should she let them know that she knew they were watching? Nah. Why spoil their fun?

Detective Flynn was settling into his chair, still cooling off from his argument. Alone in this quiet room, devoid of all distractions, Makedde noticed that he was actually quite attractive. His dark hair was thick and cropped short, accentuating a distinctive, squared-off jawline. His lips were even, his teeth straight, and something about the way they were formed was strangely sensual. But handsome wasn't quite the word for Detective Flynn. His nose was a bit crooked, his ears a bit too big. His green eyes seemed world weary and sceptical under dark brows. Somehow though, when you put the features together, and added his impressive height, the effect was appealing. Especially to Makedde.

Admit it, that's why you wanted to see him in person; because you think he's attractive.

His face was still a bit rosy, and she could have sworn she could feel the heat his body was still giving off. Makedde continued to dwell on minute details of Andy Flynn's appearance—like the little scar on his chin that she felt the urge to touch. She suddenly imagined the police issue handcuffs he would wear on his belt, and felt a naughty tingle of sexual excitement. The sensation made her so uncomfortable that she became suspicious of her hormones, or the moon.

"First off, let me just apologise for not being able to

make a positive ID on Friday," Makedde began. "Obviously I was in no state to be of much use in that regard. But even though she looked . . . *different* at the morgue yesterday, I—"

Condescendingly, he cut her off, "The autopsy was completed before your ID. Standard procedure when the death is suspicious. Bodies look different after death, Miss Vanderwall, they . . ." He trailed off, his hands making a gesture to indicate the unpleasantness of posthumous bodily functions.

The tiny hairs on the back of Makedde's neck bristled. Was he playing up to the watching detectives, trying to assert his manly superiority over a female?

"I'm not totally ignorant, Detective," she replied calmly, for she was accustomed to being underestimated. "I'm quite familiar with autopsy procedure, and rigor mortis and that most unpleasant swelling you so enjoyed illustrating for me just then. My father was a Detective Inspector, and—"

"Really?" She caught a flicker of interest in his eyes. "He's retired now?"

"Yes, but that is not the point here. I'm not asking you for a lesson on post-mortem methodology. I am simply clarifying that the ID was positive. Now, to get to the point, I think I may have some information that could prove central to the investigation." Andy leant forward. She seemed to finally have his attention. What should she say? Perhaps there was nothing more sinister about the relationship than a common cheating spouse?

"Catherine Gerber was involved in an affair," she began. "One which she was sworn to secrecy about."

Andy leant forward even further. There was an intensity about him that frightened her a little, particularly when she pictured him smashing that chair against the wall. Makedde pushed back her chair casually, separating them another inch.

She swallowed hard. "Catherine had been telling me about this affair for approximately the past twelve months. She wouldn't divulge any specifics; however, she did allude to the fact that the man was powerful, wealthy, and older than she was. With her being nineteen, I would assume he was considerably older. I also had the impression that he was married, and the whole affair was certainly considered top secret."

Flynn had moved back a touch, his body language subtly expressing a disappointment in the information.

"Well, we'll look into that." He gave her a patronising, fixed smile, and said, "Is there anything else?"

Makedde couldn't quite believe that he'd just brushed her off. She sat and studied him for a moment, analysing his position.

I should have waited until I had more to come in with; a name, dates, places.

She felt the need to fill the uncomfortable silence. "I don't know why I thought you'd care, but you *did* say that I should come to you if—"

"I do care. I care in so much that every bit of information is important, and even the most seemingly insignificant detail can take on important meaning in the big picture."

"Insignificant?" Makedde said, incredulous. She knew she should just walk away, that she wasn't going to get anywhere with him, but she couldn't contain herself. "Let me just give you a possible scenario, so you can get some idea of the *insignificance* of this. Say this guy is married. Say he has even more at stake . . . he's a politician, someone with a high profile, whatever. I'm getting these letters," she pushed the neatly folded correspondence in front of him, "where Catherine is saying, 'It won't be a secret much longer.' What if she's telling *him* that? What if she's threatening to expose him? Motive for murder, perhaps."

Detective Flynn was poker-faced as he stood up, and Makedde was further enraged that he didn't even respond to her. She watched him move towards the large mirror with his back to her. With a mixture of fury and humiliation she suspected that he was rolling his eyes for the benefit of his colleagues. Obviously she had wasted her time coming in.

"Miss Vanderwall, we don't believe this is an isolated revenge murder. Believe it or not, we think this guy does this stuff for kicks. Thanks again for the information, now let the professionals take care of it."

"You *have* a suspect. Is that it?" she said with surprising calm. "Someone you've really got it in for?" *To the exclusion of all others? Gosh, I'm just so sorry for threatening to complicate your investigation with a new lead, Mister Hot Head Detective.* She held her tongue.

"Can we keep these letters?"

"I would like copies, please. And I'd like the originals returned to me at the earliest possible time," she said firmly.

"We can arrange that."

He escorted her with exaggerated politeness out of the office to the elevator. "Thank you for your help, Miss Vanderwall."

She left the building seething. She felt foolish, and underestimated. More than anything else in the world, she *hated* being underestimated. One look at her blonde hair and model-appearance, and people just stopped listening. She could be talking quantum-mechanics and they'd be staring at her breasts, nothing but air passing between their ears. Did the detectives laugh when she left too? Sure they did. "Fuckin' women," he'd said. *I guess I was just another one to him*. It wasn't a reassuring introduction to the man in charge of Catherine's case.

The taxi snaked slowly through the city. At odd moments Makedde saw vaguely familiar buildings silhouetted by a sun already low in the sky. Directly ahead of her, an enormous full moon hovered silently. The driver snuck glances at her in the rearview mirror. Irritated, she urged him to step on the gas, and soon they reached the open water of Bondi Beach.

She entered the lonely flat. Tossing her keys on the tabletop, she mimicked her own voice, "I think I may have some information . . . blah, blah, blah. *Idiot*."

The empty room replied with silence.

7

On Monday morning the alarm clock buzzed with military authority—4.45 a.m. glowed in angry red neon on the digital face. An inhumane time to be conscious, but a cheap time to make international calls, and Makedde could catch her father before he left for the weekly Sunday lunch he enjoyed with his fellow retired cops.

She settled in by the bedroom phone and dialled the seemingly endless digits that would put her in touch with Canada. After several clicks and pauses, she could hear the phone ringing. There was a slight delay, and the line had a bit of static. ". . . Makedde?"

"Hey, Dad."

"You sound like you're a million miles away. How was your flight?"

"OK. Great service. I loved the green tea, but it was all a bit long."

"You couldn't pay me enough to get on one of those flights," he said.

That was probably true. Her father preferred the familiarity of the city he had lived in all his life. Even on holiday

51

he didn't like to stray too far anymore. She called him every second Sunday, without fail, no matter where her travels took her. She'd been especially careful to do that since her mother had died.

"How's my daughter?"

"I'm fine. Well . . . sort of. We'll get to that. I arrived safely, anyhow. How are you?" she asked. She was aware that she was stalling. Mak hated giving him bad news.

"I'm good," he said. "Going out with the guys in a few minutes—"

"I guessed as much."

He went on, "Theresa is getting huge. She's almost seven months pregnant now."

"I know. I only saw her last week." Makedde often had a vague sense of guilt and inferiority when anyone mentioned her sister. There was something about Theresa's settled, married life that seemed so laudable. It was proper, predictable and good, and Makedde's life was so, well . . . not. A bouncing, gurgling, grinning bub would only make things worse.

"You really should give your sister a call once in a while."

She rolled her eyes. "Yes, Dad. I'll call her. I promise."

"They've decided not to find out if it's a boy or a girl." He paused. "Such a shame Jane never got to see her daughters have children."

Makedde had become engaged to a local boy shortly after her mother was diagnosed with cancer, when Mak was twenty. However she soon realised that she'd only wanted to be Mrs. Purdy in a desperate effort to make her family happy. It didn't last long. She dumped George in a supermarket at the checkout counter, flipping his ring into a shopping bag full of milk cartons and cans of baked beans.

Mak didn't find Mr. Right in time for her mother to

meet him, and she certainly didn't have children in time for her mother to be a grandparent. It was her sister who'd thrilled them with the white wedding and the pregnancy news. Her perfect sister.

"Dad, I have some tragic news . . ." She told him about Catherine. As expected, he was horrified and saddened. He had watched her grow up, too.

"I hope you're getting on the next plane home. You don't want to be around when some sicko like that decides he has a thing for models."

"Dad, I'll be fine. I can protect myself. You know as well as I do that Catherine doesn't have anyone else. I can't leave until this is sorted out."

"You have to look out for yourself now, Makedde. God, that's so horrible. Have her foster parents been contacted?"

"Yes." The thought of the Unwins made Mak angry. They had been neglectful guardians, and Catherine had spent most of her time trying to get away from them. "I'm sure they're secretly relieved they don't have to look after her anymore. I wouldn't expect much of a service."

"That's an awful thing to say!"

"You know it's true."

"I'd like you to come home, Makedde." He paused. "You can take some other classes, or maybe do some modelling here for a month or two. You can't still be stubborn about your tuition after this has happened? I'll pay for it."

"I don't mean to hurt your pride, but I know you can't afford it, Dad." Her mother's death had been protracted and painful, and the medical bills wouldn't go away for a long time yet. Multiple Myloma was rare, and mostly found in fragile old men, so it wasn't often treated. But Jane was still young, so they tried every imaginable form of alternative therapy and chemotherapy over the years, and when those methods had been exhausted, a bone marrow transplant was the only option. Jane died of pneumonia in the end, when living in a bubble wasn't enough to protect her weakened immune system.

"Besides," Mak continued, shaking off the image of her bald mother hooked to machines, "I just got here. I don't think I could hack the flight back so soon. And even if you could pay, you know I wouldn't let you. Anyway, this isn't about scraping up some cash anymore. I can't leave until Catherine's killer is caught."

She heard him mumble, "Stubborn," under his breath before he said more clearly, "Is there anything I can do at this end?"

"Nothing. Please do nothing. I hate it when you meddle."

He ignored her reference. "Why don't you model somewhere else for a while? New Zealand is close."

"Nice try. You know I have to be here. Catherine was always there for me, and there is no one here for her now."

A barely audible sigh told her that she had won the debate, for now. She had always been too strong-headed for him to control. Their battle of the wills went way back. Although he had revelled in the undivided attention she gave his cop stories, even as an eight-year-old her boundless interest in crime worried him, as it did the rest of the family. He was perversely relieved when she started modelling at fourteen. Perhaps he was baffled now at her desire to pursue forensic psychology. Women were homemakers and supermums to his generation, not career types with Ph.D.s and a passion for the criminal psyche.

"Please be careful, Makedde. Don't take any chances. Promise me."

"I'll be fine, I promise," she assured him. "Anyway, I'm an Amazon. Any psycho would be crazy to mess with me."

"They *are* crazy, Makedde. That's the point."

"Not legally, they're not. Psychopaths may have a predatory, manipulative and violent predisposition, but they aren't legally insane."

"Knock it off."

She laughed. "Just buggin' you. I'll call soon and let you know what's happening. I love you, Dad."

"You too."

She hung up the receiver and drifted back into a fitful sleep.

She dreamt she was standing in tall grass, looking down at the bloodied, naked corpse of a young woman. Hair obscured the face, and as she pulled it back, she came face-to-face with her own lifeless features.

"*Makedde*," the wind whispered, "*I'm coming for you.*"

Makedde walked up the flight of stairs towards Book agency's huge, glass double doors, stopping briefly to preen in the mirrored wall that lined the stairwell. She studied her made-up face, noting the tired eyes and pale, stressed complexion. She practised a smile and was relieved that the effect was pleasing. Instantly she looked healthy, happy and confident. Looks were deceiving.

She stood outside for a moment and wondered whether she would be able to pull off the appearance of a successful model unaffected by a personal tragedy. No sense in letting them know she was devastated; they would probably insist she take some time off, and that wouldn't pay the bills. Lengthening her body, pulling her stomach in and fixing an indestructible smile, she stepped inside. She received a noncommittal raised eyebrow from the receptionist, who obviously didn't know her from a hole in the wall. Makedde could hardly have been offended; she didn't know the receptionist's name either.

"Is Charles Swinton in?" she asked.

"Yes, go on back." The nameless receptionist resumed reading a *Vogue* magazine on her desk.

Mak clutched her model bag and strode to the back area where ten booking agents, or "bookers", sat at a long oval table, handling various phone calls and dealing with the hopeful young things hovering about them. Each booker had a computer screen and keyboard, and a young model staring eagerly at the screen as they pushed buttons to determine who was working, and who was not.

Stacks of composite cards in holders lined every wall. An impossibly flawless face shone out from the cover of each card, with the words "Book Model Agency" printed boldly across the top, and the model's name printed across the bottom. The cards appeared to be organised in sections. The "Linda", "Christy", and "Claudia" type cards were in one section and the "Anna", "Louise", and "Makedde" type cards were on another wall. The categories may have represented who was in town and who wasn't, but Makedde suspected it indicated who would, or would not, get out of bed for less than ten thousand dollars.

In vain she tried to get Charles' attention but for the next fifteen minutes he remained resolutely absorbed in a constant stream of phone calls. He was a slick operator; smooth-talking and complimentary, but firm in negotiation. Charles had a reputation for being able to make or break a model's career. Such was his pull, many top models had followed him from another big agency when he quit and started up Book with a mysterious business partner. Mak was undecided as to whether or not Book would be good for her, but her mother agency, as each model's hometown agency is called, was quite enthusiastic about the arrangement. It had been a bit of a coup to have

Charles on-side, because he only handled the top girls. Her old *ELLE* and *Vogue* covers must have done the trick.

Finally he turned to her, the phone still glued to one ear. "Ah, Makedde. How did Friday go?"

It wasn't exactly the question she was expecting.

"Uh, fine. Except for my dead friend lying in the grass. Otherwise it was a breeze."

"Oh," he seemed embarrassed, "that's right. Poor Catherine. It's such a shame, she would have done so well. By the way, *Sixty Minutes* wants to interview you. Here's the number."

"Thanks," Mak answered bluntly. She took the slip of paper and tossed it into the wastepaper basket as soon as Charles turned his head.

"The client's not very happy," he went on. "They say they need to re-shoot now, and they're giving us grief about the money."

She felt her anger rise. *Catherine's dead, and they're mad because they didn't get their precious photo!*

Charles answered another call.

A female booker intervened, "I couldn't believe it when I heard what happened. How awful! She was so sweet."

Mak extended a hand. "I'm Makedde."

"Skye."

"I was just about to introduce you," Charles said absent-mindedly, and continued his phone conversation.

Mak flashed him a wooden smile and turned her attention to Skye. "You left a message on her answering machine. Were you Catherine's booker?"

"Yes."

"What was the message about?"

"She didn't make it to her last casting at Peter Lowe's studio. I wanted to reschedule the appointment."

"Did anyone see her leave for the casting?" Makedde pried gently. "Did she get a ride from anyone?"

"The cops asked me that, too. A few people saw her leave Saatchi's. She probably caught the bus."

"Did you see her much?"

"Not really. She spoke to me when she called in for her bookings, and I saw her every couple of weeks when she came in for a cheque. She was always kinda bubbly, but she never told me much about her goings on."

"Did she ever mention a boyfriend?"

"No. But we reckon she had one."

Mak perked up. "Why is that?"

"Oh, she didn't hang out with the other girls much. She had some nice jewellery, too. I don't know. We just figured." Skye seemed a little overwhelmed by the whole thing. "Did you know that Tony Thomas is being hounded by the cops? Probably because of that exhibition of his. It's pretty full on."

"What exhibition?"

"Oh, his S&M photo exhibition. I went to the opening. It's not my style, but some people think it's art."

Oh, really? "Is it still on?"

"It's at The Space in Kings Cross for a few weeks."

Makedde decided to give the exhibition a look.

It took her another ten minutes to get Charles' attention long enough to check her details for the following day. She found that she had no work to go to, but Charles suddenly remembered that they had just received a fax from her mother agency, Snap! Models back in Canada. He pointed to a tray full of faxes beside the machine.

She walked over and picked it out of the pile. Her name was scrawled in huge letters across the top of the cover letter. Barbara, the owner, was sending Mak condolences on the loss of her friend. It was a kind gesture, but how could she already know?

"Did someone tell them what happened to Catherine?" Makedde asked, puzzled.

"No. I don't think so," Skye said. "Catherine wasn't even with them, was she?"

"No she wasn't." So how did Barbara know already?

Dad.

She supposed he was already spreading the word to the appropriate people. He was taking care of things; looking out for his daughter, pooling resources. He was probably checking up on her, too.

Makedde took the fax with her and left. With the exception of a few of her favourite agencies, she knew that without ten thousand dollar bookings or a recent *Vogue* cover, a model becomes invisible. After thanking the table of bookers, the invisible woman made a quiet exit.

8

Catherine Gerber's lover was relieved to shut the door at midday and take his phone off the hook. He needed time to think. His daily lunch order sat untouched on the desk. He couldn't eat a bite; not out of grief but annoyance. They had not prepared exactly what he had asked for—a smoked salmon sandwich with capers, horseradish and lettuce on rye. Not on brown, on *rye*. It was simple. On any other day he would have complained bitterly about the brown bread. Today his appetite had been quashed when he glimpsed the morning paper. He couldn't think about food. His mind was on that photograph.

Catherine Gerber.

There had been an article about the murder every day since Catherine's body was discovered by that Vanderwall girl on Friday. That was fine. That was to be expected. It wasn't the article itself that worried him. It was the photo.

Stupid little bitch!

He had always been so careful, so meticulous. He had made sure that nothing could trace Catherine to him. He was sure no one of any importance had seen them together. It was crazy that such an ignominious little hussy could end up as such a threat.

He opened the newspaper, flipped it to page three and stared at the large photo featured in the article titled *Canadian Model—Third Victim of Stiletto Killer*. There she was, photographed at some social event, smiling innocently, wearing a low-cut dress with a thin necklace dangling around her throat, a dainty necklace with a man's diamond ring suspended from it.

His ring.

Lying little slut!

He'd assumed he'd lost it, but evidently that was not the case. It must have been when he met up with her in Fiji during the autumn medical convention. He had been careful, as always. He gave her cash for the ticket, they stayed in different hotels, and he snuck over to hers in the evening. When he left, he must have forgotten the ring by the sink. It was days after the convention before he realised it was gone. When he questioned her, she swore she'd never seen it.

Conniving, scheming tart . . .

It was an important ring. His father had awarded it to him and a precious few other top brass at the company. It meant that he had proven himself. Unlike his parasitic brothers, he had a future. One day it would all be his, and the ring proved it.

The ring . . .

He had even phoned the hotel and asked them to search everywhere. When his colleagues noticed that it was missing he had to make an excuse. "I lost it scuba diving in Fiji," he had told them. "Don't tell Dad."

No, I took it off to wash my hands in a hotel room, and the little trollop stole it.

A droplet of sweat rolled down his throbbing temple.

His pulse was racing. Everyone would see the article. If anyone looked close enough, they would recognise the ring. What if they made the connection? And the police; what if they found his ring among her possessions?

It has my damn initials engraved on it!

He wiped the sweat away, his blood pressure soaring.

Something had to be done. He needed to get that ring back.

9

There was no such thing as an "unintrusive" search, Makedde decided. The flat still felt like a crime scene. Any attempt the police had made to return the place to its original state had not been at all successful. Every object in the room was just a few precious inches out of position, the dark coffee table was grimy with white Lanconide and the cream-coloured kitchen cupboards were still sooty with carbon powder. Makedde was grateful that the flat wasn't her own. Cleaning it up would have been a far more traumatic process.

Mak set about rearranging the place and packing up Catherine's belongings. She started with the walls. One by one, she tore the magazine pin-ups down. Sticky tape ripped off in loud strips, leaving a tacky residue in their wake, the airbrushed faces of starry-eyed models shredding into meaningless ribbons of colour.

Catherine had naïvely aspired to become a "super-model". Of the many that tried, few lasted very long on the international scene, and even fewer made it to the big time. Mak had been the flavour of the month in Italian *Vogue* at one point, and enjoyed fleeting moments of fame as the face of numerous fashion and cosmetic campaigns, but she'd never quite fit the title of "super".

With the exception of Carmen, and perhaps Lauren Hutton, who both continued to do the occasional photo shoot several decades after they began in the business, a model's career was spectacularly brief. The transformation from fresh-faced fourteen-year-old to jaded twenty-five-year-old was as cradle to the grave to most in the industry. Makedde had seen countless girls come and go. In their fleeting time, some sacrificed more than others, and some achieved more than others, but for most the trip was ephemeral, and the fickle industry moved on. The trick was to take the money and run, but it was a strategy few young models understood.

Makedde reached up and tore another face from the wall.

When fifteen-year-old Catherine reached five-foot-nine, she had wanted to give international modelling a try. Mak had mixed feelings about her friend's aspirations. It would forever be a misunderstood lifestyle, reinforced by movies like *Prêt à Porter* and *Unzipped*, which portrayed the industry about as realistically as *Pretty Woman* portrayed prostitution. The international fashion scene could be harsh and confusing to a teenager, and the combination of a mismanaged career and a misguided soul could be disastrous. Everyone knew a horror story—sixteen-year-olds gliding down the catwalk zoned out on heroin; cigarette and coffee-dieting anorexics; bulimics; chronic diet pill—laxative pill—diuretic pill—upper—downer—*everything* pill poppers. The casting couch. It could become a deadly obstacle course for unchaperoned kids with poor self-images or little self-control.

On the flip side, many models enjoyed great experiences—travel, culture, new sights, new languages, new people, and occasionally, lots and lots of money.

Knowing all that, what do you do when someone you know wants to give it a shot?

In Makedde's case you help in every way you can, and try to guide them away from the pitfalls. With a six-year gap in age and experience, she showed Catherine the ropes, leading her through the bizarre maze of international modelling. She bailed Cat out of trouble on several occasions, but it seemed she wasn't there for her when it really mattered.

One day too late.

She crunched the magazine photos tightly in her hand, shoved them into a large garbage bag and walked over to the neat stack of Catherine's clothes. The Unwins, Cat's foster parents, had made it clear that they had no use for the clothes. The police had no use for them either. Mak would take them to a women's charity and ship the remainder of the belongings back to Canada.

She had never met Catherine's birth parents, and was thankful they never lived to see their only child cut up like that, cold and lifeless on a morgue tray. With her eyes closed, Makedde placed the stack of garments into a fresh garbage bag. She didn't want to see any familiar clothes. One glimpse of a moss green jumper had brought memories flooding back of Catherine smiling and laughing in Munich, treating herself to a shopping spree for landing her first big hair commercial.

With the clothes ready in bags for charity, she turned her attention to the ornate, antique jewellery box that sat beside the mirror. Catherine's cherished jewellery box. It was made of wood, intricately carved and embellished with swirling designs and bright, luminous semi-precious stones. It was a sentimental reminder of Catherine's true mother, one of the few tangible things which had remained of her. It was small, and Catherine had travelled with it wherever she went. Alison Gerber had given it to her daughter only months before she and Catherine's father drove over the Malahat to visit a friend. The Malahat cuts for miles through the mountains of Vancouver Island in a steep and winding highway. Sometime during the night, as they made their way home, their car hit black ice and slid off the road, rolling down the mountainside for five hundred feet before lodging in the pines. Both parents died before the wreck was discovered. Catherine was being baby-sat at home. She was five.

Makedde sat cross-legged on the hard wooden floor, placed the jewellery box in her lap and opened it. It was small, and its contents few. Some thin necklaces, silver and gold, were tangled inside. A pair of delicate, diamond stud earrings, and a turquoise and silver ring were jumbled underneath. But it was the thick diamond ring that immediately caught Mak's attention.

She fished the ring out. It was a chunky men's style, with a pattern of diamonds set in its square design. The gold was smooth and unmarked. It couldn't have belonged to Catherine's father; it was too new. Where else would she get a ring like this?

The lover.

The lover's ring. A souvenir. She turned the ring over and looked inside its band. She couldn't believe her luck.

JT.

The initials were engraved on the inside of the ring. She recalled the notepad message she had seen when she first arrived.

JT Terrigal
Beach res
16
14

Makedde slipped the ring on her thumb. It was solid proof of the relationship, but she was no longer sure that she cared to share it with Detective Flynn. She placed the jewellery box on her bedside table and leant her favourite photo against it. Makedde's face smiled out from the photo, standing beside a happy, living Catherine.

10

He licked his lips distractedly, one hand flexing slowly while the other held the photograph.

Makedde Vanderwall.

Makedde.

Mak.

She was the blonde in the photograph. Beautiful. Special. She was the one who'd written the letter. The one who had found his handiwork at the beach. Her eyes were light, although from the photograph he could not tell if they were green or blue. Her nose was slim and straight, her body curvaceous, and she was *so* familiar.

And her skin. Her skin looked so . . . perfect.

Utterly perfect.

He was annoyed that he couldn't tell what her feet looked like from the photo. She was cut off at the hips. But she looked so tall standing next to Catherine that he convinced himself she was wearing high, vermilion stilettos. He just knew her feet would be as perfect as the rest of her.

Her familiarity drew him in; she was magnetic, more special and important than any of his other girls.

Makedde was the one.

He traced his finger slowly over the face of the photo-graph. Destiny brought the dark-haired whore to him. Destiny brought Makedde with her.

11

Makedde held a black skirt in front of her at the full-length mirror, trying to decide what to wear to The Space nightclub. She cocked her head to one side and eyed the hem.

Too short?

If she wore opaque stockings with it, the skirt would be fine. With a miniskirt and her shimmery, deep blue top, she would blend into the clubbing atmosphere. She slid dark stockings over her bare legs, careful not to catch them on her nails, and pulled the skirt over her hips. To complete the look, she chose a pair of comfortable, mid-heeled boots that laced up to her calves. She threw a coat on, checked her pockets for cash and switched the lights off. Venturing into the night alone made her a little nervous. She would have liked a good can of Canadian Bear Spray to carry with her, but that was illegal in Australia. She'd have to rely on quick thinking or a wicked snap kick.

Makedde followed the thundering dance music from almost a block away, arriving outside The Space close to midnight when things were just starting to heat up.

The hip and nocturnal had come out of the woodwork,

rowdy and ready to play. Leather, PVC, micro-minis and fishnets appeared to be the uniform of the moment. Mak felt pretty tame in her carefully chosen apparel.

A queue of about thirty clubbers snaked away from the entrance. As soon as Makedde joined the end of the line, a tall hulk of testosterone with a buzz cut called her up to the front. After glancing around to confirm that it was indeed her that he was motioning to, she sashayed up to the door and gave him a sultry smile. There was no sense in waiting in line if it wasn't necessary.

"You a model?" he grunted. He stank of cigarettes and cheap cologne.

"Yes."

He eyed her approvingly, which made her skin crawl, but her smile never faltered.

"Which agency?"

"Book," she replied.

With the magic words spoken, he opened the door. As she stepped cautiously into the smoke-filled nightclub, he mumbled something incoherent and shut the heavy door behind her. Her senses were immediately assaulted by a high decibel pounding dance mix and a throng of sweating bodies grooving to its beat. A long, neon illuminated bar held four busy, steroid-inflated bartenders in skimpy black leather vests. She wondered for a moment whether she had stumbled upon a real S&M party, but on surveying the dancing crowd she determined that it was probably just a trend, and she would not at any moment be whisked away for a spanking.

Squinting through the smoke she spotted what she had come for—the photos. A display area towards the back presented large black-and-white prints. She weaved through the whirling crowd and made her way towards them. When she looked down to pull her skirt further down her thighs, she caught a flying elbow hard in the jaw. It could have been any one of a number of the flailing limbs of several people crushing against her. Fists up at her face in a protective boxing position, she continued towards the far wall. When she finally broke through the other side of the dancing mob she discovered more people, seated at a series of tables, attempting conversations that consisted of little more than hand movements. It was a relief to stop moving, so she simply stood still for a moment, and instantly regretted it.

Someone grabbed her by the shoulder.

Makedde inhaled sharply at the surprise and spun around to look down at the man's face. Her fist was clenched and ready in case she needed it, her whole body tensed. It took several seconds to register who it was.

"Oh, Tony. How are you?" She hoped she managed not to sound frightened by his sudden appearance.

"Good. How ya goin'?" he shouted above the din, sending a cloud of stale beer breath into Mak's nostrils.

"Fine. I heard about the exhibition. The agency's raving about it," she said.

"Really?" His face lit up. "Have you seen it all?"

"No, I just got here."

"Let me take you through it."

She managed a smile, and he led her by the hand to the first of the photos. Makedde felt decidedly uncomfortable. She wanted to know why Tony's exhibit had caused such suspicion, but she hadn't expected a personal tour.

She ran through a series of excuses in her head: *I have friends waiting? I have an early morning photo shoot? I'm allergic to smoke?* Then why had she come here? *Good question.*

The first photo immediately answered her questions about his exhibition. It depicted a young, naked woman, trussed in thick rope. Her long brunette hair was brushed forward over her face, and ropes circling her head held her mane in place. The faceless body was so tightly bound that the rope bit painfully into the woman's flesh.

Makedde was at a loss for words.

"That's Josephine. She's a professional dancer," Tony boasted.

She answered his questioning look with a neutral smile. He led her to the next print.

"This one is Josephine, again."

He stared at Makedde's expression as she studied the print. It featured the same faceless physique, hands tied behind the woman's back, bound in a restricting, leather corset and impossibly high stilettos. Her feet were so arched with the shape of the shoes that her ankles seemed to bend over her toes. The woman's breasts were popping out over the top of the leather, and her naked hips bulged under the strain of the tiny corset. The body was contorted into an agonising, silent struggle with its bonds. Rather than arousing, the effect was disturbing. A little playful bondage didn't trouble Makedde. But this clear depiction of deliberate pain was troubling.

Sadistic fantasies. How far does he take it in real life?

"I love what you've done with the developing," she commented vaguely. "The sepia and tobacco tones complement the mood nicely . . ."

"Thank you," he exclaimed proudly. "I felt that it brought out the texture of the leather in this shot." He slurred his words slightly, turning the word "texture" into "testya". He didn't bother correcting himself.

The police were giving Tony trouble for good reason. He had arranged the location for the La Perouse shoot and may have known Makedde's connection to Catherine. He also had a definite predilection for paraphilia. She needed to know more.

After perusing the stylishly displayed images of bondage, dominance, and sadomasochistic sex which made up the remainder of the exhibition, she sat down with him at one of the tables. With a fresh beer in one hand Tony loudly went on about how the police "wouldn't know art if it crept up their trouser legs and bit them where it matters".

"Tony, I remember you were arguing with a detective after Catherine was found. He was holding your camera. What was that all about?" she asked him casually.

"What a prick. Detective Wynn—"

"Flynn?"

"That's right. That wanker took all my film from the shoot as evidence. The client freaked."

"No kidding? Why would he want the film?"

Tony was obviously still upset about it. "Fucked if I know." His face twitched as he spoke. "What a fuckin' prick."

What are you hiding, Tony?

"Are they still on your case?"

"Yeah." He changed the subject. "So you're from Canada, *eh*?"

"*Eh*. That's very good." If she had a dollar for every time someone had made a joke about a Canadian expression, she'd be a very rich woman. "So, did you see much of Catherine before she . . . died?"

"Nah. You out here with anyone?"

Makedde could see it coming.

"No," she said honestly.

"Hmmm," he murmured. She could see his inebriated mind slowly clicking over. "Would you be interested in doing a test sometime? We could shoot whatever you wanted; head shots, body shots, whatever."

"Oh, no. I have plenty of shots in my book at the moment. Thanks anyway." Makedde pushed back her chair. "I've gotta get goin', uh . . . early shoot tomorrow morning."

"Want to go out sometime? Maybe—"

She swiftly cut him off. "I'm involved with someone."

Myself.

"We could just go for coffee or something," he persisted.

She was up and walking away as she repeated, "No thanks."

From behind her she heard him say, "I didn't kill the stupid bitch, for fuck's sake."

She shot him a hard look over one shoulder, and hissed, "I'm leaving." She forced her way through the crowd. Behind her, she could hear Tony shouting, "I'm sorry, Macayly! I didn't mean that! I'm sorry!"

"It's *Makedde*, you jerk," she mumbled, pushing past the mass of dancing bodies. "Ma—kay—dee."

She hurled herself out the front doors and into the crisp, night air. The cool wind whipping down the street was a welcome relief. She shook her head and hailed the nearest taxi. In under an hour, Tony had managed to insert himself at the top of Makedde's growing "arsehole list".

Just after 2 a.m. the taxi deposited Makedde outside the block of flats on Campbell Parade. She tipped the driver and dragged herself out of the taxi, still brooding over Tony's flippant comment. She was too tired to think straight. Whether it was jet lag or the hour, she was running out of battery strength like an old toy winding down.

She noted the ugly odour of stale smoke hanging in her hair as she opened the door from the street and stepped inside. Wearily, she stomped up the steps, intent on the thought of her warm bed.

Wait—I didn't leave the lights on.

Makedde backed up, nearly tripping over her feet, then froze flush against the wall. Someone was in her flat. She could hear movement. Silently, she covered her mouth, as if it would somehow silence her breath. She listened.

Someone was in there.

Killer.

Who? It didn't take long to decide that she didn't want to meet her intruder alone and she tiptoed back down the creaking stairs as quietly as she could manage. What if the intruder heard her? What would he do to her? Did he expect that she'd be out this time of the night, or did he want her to be at home, sleeping?

She started to run.

Makedde burst out onto the street and ran full tilt towards the public phone booth. When she reached it she decided it was too close, and she kept on running.

At the far north end of Bondi Beach, Mak nervously dialled Detective Flynn's mobile number. She didn't feel like explaining her life story to some triple "0" operator, or perhaps she enjoyed having an excuse to wake Flynn up in the wee hours. Either way, after two rings his phone was answered. For a moment there was no voice, then a coarse, sleep-fuggy sound filtered through the line.

"Flynn."

"Detective Flynn, I'm sorry to wake you," *or not,* "I have an emergency. Uh, the detectives didn't come back to search some more, did they?"

"What? No." He paused. "This is Makedde, right?"

"Yes. I didn't think they'd come back at such a weird hour," she said stupidly. "Someone has broken into my flat. They're in there right now."

He suddenly sounded more awake. "Where are you? Are you OK?"

"Yes. I didn't go inside. The lights were on when I came home a few minutes ago. I ran to a phone in the street."

"You did the right thing. Tell me where you are and I'll have someone there in a few minutes."

Mak explained her location and hung up. She slid down the booth wall and sat on the cold, concrete floor. Her dark stockings had a long gash up the thigh. Smoky grit seemed wedged under her fingernails and embedded in her skin.

Within minutes a police cruiser pulled up. The driver was a sharp-looking female cop with short blonde hair and thin lips. Her partner was a beefy young officer with a face like a meat lover's pizza. He looked like he would be quite tall and foreboding when he stood up, which made Mak feel safe under the circumstances. She climbed into the back and the officers asked her what happened. Briefly, she explained the situation and mentioned her involvement in the Gerber murder case.

Makedde scanned the road. The streets were deserted, as one would expect after 2 a.m. on a Monday night in the middle of winter. She nestled deep into the back seat as they drove towards her building, and when they got close she saw that the lights were still on.

"Which flat is yours?" the male officer asked.

"The only one with the lights on. Number six."

"Could we have your keys, Miss?"

Makedde handed them over, and the officers locked the car and walked across the street while Mak sunk herself as deeply as she could into the seat. She rested her nose against the window and stared out, watching the two uniformed cops enter her building. The lit window revealed no figures, and she could hear no sounds of struggle. Eventually, the street door opened and the female officer stepped out. She came up to the car while Makedde got out.

"There's no one in the flat, Miss. It may have been rifled through, though. It's hard to tell."

Makedde was almost sorry that they hadn't found anyone. She felt a bit embarrassed, as if she might have been tired enough to forget whether she had left the lights on or not. She was sure she'd heard movement. *Wasn't she?*

Exhausted, she climbed the stairs, aware that the run in her stockings had ripped up another few inches. Door number six was open, and just as she was about to chastise herself for overreacting, Makedde caught a glimpse of the flat.

The place had been turned upside down.

All the bags of clothes she'd packed up were emptied out on the floor. The beds were ripped apart and every drawer and cupboard was open. Catherine's jewellery box was overturned, and it looked broken. Sweaters, jeans and underwear were scattered everywhere, strewn about with papers and jewellery.

"You weren't sure if I'd been broken into?" Mak asked in disbelief.

The blonde cop turned to her and said, "We couldn't be sure. You'd be surprised the way some people live."

12

When Detective Flynn arrived, Makedde Vanderwall was sitting on the floor of the flat. She was in a miniskirt, her legs splayed slightly in a totally unselfconscious position. She was leaning against the wall, eyes closed, with a small jewellery box in her hands.

"Miss Vanderwall?" he asked tentatively.

Her eyes snapped open at the sound of her name, and he noticed the dark, smudged make-up. She didn't appear as untouchable as she had at the police station on Sunday. Sitting there in the ransacked flat, she looked vulnerable and lonely. He regretted treating her so flippantly. Maybe his partner Jimmy was right; his wife was making him an arsehole around women.

"Hi," she said in a rough voice. "I'm sorry to have dragged you out of bed, but I wasn't expecting all this when I got home. I guess I panicked."

"No, no. You were right to call me. Tell me what happened."

She explained the evening's events in a resigned and dispirited tone.

"Have you noticed anything missing?"

"I couldn't say at the moment."

"You know, we can't assume this is related to your friend's death—"

"Murder."

"What?"

"She didn't just die, she was murdered."

"Right. Well, we can't assume the two are related. There are a lot of break-ins around here, especially in these older buildings." He didn't want her panicking any further. It was unlikely that the killer would come after her.

"Well, they didn't take the television or anything. Then again, I would have left that heap of junk too." She cracked a tight-lipped smile, then looked down at the ornate box in her lap.

He noticed that she was wearing a thick diamond ring on her thumb. He couldn't remember seeing it at the station. "Nice ring," he said. "Where did you get it?"

She eyed him suspiciously, and he had the odd feeling that she was evaluating him, deciding something. When she didn't speak, he said, "I want to apologise if I was flippant with you on Sunday."

She gave him a hard look. "Yes, you were flippant."

She was so direct, he didn't know what to say for a moment. "You look tired. Do you have somewhere else to stay the night?"

"No. I'll stay here tonight. They wouldn't return with cops crawling all over. They probably have what they want anyhow." He raised an eyebrow at her. What did she think they had? "They were either burglars or souvenir hunters after a piece of Catherine."

Flynn was a little surprised. She was probably right, but he hadn't expected her to understand that.

"We could help you—"

"No, I don't want your help," she said suddenly. "I'll stay here tonight." She glanced at her watch. "Or rather, I'll stay here the rest of this morning. I was planning on getting up in less than four hours anyway."

"Well, we'll send someone over to speak to you tomorrow. We might need to dust again."

"I doubt they would have left prints."

Andy looked at her curiously. She was reacting strangely. Did she know something? "Why is that, Miss Vanderwall?"

"The place is obviously coated in powder. Anyone with half a brain would wear gloves. You don't have to be a detective to figure that out."

"You're assuming this person has brains." He turned and started towards the door. "We'll see you in the morning."

She surprised him by saying, "Have a good sleep."

"You too," he replied, and he meant it. He was slightly unnerved by her fortitude. Or was she simply being stubborn because of how he'd treated her?

Whatever the case, it was already past 3.30 a.m. and it was time to leave the girl in peace.

Detective Flynn arrived at the office the next morning to find a huge, sixteen-by-twenty photograph of Makedde Vanderwall, dressed in nothing but a brief aqua-blue bikini, pinned to the bulletin board. Someone had circled her breasts and drawn nipples in bright red felt pen. Andy stopped and stared at it through puffy eyes. He heard restrained chortling behind him.

"Well, that's . . ." he was at a loss for words, "that's art." He admired the unbridled display of immaturity for another moment, and then began untacking it.

"No, no." Jimmy got up and walked towards him. "She stays."

Jimmy Cassimatis was Andy's partner of four years. He

was also a friend. The "Stiletto Murders", as the case had now been dubbed, was one of the biggest either of them had worked on in their careers. With three murders so far, Jimmy's delinquent sense of humour was a welcome respite from the pressure. He was known for doing the most appalling things at the morgue, so doodling on photographs was nothing.

Andy Flynn was more serious about his career in the police force. He was more ambitious. He had been raised in the safe suburbs of Parkes, where residents possessed only the most abstract concept of crime. The main concern on his block was kids nicking your tricycle if you left it on your front lawn. Like most of the public, it didn't occur to anyone that there could be a killer next door, or a paedophile teaching at the primary school.

The local cops may not have been under pressure to control any soaring crime problem, but Andy sure noticed the small town appreciation. There was a pretty girl who worked in the corner deli, and she always had the biggest smile for Sergeant Morris. All the kids wanted to catch a glimpse of his gun, and his uniform commanded respect. By then, the police already appealed, but it wasn't until a sensational case in 1974, however, that Andy's dream of joining the police force really took form. Three men were murdered and Scottish-born Archie "Mad Dog" McCafferty was brought to trial. He claimed that the voice of his dead six-week-old son had told him to kill seven men so that he could live again. People were fascinated and repelled by the case, and all that interest wasn't lost on eleven-year-old Andy. It seemed to him that the cops and the killers were playing at a different level. There was so much at stake, and such importance placed on their actions. He wanted to be part of it. He joined as soon as he graduated from school, and eventually found his way to the city, where the real action was.

"I hope you weren't planning on entertaining yourself with that for long," Flynn warned, with one finger poking at Makedde's navel. "Because the real thing will be walking in here at some point, and I'm quite sure she'd castrate me on the spot if she saw that."

"Ah, ya pousti! Don't ya like girls?" Jimmy laughed, blocking Andy's half-hearted attempts to take the photo down. "She had quite a night with that B and E."

"Tell her next time, she can call *me* in the middle of the night. I'll help her out." He winked. "Actually, Angie would have lost it. Especially if she knew it was that model."

She would have. Angie Cassimatis was a bit touchy about that sort of thing, but then, she had reason to be. Jimmy was no Brad Pitt, far from it, but he had still managed to get it on with a young constable in the not-so-distant past. It had filtered through the grapevine and Angie found out from a friend of a friend, who just happened to be the cousin of the girl he was having the affair with. It was like a game of telephone gone wrong. Big trouble. They smashed plates at their wedding, but Andy could bet that a helluva lot more was broken when Angie had found out. The young lady in question was somehow transferred to Melbourne after that, and Jimmy arrived at work with a mysterious bruise on his cheek the size of Angie's hand.

Jimmy read his thoughts. "Skata! Once, OK? Once. Are you saying you're some fucking saint? Cause I know you're not."

"No I'm not. Let's drop the subject. Just promise me you'll take the photo down before the wrong person sees it."

Jimmy didn't answer him, but a mischievous smirk flickered across his lips.

"Where'd you get it anyway?"

"The film confiscated from the photo shoot."

Andy shook his head.

"I've just been to forensics," Jimmy began, getting back to business. "They're satisfied we've got the same killer in all three cases. No copycats. So maybe we're finally gonna get somewhere with Kelley."

Detective Inspector Kelley had rejected their request for more backup, even after Catherine, the third victim, was discovered. Luckily, all three fell into their jurisdiction, so the connection between the crimes was made early. Once a pattern was established, the added resources could be more easily rationalised. Inquiries were still being made in search of similar offences in other states, but so far, nothing conclusive had come up.

"Same hammer type. Plus, as you said, same signature. We all agree, at least unofficially, that we've got some serial psycho on our hands," Jimmy said.

Andy nodded and paused. *A serial psycho.* All the DNA evidence in the world wouldn't help if the killer was random, as signature killers often were. He had to hope there was some relationship between the girls, some common link.

"Roxanne Sherman; eighteen, prostitute. Cristelle Crawford; twenty-one, prostitute and stripper." Andy looked at the victims' photos as he spoke, and their eyes stared back at him in a silent communication that he could not decipher.

"What were they like?" he said to no one in particular. "Aggressive? Passive? What turned him on?"

Andy had the habit of talking to himself from time to time, and it was a bit of a joke around Homicide. He supposed it had started with sleeptalking and an active imagination as a kid, but in brainstorming sessions like these, when major crimes needed to be solved, he found that verbalising his mental gymnastics worked well. Sometimes a detective would take him to task on a theory he wasn't even aware he'd said aloud.

"Attractive," he mumbled under his breath, still staring at their images. Pretty, smiling photos of each girl contrasted with their gory crime scenes—photographs of blood and mutilation. Decomposition. Wasted flesh. Wasted lives.

"Some would have wanted to take them under their wing, but our guy wanted to violate them." He thought about that. The victims were practically kids. Kids in heavy make-up. He spoke aloud as much for his own benefit as that of his partner. "The ages and professions are all similar. Late teens/early twenties. Then he goes for an overseas model. Does this blow your hooker-hater theory out of the water?"

"We haven't found the clothes, apart from the shoes," Jimmy replied. "The model one could've been dressed sexy and he thought she was for sale. She rejects him, and *whammo*," Jimmy slammed his thick palms together to illustrate one of his favourite words, "the malaka grabs her."

Andy considered the scenario. "He gets her alone without anyone seeing anything suspicious. The other two might have gone somewhere with him willingly if they thought he was a legitimate John, but not this one. Plus, she was young and healthy. If she put up a fight someone might have seen or heard something. She had no defensive wounds, only the ligature marks on her wrists and ankles. So it appears he got her into those binds without much trouble. Maybe we're looking for someone in a position of trust." He reached for a steaming cup of black coffee; his second of the morning. "Or a charming Bundy type. Did Colin find anyone at the dump site?"

"Ah, just a few residents, people walking their dogs, nothing unusual."

He was disappointed. They had hoped the killer would return to the site to relive the murder.

"Let's say they're strangers," Jimmy suggested. "What makes him choose *them* over all the other birds walking around?"

"The shoes?"

"Lots of 'em wear heels," Jimmy pointed out.

"Contact the model agency and find out if Catherine frequented any nightclubs, bars, anything like that. Maybe he spotted the girls in a common area, followed them home, waited for the right moment. Maybe he hunts in a certain patch and Catherine walked down the wrong street."

"My guess is the Cross. That's where The Space is."

"Possible."

Jimmy scribbled in his notebook, then looked to Andy, his face unusually serious. "Do you think there are more?"

"The violence has escalated, the mutilation has escalated, and there doesn't seem to be a pattern for the dates that he kills. He could be on a spree, so I wouldn't be surprised if he's killed before but he covered his tracks better. There are more than a few missing persons that fit his victim type."

"He won't stop."

Andy nodded his head in sad agreement. "Not unless we catch him first."

13

Makedde shifted on the bed. Not in it, but *on* it. She hadn't slipped between the sheets, and she hadn't slept a wink. Since the cops left hours earlier, she had sat on top of the bedclothes, practically motionless, fully dressed, and unable, or unwilling, to rest.

She's dead.

It seemed at that moment that there wasn't a single safe place in the world. Not a fortress, not a room, not a corner, not one single square inch of security.

If it isn't a killer, it's a disease. Your own body killing itself off. Eating itself up.

Perhaps that was why she didn't feel the urge to go home, or move. What would it change? The world would still be the same, wherever she was. She had decided not to tell her father about the break-in. He would be worried enough as it was. Like the cops said, it was unrelated. An unfortunate coincidence. Just another attempt by the world to rip her away from her carefully preserved sanity.

I'm not going to do it. I'm not going to freak out.

She realised that sitting for hours on the bed, staring

into the dark room had perhaps been a bit self-indulgent. Then she snapped out of it. It was morning, the sun was up, and she should run. She would get her blood pumping and deal with it. She would deal with it like she had everything else. There was no choice.

It was a beautiful, still morning on Bondi Beach, and Makedde ran hard, cutting a determined and cathartic swath through the serenity. Her legs churned up the pavement beneath her, faster and faster as if she could somehow escape the world crumbling around her. She felt as though she'd lost everyone; everyone except her father. Her privacy had been invaded. She wasn't sure about what to do, or what to think, but she knew she didn't want to run away.

No obvious forced entry.

That fact rattled her. It seemed odd, but the cops assured her that it would be fairly easy to break in cleanly. They said the locks were cheap. But why would anyone break in and not take anything? It just didn't make sense, unless it was someone hunting for souvenirs. Some weirdo who was willing to go to great lengths to get a piece of Catherine. Crisp, salt air filled her lungs as she ran the last leg of her rapid circuit from Bondi to Bronte, and a stunning view rewarded her efforts as she came up over Mark's Park. Despite her lack of sleep, her body responded well to her commands. Running was like a meditation; a chance to think, and at least try and piece together life's little mysteries.

She was sure the dipsomaniacal photographer Tony Thomas was hiding something when they talked at The Space. She wondered whether the kind of man who murdered and mutilated young women was also the kind who blatantly displayed his fetishes in public. In fiction, Tony wouldn't have been the prime suspect to a seasoned reader;

he was too obvious. But in real life, criminals were not always so clever. Whether it was lack of intelligence, or lack of discipline, they often left the proverbial bloody trail to their own front door. She would have to consider Tony very dangerous.

And what about Detective Flynn? On Sunday she could have wrung his neck, but now he didn't seem to be quite such an arsehole. How much would Flynn be willing to divulge about the progress of the investigation?

Makedde advanced swiftly past the Bondi Icebergs swimming club and cut left across Campbell Parade. On this Tuesday morning traffic was slow, and the brisk winter day attracted only a handful of hard-core surfers to the beach. She slowed down to a fast walk on the footpath, stretching her arms in big whooping circles. It felt good to sweat out her frustration—and her fear. She let herself into the block of flats, leaping up the stairs two by two until she reached the front door. A wildly flashing answering machine greeted her as she entered.

"Oooh," she breathed, "somebody loves me."

She wiped the sweat out of her eyes and pressed the "messages" button, then walked in lazy circles to cool off. The first message consisted only of a series of nondescript noises and the sound of a receiver hanging up. A beep declared message number two, which sounded the same. This repeated itself several times until she finally found a voice on the recording.

"Makedde, this is Charles. *Weekly News* magazine have been trying to reach you for an exclusive interview. If you're interested, call Rebecca on her mobile . . ."

Poor Catherine is still selling magazines, she thought sadly. The machine clicked to the next message.

"Makedde Vanderwall? This is Tony Thomas."

Oh no.

"Hey," the message went on, "I'm sorry about last night. I get a bit stupid when I have a few drinks . . ."

How did he get this number?

He sounded just as relentless when sober. "Could we meet for lunch today? Please? I know you're not working."

"Thanks Charles," Makedde said, fuming.

"We've got to talk. I insist. I'll be around at 1.30 p.m."

What?!

Maddeningly, the message ended without him leaving a phone number so she could tell him off. Makedde was furious. How dare her agency give out her number and let Tony know where she was staying! She yanked her running shoes off and hurled them across the room. The phone started to ring, and by the time she picked it up she was practically foaming at the mouth.

"I don't know who the hell you think you are, but you can't just invite yourself over to . . ." she trailed off as doubt crept into her mind. The caller was silent on the other end. "Uh, to whom am I speaking?" she asked with a hint of cautious embarrassment.

"This is Detective Flynn."

Now she was really embarrassed.

"I was expecting someone else."

"I sure hope so," he said with a laugh. "I'm just calling to thank you for coming in with the information about the affair. I also wanted to see if you're OK after last night."

To what do I owe this back flip? "Oh. Yes, I'm fine. Tired but fine. Any news?"

"No. No news."

He sounded a bit too friendly, and he didn't seem like the social type. She took a wild guess. "You're about to tell me something I won't like," she said.

"Well, we aren't dusting again. We figure it was a standard break-in. There's been a rash of them lately."

"Uh-huh."

"And we'd like you to come in for a set of elimination prints."

"No great surprise. So what you're telling me is that the priority has shifted and any possibility that the break-in may be related to Catherine's death is not going to be explored at all. Brilliant. My confidence is growing daily."

"It's highly unlikely that the break-in is related. There's not much we can do, and considering that you didn't lose any valuables . . ." He changed the subject. "Can you come in to be printed today? I'll be here until quite late."

"Yes. I can make it in the late afternoon."

"Great. I'll be here. Thanks again—"

"So," she quickly interjected, "you confiscated the film from Tony Thomas' camera?"

"Yes," he answered cautiously.

"Anything unusual on the film?"

"I can't discuss the details of the investigation, Miss Vanderwall."

Makedde rolled her eyes. "Look, I'm a model. I've got to work with this guy. If he's a sicko, I want to know about it. Besides, you owe me one. Quid pro quo, Detective."

There was a long pause, then he said with a touch of mirth, "A Thomas Harris fan, I see. Only, I'm hardly Hannibal Lecter. I can only pass on what I am permitted to, and I don't require your darkest secrets in exchange. There is a certain protocol."

"Well, thanks," she said sarcastically. "Anyway, I'm off to a photo shoot now. Shooting some lingerie with Tony Thomas . . ." She waited for a response.

The line was silent, then in a near-whisper he said, "He took photographs of the body before the police arrived."

Makedde's jaw dropped. "My God."

"We're doing all we can," Andy continued, clearly deciding that he'd said too much. "That's all I can tell you." It sounded like a pre-recorded statement. She knew she was getting to him, just a little bit, and she wasn't willing to let go.

"I just want to know that this guy will be stopped. If he's killed like this twice before, he'll do it again."

She heard a barely audible sigh.

"Don't believe everything you read. We don't know anything for sure at this point."

"Bullshit. You *know* he's done this before," she challenged angrily, "probably more than twice. It takes years to build up to that sort of mutilation. Clearly this is a signature case. Guys like this don't just stop; they perfect their MO and find new ways to get off."

"It's possible—" he paused. "What sort of books do you read in your spare time, anyway?"

She ignored his query. "Catherine was a friend. I saw what was done to her. I won't feel safe until *you* find this guy." The line was silent. She had hit her mark.

Andy's voice was slow and resolute. "We'll do everything we can."

She wanted to believe him.

14

There were several unusual elements in the "Stiletto Murders", and as the days dragged on, Detective Flynn had become more and more obsessed with re-analysing and re-interpreting the evidence. He knew that in signature killings, every violent and perverse detail of the crime scene and victimology offered potentially valuable insights into the killer's personality. However, Catherine Gerber's murder provided few clues, and many more questions.

He had spent all morning poring over the facts yet again, trying unsuccessfully to join up any personal or professional link between the three known victims. It seemed that they had a random killer on their hands; the hardest type to catch.

"Any thoughts on the condom thing?" Andy asked out of the blue, as Jimmy walked past his desk carrying his lunch, which reeked of garlic and onions.

"I reckon this malaka plans to kill 'em the moment he lays eyes on 'em," Jimmy replied. "So he's using the skins for his own reasons." He stopped and leant on Andy's desk, biting into a gyro sandwich. Tzatziki oozed out of the pita bread, down his fingers to his wrists. Jimmy was oblivious. "If my hooker-hater theory is right my friend," he said with his mouth full, "maybe he's afraid of AIDS. That could be another reason he likes them young."

"There's blood everywhere," Andy pointed out. "If STDs or HIV was his concern, he would take other precautions as well. Maybe he does. I've got the feeling he doesn't want to leave semen because he's familiar with forensic procedure. Half these guys study fuckin' law enforcement and forensics when they're inside."

"Yeah. Such a wise use of their time."

"And our money. So you figure he's got a record."

"Possibly."

The two detectives stood silently.

"Where does he do 'em, Andy? He'd look like a fuckin' abattoir worker by the time he was finished. He can't have a wife, I wouldn't think."

Andy stared at the running board; at the dead faces of Roxanne, Cristelle and Catherine. Makedde's impressive physique threatened to distract him completely. Suddenly the red pen marking her body looked like blood. He turned away.

"He doesn't bother taking the jewellery, which is a common souvenir, and he only takes one shoe, not both. So he's not giving them to his wife as a sick gift or anything. You're right, he probably lives alone. But we can't assume that. The other clothes are missing. What does he do with them?"

Jimmy didn't have an answer.

"There's some parallel here to the Jerome Brudos case," Andy said.

"Brudos?"

"Jerome Henry Brudos. As a pre-teen in Oregon in the States he abducted younger girls at knife-point. He dragged them off to the family barn and made them strip. Then he'd take some photos. He'd lock them up in some shed, and a few minutes later he'd come back and pretend he was his twin brother Ed. He changed his clothes, hair, everything for this, and then he'd pretend to be horrified at what his 'deranged sibling' had done. He'd even make a big show of destroying the film in the camera, and he'd make the girl promise she wouldn't tell." Andy paused. "There's bound to be some infraction, however minor, to indicate deviant tendencies in our killer's youth. I'm surprised Tony's past didn't bring up anything."

"Best precursor of violence is past violence," Jimmy said. "Most people wouldn't know what to look for, though. Getting into fights after school attracts a lot more attention than quietly dissecting household pets."

Andy could hear Jimmy's stomach rumble. "Finish your sandwich."

Jimmy took a fist-sized bite out of one corner and more tzatziki flowed down his chin. Chewing lustily he said, "So what'd this Brudos guy do when he got older?"

"He became the Stiletto Killer," Andy said, grinning.

Jimmy laughed, and gestured at his groin. "Here, mate. Right here."

"Actually, he advertised for models to come and model shoes and pantyhose for him. They ended up dead, hanging from his garage. He'd photograph them nude or in frilly clothes and high-heeled shoes. Always high heels."

"Parallels? You're not kidding. Our photographer would have all kinds of young birds around, willing to have their photos taken."

"Exactly. 'Trust me, I'm a photographer'."

As Jimmy started to walk back to his desk, Andy said, "The weird thing about Brudos, well, apart from the obvious, is that he *did* have a wife. She never went in the garage."

"Sounds like Angie."

"He kept souvenirs . . . body parts. I bet our guy does too, but what does he do with them?"

Jimmy shook his head.

"Just goes to show you, you don't always know who you're living with."

Jimmy wandered off to his desk and left Andy to his laptop, concentrating on his notes:

Roxanne. Cristelle. Catherine.

June 26. July 9. July 16.

More torture. More mutilation.

This guy's picking up speed.

By 1.30 p.m. Makedde stood before the window dressed in black pants and a fine knit sweater. Her fingers played absent-mindedly with the diamond ring on her thumb.

JT?

The two-letter puzzle had been on her mind for hours. She couldn't recall any JTs that she knew. Perhaps it was a nickname or abbreviation. But for what? Speculation was pointless. She had more pressing matters to deal with. Soon Tony Thomas would arrive, and she would have to do her best to decipher his guilt and level of dangerousness. Her study of psychology might assist her if she was observant, but if Tony was a psychopath it would be impossible to detect the usual signs of perjury.

She slid a sharp paring knife into her purse. "Wish me luck, Jaqui," she said under her breath with an almost superstitious intensity. Jaqui Reeves was Makedde's Canadian self-defence instructor and friend. She was well versed in martial arts, street fighting and the use of weapons, and was an enthusiastic teacher. She also had a notorious disrespect for some of the technicalities of Canadian law, particularly with regard to concealed weapons. Among other gadgets, she kept a small folding knife in her bra at all times, which she affectionately called her "booby trap". Knowing Makedde's obsession with ongoing training, she had referred her to Hanna, who taught Friday afternoon classes in Sydney. It seemed that Mak needed to be on her toes more than ever, and she looked forward to attending.

She planned to take Tony to a café where there were lots of people around. She would confront him and scrutinise his every response. And if something went terribly wrong, she'd have the knife. She wasn't afraid to use it. It was better than nothing.

She crossed her fingers.

By 1.50 p.m. Mak hoped that Tony had changed his mind, or better yet, had been hit by a car on his way over. Four minutes later a hard knock shook the front door.

Doesn't anyone use the buzzer downstairs?

She peeked through the spy hole and saw Tony's round face peering up at her, sporting a freakishly large nose in the warped glass image. He was carrying a bouquet of flowers. With the knife in the purse clutched at her side, Makedde reluctantly opened the door.

Tony barged straight in. "Do you have a vase for these?" he asked, heading straight for the kitchen.

"Tony—"

"I'm sorry about last night," he shouted from across the room. "This place is a box. A pretty girl like you should be staying somewhere upmarket," he continued as he wandered around, touching things. "Nice to be down at Bondi, I guess. But still—"

"It will do," Makedde said sharply.

He was already examining the kitchen. "Your cupboards are filthy, you really should get a cleaner."

"It's carbon."

"What?"

"Never mind."

"I've got a place," he persisted. "I rent it to models occasionally. Sarah Jackson stayed there for a while, until her career really took off."

Sarah Jackson was on the cover of the latest British *Vogue*.

"No thanks."

"You should at least see the place."

She gave him an icy look.

"You know, you could be a really top model if you got your lips done. You've got a great face."

"Thanks for the advice. Can we get out of here now? I'm starving."

"Just a second. We've gotta talk."

"We can talk while I eat," she insisted.

It didn't work. Tony sat on her couch and started complaining about the police, and how they were treating him like a criminal. "They're pulling apart my files, looking at all my negatives. You have to believe me."

"What do I have to believe, Tony?"

"I didn't kill anyone, I swear."

"What was on the film then?"

"What film?" he said stupidly.

She gave him a hard look, and spoke slowly, emphasising every point. "The film the cops confiscated."

His face went red. "I . . ."

"Why did you take photographs of that poor girl's corpse?" She stared unflinchingly at Tony as he sunk deeper and deeper into the couch, like an ostrich without the necessary sand. "Did you know we were friends? Did you know I would find her?" she pushed. Tony began blubbering incoherently. "What made you choose that location? Out of all the beaches in Sydney, why did you choose *that* location, on *that* day?" she demanded.

98

"I always shoot at that damn beach! I must have shot there twenty times this year. No one is ever around, so you can get away without paying the permit. They charge a fortune to use the beaches these days. It's the truth!"

He was pathetic. She couldn't help but feel sorry for him, at least for a moment.

"Give me one good reason why I should believe you."

As it turned out, Tony couldn't give her a single reason. With his pathetic Don Juan façade ripped away, he become so flustered that he made a hasty retreat, begging her not to tell anyone in the business about the photos of Catherine's corpse. It was a pitiful display. No alibi could be as poignant as his feeble ramblings for forgiveness.

Later that afternoon Makedde sat alone at the Raw Bar, a great sushi place on Bondi Beach. She watched as sizeable sets of waves rolled in, dotted with wetsuit-clad surfers, and then crashed back onto themselves, sending boards and bodies flying. She smiled as a plate of fastidiously designed sushi was placed in front of her. The salmon onigiri melted in her mouth, and the California rolls were fresh and delicious with a subtle bite of wasabi. An unconscious "Mmmm" escaped her lips as she ate.

Never keep a Vanderwall from her lunch.

She couldn't picture Tony Thomas smashing someone's skull in, unless he was drunk. Let alone slicing them open. Disembowelling? She was pretty sure he couldn't stomach it. He had access to beautiful, impressionable young girls, and he obviously took advantage of it as best he could. But was he a killer? Mentally, she crossed him off her suspect list, but reminded herself not to be too sure. A clever psychopath could play any role they liked to assure you of their innocence. She had to keep her mind open, and she had to find the identity of the elusive JT.

15

Detective Flynn was immersed in the data on his laptop when the loud, deliberate coughing of one of his colleagues made him look up. Cassandra, his soon to be ex-wife, was striding into the office with a briefcase and a stack of papers under her arm. Jimmy was behind her, waving his hands and mouthing the words, "The picture! Get the picture down!"

It was too late.

Cassandra paused in front of the bulletin board and scowled at the poster-sized photo of Makedde. He watched uncomfortably as her eyes rested on the breasts.

"I can see you've grown up, Andy," she snarled, flicking her dark hair back. Anger was an unattractive emotion, and one he had seen from her all too frequently in recent years. He didn't even attempt to explain.

"What do you want, Cassandra?" he asked, leaning against his desk with his arms folded.

She looked at him with disgust and threw a wad of papers onto the desk. "Sign these."

Jimmy was watching quietly.

"Let's do this somewhere private," Andy said, pointing to the interview room. "Shall we?"

Cassandra led the way, making a wide berth around the photo. Andy followed. Before he shut the door, he stopped to show Jimmy a clenched fist, mouthing the words, "I'm going to kill you."

They sat down at the table and he began reading the lawyer lingo.

"Just sign it," she insisted.

"The car?" He gave her a steady look, but she wouldn't meet his eyes.

"I need the car," she said.

He could feel his blood starting to boil. "*You* need the car? I need the damn car. What I've got is a heap of crap. Jimmy's gotta pick me up half the time."

"Tough."

"Tough?" He tried to restrain himself. "You have a car. You have two! What's wrong with the Mazda?"

"It's an old piece of shit. I want the Honda. *You* can have the Mazda."

He began drumming his fingers slowly on the Formica tabletop.

"You know how I love that car."

She said nothing.

He pleaded, "Cassandra, you've got our house. You've got most of the furniture. I just want the Honda ... please."

She stood up. "When did you ever do anything for me? The whole time we were married it was you, you, you! Your career. Your life! Are you happy," she jeered, "now that you're a big senior sergeant with a big badge and a big gun, and a bunch of losers to laugh at your infantile jokes?"

"You knew my lifestyle before we married," he said quietly. She was doing it to him again; pushing his buttons. It was as if she actually wanted him to lose his temper. But he stared at the table with determination, gripping its legs with whitening knuckles.

"Well, I didn't know *you*! You petty little shit!" With that she ripped open the door, leaving him still gripping the table, and marched past the silent detectives in the office like a prize prima donna. "You'll hear from my lawyer!" she yelled out as she disappeared into the busy hall.

He let go of the table and slammed his fist hard into the wall. Once. Twice. Three hits.

Damn that fucking bitch!

A cut opened up across his knuckles.

God, she made him angry. Why was she so damn greedy? Nothing would satisfy her. Nothing. Not when they were married and not now. Andy stormed back to his desk, brooding, aware of the silent pity from the other detectives. They weren't laughing this time, probably because most of them had been in the same position at one point or another. It was an occupational hazard.

They could have worked on their relationship, he believed that. But she didn't want to. Cassandra had become worse over the four years they'd been married. Now that she had found success as a real-estate agent and was doing well, she wanted to get him out of her life. Yes, he worked long hours. Yes, he was wrapped up in his job. But when some guy is running around slicing women from head to toe, it's hard to care about getting home on time for dinner. He flexed his hand and a trickle of blood flowed down from his knuckles into his fist.

A rookie constable, whom he didn't much like, noticed it. "Hey, sarg, whatcha done to yourself?" Hoosier asked, reaching towards his hand.

"Fuck off," Flynn spat. "Go arrest some fucking jay

walker, will you?" Hoosier cringed back and slunk quietly away. Andy turned and ripped the photo of Makedde off the board and threw it in the garbage. His veins were pumping so hard, a thin spray of blood spattered the rubbish. He'd had enough. He wasn't planning on copping any more crap over Jimmy's pranks.

Makedde arrived at Central Homicide in the evening, as arranged. She had her shirt sleeves rolled up, ready to be fingerprinted for the first time in her life. The duty sergeant had been expecting her and gave her an approving once over.

"You can head on up, Miss Vanderwall."

She stepped into the elevator, which carried her noisily to the fourth floor. When the doors opened, she was struck by how quiet it was. Most of the detectives had gone home or were out on assignment, but she found Flynn glued to the laptop on his desk, surrounded by files and papers and tagged and pinned city maps. His jacket had been discarded, his tie loosened and his pale blue shirt was rolled up at the sleeves, just like hers. She noticed his right hand was decorated with skin-toned plasters.

"Good evening," she said simply.

He jerked his head up at her greeting. She had startled him. "Miss Vanderwall, I'm glad you could make it in. This won't take long." He was all business as he rose to his feet.

"Any updates on the case?" she asked.

"No."

"Now, there must be *something* you can tell me. You don't sit hunched intensely over a laptop like that without something on your mind."

"I'll let you know of any progress."

Makedde didn't believe that for a second.

He rose and she followed him back to the elevator and

stood with her arms crossed on the opposite side as it took them down several floors. As they rattled down in the otherwise quiet building, Andy turned and smiled weakly at her, shaking his head at the noise. She offered a thin-lipped smile in return. When the doors opened, he led her to an area housing a series of uninhabited holding cells. Along one wall she saw the fingerprinting station; the large black ink pad, and clips for holding the fingerprint forms in place. The wooden surface of the printing table was smeared with the efforts of uncooperative offenders, and the large sink which sat beside the set-up had no doubt once been white, but was now a grimy grey.

"How many separate prints were picked up in the flat?" she asked, throwing her coat over a clean table.

"Several."

"Several as in . . . three? Four? Sixteen?"

"We picked up at least four different clear sets. Happy now?"

"Happier. But I'd be much happier if you," *stopped treating me like an airhead*, "could tell me more about the progress of the investigation."

"You were wise to roll up your sleeves," he said, ignoring her comment and taking her by the wrist. His grip took her by surprise. She didn't pull away, and let him lead her towards the ink pad. He had a form already sitting in its clips, ready for her prints.

He took her wrist in his left hand and held her thumb with the fingers of his right. He pressed her thumb to the ink pad and rolled it from one side to the other, thoroughly coating most of its circumference.

"I don't think it's necessary to—" Mak began.

"To get proper prints, I have to do this."

"Don't I seem like a cooperative criminal to you, Detective?" she asked.

She sensed subtle embarrassment. "Cooperation has nothing to do with it," he stated. "I've had to redo loads of fingerprints when they weren't done correctly."

He twisted her thumb to one side and placed it on the sheet, slowly rolling it across until the complete print was accomplished. They shuffled over to the ink pad together and he thoroughly smeared her index finger in the same way.

Surely I could ink my own hands?

"How do you ever get actual perps to do this?" Makedde asked.

"Crims? Sometimes it takes a few of us."

"And some considerable persuasion I would imagine." He looked like he could be quite persuasive when he chose to be. She gazed at his hands as he manipulated hers. She hadn't noticed before, but his left knuckles were scarred, precisely where the Band-Aids covered his right ones. An ambidextrous bruiser?

"Is that how you cut your hand? Persuading someone?" she asked.

He stiffened. "Nothing like that."

"Uh-huh." She wasn't convinced.

They were both silent as he inked and printed her middle, fourth and pinkie fingers. When Senior Sergeant Flynn went to ink her left palm, he moved in closer, his chest pressing into her shoulder, and his face tilted in front of hers. She glanced at his wrinkled shirt collar and the smooth olive skin of his neck, recalling the way he had affected her in the interview room under the mad full moon.

And the way he brushed me off.

"So, you're the daughter of a Detective Inspector?"

"Indeed."

"How long have you been modelling?"

"Started at fourteen, and a couple of years ago I began studying for my Ph.D. in forensic psychology."

105

"You're pulling my leg."

"No, you're pulling my arm."

He let go.

"Right now I need to continue modelling between semesters to pay my way through. Besides, I like the travel."

He swallowed hard, then smiled. "A shrink, huh?"

"I doubt that shrink is the appropriate term. But I'm not yet a qualified psychologist, no."

He seemed to muse on that as she inked her own right thumb and brought it over to the sheet. He let her print it herself, then said, "May I?" before helping her print her index finger.

He was leaning close to her when he said, "So, you're studying to find interesting ways to get the crims I catch off with some screwy psychobabble?"

"You've been watching too many movies. You should know as well as I do that few offenders go for the insanity plea and fewer still are acquitted. No, I'm more interested in criminal justice personnel psychology, so I can stop people like you from jumping off buildings after a bad homicide."

"Very cute."

She smiled.

After printing her right hand, she walked to the sink and examined a peculiar gritty soap, also smudged with black ink.

"That should get most of it off," Andy offered.

"I'll bet," she countered sceptically, and started scrubbing her hands. "Flynn's an Irish name, isn't it?" she asked casually.

"Yup. My family's been here for a couple of generations, but I've got a bit of Irish from way back. Scottish, too."

"Really? Can you do a Sean Connery?"

"Well, Miss Money Penny . . ." he said in a rounded Scotch accent.

She felt herself go weak at the knees. She had to get him to stop, or she would be jelly in his hands. "Beautiful countries; Scotland and Ireland," she managed to say, grateful that her back was to him. "Have you been?"

"Nope."

"I guess your work makes it hard to take time off."

He didn't respond.

Makedde scrubbed until her hands felt raw before deciding to give up on making them clean. Her skin was pink in spots and vaguely grimy in others. Her nails looked like they'd been done with a black French manicure.

"Since I've been so cooperative, maybe you can put a little more effort into finding Mister Wrong," she said. "I know you don't have much to go on but—"

"I assure you, we're on to it."

"No new leads to his identity?" *The ring?*

"No."

"OK." She let it rest for the moment. "Just let me know what comes up." She knew it was pointless to mention the ring before she had any more information. They would have found it in the search and had obviously thought nothing of it. Makedde picked up her coat, grateful that it was black, and started towards the door. What the detective said next stopped her dead in her tracks.

"Would you like to go out sometime?"

For a moment she simply stared at her hand fixed around the door knob.

"Do you ask out all of your witnesses, Detective, or just the ones who are models?" she asked.

"First time, actually. I guessed you probably didn't have a lot of friends here."

"I have plenty of friends, thank you," she fibbed. "So do you, by the looks of things."

He smiled. "Yes, I suppose you're right. I'm sorry."

Detective Flynn escorted her politely to the elevator.

"Thank you for your help, Miss Vanderwall," he offered coolly as she stepped out.

Makedde felt the urge to apologise for being so terse, but suddenly he was gone. He had taken her completely off guard. What was it with that guy? One minute she wanted to wring his neck and the next moment she wanted to kiss it.

She threw her coat on and walked out to the street. "Do you ask out all your witnesses or just the models?" she mumbled in an irritating impersonation of herself. "Blah-blah-blah. *Idiot.*"

16

Detective Flynn braced himself. He had seen Wednesday's paper, and instinctively knew his boss wouldn't be happy. He rubbed his red-rimmed eyes and strode into the office, carrying under one arm the files he had stayed up all night with, and under the other the offending morning paper. He was met at his desk by his eager partner, performing his worst female-secretary impression with deadpan humour.

"Detective Inspector Roderick Kelley wishes to see you in his office, sir," Jimmy crooned.

"Has he talked to you already?"

"Oh, yeah. Actually, it's surprisingly good news."

Andy unconsciously straightened his tie and ran a hand through his hair as he made his way to Kelley's office.

The door was open. Kelley was waiting.

"Flynn," he said, leaning back in his chair. "Come in."

Detective Inspector Kelley was a lean, grey-haired man in his early fifties. He had slate-grey eyes, thin lips and an angular, clean-shaven face. He was tough and economical in everything he did and said, and he was very intelligent. Andy respected him enormously. The morning newspaper sat open on his desk. It was facing away from Andy, but even upside down it was easy to read the bold headline. *SYDNEY SERIAL KILLER, POLICE CLUELESS.*

"What do you make of this?" Kelley challenged as Andy took the hot seat.

He paused, searching for the right words. "Well, sir, we tried to keep a lid on it, but someone picked it up and ran with it, which is not surprising. We've been getting a lot of calls, none of them useful."

"And *do* we have a serial killer on our hands?"

"I believe we do."

"Tell me about it."

"These are clear, almost textbook, signature killings with distinct patterns of mutilation. Unfortunately, no connection has been found between the victims at this point. Just general age, appearance, that sort of thing. He's not leaving a lot of clues. Just the shoes."

"He's leaving clues, Flynn. They always do. It's just a matter of finding and interpreting them."

He knew Kelley was unhappy with him when he called him "Flynn". "Of course—" Andy began.

"And the shoe is the victim's in each case?"

"Cristelle was seen leaving the Red Fox wearing similar shoes. With Roxanne and Catherine, we don't know."

"What else have you got?"

"Head wounds inflicted with a heavy blunt instrument, probably your average garden variety hammer. Thousands bought in Sydney."

"And . . ."

"The other injuries took time. A doctor or a surgeon might cut in that way, but then again, any sicko might as well. We've learnt that since the Whitechapel days."

"I'm listening," Kelley pressed.

"No one unusual at the dump site of the Gerber girl,"

Andy continued his spiel. "He doesn't seem to have come back. I'm still suspicious of the photographer. He seemed more affected by us wanting to see the film in his camera than he was by having just come across a slaughtered girl. He had worked with Makedde Vanderwall before and may have set her up to discover her friend. The ultimate thrill."

"Does he have an alibi?"

"No."

"And this mystery man the last victim was involved with?"

Andy hated being confronted with questions for which he had no satisfactory answers. "Could be anyone at this point. They kept it pretty quiet, and nobody has come forward. I doubt it's related."

"Physical evidence?"

"Nothing pointing to a specific suspect at this time. The killer uses condoms. No semen has been found at all, which I find unusual with this amount of violence. Our killer could be worried about disease or, more likely, leaving DNA. The traces of disinfectant found on the bodies fits with that."

"So he could be familiar with forensics. Someone who's done time. Or maybe he's just a clean freak. What else?"

"On all the victims we found dark fibres consistent with a thick material like a blanket, not carpet fibre."

Kelley stared out his window. "A material used to transport or hide the body?" he asked.

"That's what I suspect. A few hairs were found in the wounds as well," Andy said.

"The killer's?"

"Miss Gerber was dead for at least thirty-six hours before she was found, and it was windy, so a lot of fibres and hairs appear to have blown over from somewhere else. We've got a few hairs, all vastly different. Long blonde, long brown, short brown, red, curly, you name it. They're working on DNA tests. There's a theory that some of the hairs belong to the previous victims."

Inspector Kelley was silent. He turned his back to Andy and stared out the window. The inspector unconsciously picked at his fingernails while his hands were clasped behind him. The skin around the cuticles was raw; the result of a nervous habit. A small clock ticked on the inspector's desk.

Finally Kelley spoke. "Now that we can assume we're dealing with a multiple killer, I'm giving you more backup. You'll head a small task force. I'm giving you Hunt, Reed, Mahoney, Sampson, Hoosier, and you've got Bradford full-time now along with the rest of your crew. You won't have much difficulty authorising what you need from now on. The media is scaring the daylights out of every citizen in this city. If there's a serial killer out there, I want him stopped."

Andy was impressed; Kelley was usually a tightarse.

"Thank you sir. But um . . . about Hoosier—"

Inspector Kelley cut him off. "You get who I assign to you." Subject closed. He stood and walked back to his well-earned window. Andy knew he had put in a lot of years to get that precious view. Without turning around Kelley said, "Get busy. Oh, and take that pin-up off the board. It's distracting."

"Yes, sir . . ." He paused. "Wait . . . it's up again?"

Andy assembled his team. It felt good to have the freedom to properly handle the investigation. Budget cuts had made everyone's job increasingly difficult over recent years. Unfair though it was, if the victims had been the daughters of politicians, instead of two hookers and a foreigner, money would have been falling out of the sky from day one.

He kept the usual group on their research duties, and

said, "Constables Hunt, Mahoney, Reed and Sampson; you're on surveillance of the photographer. Groups of two. Twelve-hour shifts. We don't have enough for a search warrant but we'll sure as hell watch this guy. I don't want Tony Thomas leaving your sight."

Andy turned to Jimmy. "Keep Colin Bradford on the dump site. You never know who might turn up."

"I'll talk to our men in the Cross," Jimmy offered, talking over the chatter as the room dispersed. "If this malaka is hunting the area, maybe somebody has seen something, heard something."

"Good idea. And check the personals for ads asking for girls to model shoes."

Jimmy paused for a moment. "The model doesn't strike me as the type who'd go for something like that."

"I know. But she could be the exception. Maybe he's got himself a nice little system, but she was a victim of opportunity. There are no set rules here."

"Y'asou. I'll get on to it," Jimmy assured him.

Andy was surprised when a small voice spoke up from the back of the room. "Uh, what about me, sir?"

It was Hoosier again.

"Ask Colin if you can do anything useful," Andy said offhandedly, brushing off the junior officer like a summer blowfly.

17

"What do you mean you didn't find it?!" JT exclaimed with thinly veiled panic.

Luther's expression did not change. In his usual deep monotone he said simply, "No ring."

Luther was built like a gnarled and immovable two-hundred-year-old tree stump. His chest rose above JT's eyes, and his head towered above everyone else's, planted stiffly atop wide shoulders on a knotted, muscular neck. Lank hair fell over his eyes, but disappeared with a close shave from his temples to the back of his head. His leathery, pockmarked skin read like a road map, and his small eyes languished motionlessly in their sockets. Thankfully, JT had only ever had to meet him in person once. Luther was supposedly the best, but JT would have much preferred an arm's-length, rather than face-to-face, business relationship.

"You drag me all the way out to this crappy bar to tell me news like this?" JT continued, trying to make his point as firmly as possible. "I don't want bad news. That's not what I pay you for."

Luther had no response.

The dimly lit bar was a forgotten dive, an alcoholic's refuge with faded red-patterned carpets that reeked of hops, hardship and cigarette smoke. JT looked around furtively, his nose pinched against the distasteful smell. A neon beer advertisement flickered on the back wall. This certainly wasn't the type of place he usually frequented and was a far cry from his Macquarie Street club.

The bartender offered him peanuts, but although he was starving, JT couldn't bear the thought of eating from a bowl that patrons at this kind of establishment would have put their hands in. He imagined salmonella or hepatitis A festering over every nut. He wiped his hands on his pants again, hoping he wouldn't pick up some heinous and unseemly disease from the door handle or stool.

"Look Luther," he said resolutely, "I want the ring, and I want the girl out of the picture. Do I need to pay more?"

"You want 'er whacked?" Luther watched him expectantly, one huge, callused finger making an odd caressing motion against his scarred palm. JT suspected Luther would take great pleasure in executing that particular errand.

"I don't need you to do that. Just put the pressure on and scare her out of town."

Luther nodded.

"I don't like meeting in person like this. Keep me posted as you have been. Only call from public phones, right?"

"Of course." Luther stared at JT from his towering perspective. "The money?" he asked.

JT fumbled in his pockets. He was reluctant to hand over such a large investment for such a small return. "There'll be more on completion," he said gruffly.

Luther took the envelope, shoved it down the back of his dark jeans, skulled the remainder of his beer and walked out without another word.

18

Makedde tiptoed from the bathroom still dripping from the shower, and began humming along to the familiar tune playing on the radio. She tried hard to ignore the remains of the dark dusting powder that covered most of the surfaces in the flat. Her sunset run had been exhilarating, leaving her rejuvenated and she felt that she was finally being released from the heavy burden of grief. Clean, wet feet squeaked on the floor as she broke into a spontaneous bit of dance. Mak wasn't about to let fear and misfortune get the better of her. She needed to release her tension, turn up the volume and escape.

Makedde whipped the towel off and struck an exaggerated rock star pose. After a moment grinning in her birthday suit, she felt an inkling of self-consciousness, and started towards the wardrobe. She kept humming along. The beat was uplifting, and eventually the last chorus was sung, and a radio host reminded her she was listening to Triple J. "*And in today's news,*" the host continued, "*more public panic that a serial killer may be loose in Sydney . . .*"

She turned and quickly strode back across the room to-

116

wards the radio. The floor was wet, and in an instant she had slipped. She landed with a thud on the unforgiving floorboards, her legs splayed out, a tangle of wet hair strewn across her face.

The DJ went on, "*The latest victim, nineteen-year-old Canadian model Catherine Gerber . . .*"

Makedde lay bruised on the floor, the smile wiped from her face. *Catherine*. There was no escaping the constant reminders. Radio. Television. Front page headlines. She brushed the hair away from her eyes and looked down at her naked body. Fresh blood left long, red streaks up her legs, and little, damp smudges on her buttocks.

Just like Catherine.

"*. . . third woman found brutally slain . . .*" the announcer went on.

Makedde tried not to listen. Her face was ashen. Small smudges of blood led across the floor. Beneath the sound of the radio, the telephone started to ring, but still she sat there, immobilised by the sight of the red blotches on the floor. It coated her body and pooled out all around her, smelling sharply of metal and decomposing flesh. It was so frightfully red, so like the blood that had covered Catherine's corpse. She looked at her body as if she were bathed in the crimson of her insides, but then she blinked again and the blood was practically gone; just a couple of harmless streaks. The trail of tiny blood drops led straight to the shower. "Damn razors!" she cried out when she realised its source.

By the fifth ring she managed to stand up and carefully cross the room. She didn't care about answering the call. Before anything else, she had to turn off that wretched announcer.

"*. . . police say . . .*"

The radio signal mercifully faded away as she switched

the dial. When the phone rang once more, Makedde picked it up.

"Hello?"

Click.

She hurled the infuriating machine across the room. It sailed through the air, hitting the back wall with a clap and a tinkle. Breathing slowly and deliberately, Makedde reached for the towel and dried her feet, mindful that she didn't stain it with the bleeding cut on her ankle. Just as her heart was slowing to a regular pace, Makedde was startled by a loud, unexpected buzzer. It took her a few moments to register what it was—it was the first time anyone had used the intercom.

"Hello?"

"It's Detective Flynn. May I have a word with you?"

Detective Flynn? "I . . . this isn't the best time."

She suddenly felt very naked.

"Do you have company?"

"No. I just came out of the shower." She looked at her watch. It was almost 9 p.m. "Isn't it a bit late?"

He paused. "I can wait till you're decent."

"Is it important?"

"Yes."

Oh, stop being such a bitch to the man, Makedde!

"That's all right. I'll quickly throw something on. Just wait," she told him. Makedde hung up the intercom and ran over to pick the phone off the floor. She propped it up in its normal spot and raced to the bathroom to quickly wet some tissue and wipe the streaks of blood off her legs. She pulled on a pair of Levi's and a sweater out of the chest of drawers beside the bed, and did up the last button on her jeans as she walked back to the intercom.

"You still there?" Makedde asked the street.

"Yes," Flynn's voice came back.

"Come on up."

As an afterthought, she looked in the tiny wall mirror and checked her residual make-up and wet hair, which she'd tied into a quick knot. It was obvious she had been crying and the mirror was far from complimentary, but she didn't look quite as terrible as she felt. When she opened the door, Andy smiled at her. He wore an attractive, though slightly wrinkled, single-breasted navy suit.

"Sorry to bother you. I was in the area and I . . . um—"

"Please come in," she said, then stepped back and turned away, so that he wouldn't have time to register her puffy eyes. His timing was bad. She didn't want him to know she had been crying. "I'm sorry if I responded a bit harshly the other night," she said over her shoulder as she walked towards the open kitchen.

"That was just something stupid that popped out. It was totally inappropriate. I apologise," he said.

"Good. Well, I'm glad we . . . uh, understand each other." She walked to the kitchen counter and pretended to be busy arranging the dishes. "How can I help you then?" she said.

Andy walked over to the entrance of the kitchen and leant against the wall. "Well, like I said, I was in the area and I had some questions for you. Tony Thomas has been hanging around your door. I wanted to know if he's been bothering you."

"Not really," she said with her back to him.

"*Not really?* What does that mean?"

She was silent.

"Hey? Are you OK?"

She brought her hands down to rest on the countertop, and turned her face to look at him. "Not really," she said simply.

Andy's composed expression lost all of its hardened professionalism when their eyes met. He moved to her side, and carefully put a hand on hers. "Hey, it's OK. You're coping really well."

"I'm not so sure," she said, annoyed that her lip was trembling and she couldn't make it stop.

"Trust me, you are. I've seen good cops go to pieces over stuff like this. You're very strong."

Her thoughts were confused, her body urging her to do things that were inappropriate. She wanted to move into his arms and let them close around her. She wanted to tilt her head up, taste his lips.

"I uh . . ." She pulled away from the temptation, away from his comforting hand. "I'm OK, really. What else did you want to ask me?"

Andy responded in kind, moving back and putting his hands in his suit pockets. "Makedde, what's Tony Thomas been up to?"

"Well . . ."

His expression became serious. "Makedde."

"Fine," she said. "If you really want to know, he invited himself over for lunch yesterday, barged in with some cheap flowers, lived up to his reputation as a half-wit sleaze and left crying."

"Crying?" Andy looked shocked. "Jesus, Makedde. He's a suspect. Whatever you're doing, just stop. I don't want you involved in this."

"Excuse me? How am I *not* involved in this?" she asked.

"Just don't get yourself into trouble."

Mak raised herself up slightly, so that she was his height. Her face was close to his when she said with renewed confidence, "I can take care of myself, Detective."

He gave her a long, steady look, which she returned unflinchingly.

"So, did you find anything out?" he finally asked.

"He seemed pretty anxious about the police going through his files. He did admit to having chosen the photo shoot location, but he claimed he chose that particular beach to avoid paying a hefty permit."

"That's all? No confession?"

She gave him a withering look.

"If you ever thought of becoming a detective," he said matter-of-factly, "well, don't. It's not very glamorous."

"Did you just come here to underestimate me, or did you actually have something valid to say?" she snapped.

"Just stay out of this investigation and keep away from the suspects."

"Thanks for your advice. Have a good evening," she said bluntly. "Unless there is something more you wanted to ask me?"

"No. Nothing else," he said, but his eyes contradicted him. "Tony could be very dangerous. If he tries to contact you again, let me know right away." Detective Flynn resumed his mask of professional detachment. "Thank you for your time, Miss Vanderwall." He turned to leave but his eyes caught something in the main room and widened. He walked over to it.

"There's blood on your floor."

She felt herself blush as she followed him out of the small kitchen. "Oh, it's nothing . . . girl stuff." As soon as the words left her lips, she knew how it would sound.

He grimaced and stepped back.

"No, no. Not *that* kind of girl stuff," she assured him. "I cut my ankle shaving."

"Oh!" he said with a laugh. "Well, are you OK?"

"Yeah. It just bled a bit because of the hot shower. The cut's small. Nothing really. How's your hand?"

"Oh, fine." He looked down at the Band-Aids on his knuckles. "OK. Well . . . I'll be going then."

An uncomfortable silence hung in the air but a second later the moment of awkward intimacy was broken and he turned and walked to the door. She said good-bye and watched him disappear down the stairs and onto the street.

19

He didn't need to consult the phone book. The numbers, along with her name, were indelibly etched into his memory. He dialled slowly and deliberately, savouring the clicks and tones like a lover savours foreplay. He could reach her just like that and she would stop whatever she was doing for him.

"Hello?"

She sounded tired. She was still alone in her flat.

"Hello? Is anyone there?" she asked.

He listened to her breath; passing in and out of her lungs, her throat, her mouth, flowing over her soft lips and into his ear.

"I'm hanging up now . . ." she said irritably.

Was that disappointment in her voice? Did she want him to come to her? Or should he wait?

When she hung up on him, he replaced the receiver and crossed to the other side of the bed, where a thin blade glinted in the glow of his lamp light.

Tonight?

No. She was so special. He couldn't rush.

Tomorrow will be right.

He wanted to hear her breathe for him one more time. He held the cold blade in his hand, and dialled her number with its razor-sharp tip.

20

A throng of preoccupied business people rushed past Makedde as she made her way to the imposing city department store on Elizabeth Street. She scanned the industrious crowd with heavy eyes, wanting nothing more than to crawl right back into bed. A crank caller had kept her phone ringing into the night, again robbing her of precious shut-eye. She may as well not have bothered fixing the phone cord. Eventually she had taken the damn thing off the hook and had managed to drift off.

Several windows of the department store had been given over to Becky Ross publicity—larger-than-life posters of the twenty-one-year-old soap star and other information about the launch. Everything about Becky's carefully crafted image was easily masticated fodder for the Australian and English tabloids—what she wore, what plastic surgery she supposedly had had, and of course, who she was currently sleeping with. The media had gone temporarily mad when she dated a certain famous rugby player, but lost interest when a newer sensation came along. The rugby player was soon after unceremoniously dumped.

Becky had a penchant for severe hair-colouring faux pas-platinum, then red, then platinum again—and cleavage-revealing, see-through designer outfits that endeared her no end to the paparazzi and the glossy gossip magazines. Since Makedde had arrived, she had seen Becky countless times on covers and in television ads for fast food. Somehow she had convinced the conservative department store crowd that she was a fashion item.

Wearily, Makedde pushed open the elegant doors, lugging her heavy black model bag on her shoulder. It was her first job since Friday's grisly discovery, and she wasn't feeling quite up to it. A few shoppers turned and watched Makedde stride through the store. She made her way to the escalator, past make-up counters gleaming like lollyshop shelves with polished glass and shiny gold and silver surfaces covered in rows of colourful lipsticks and eye shadows. A heady, slightly sickly floral scent permeated the entire ground floor; a mixture of hundreds of brands of expensive perfumes and cosmetics.

After seven scenic escalator rides, which left her wondering why she hadn't just caught the lift, she eventually located the fashion show salon. At the head of a long, thin, T-shaped catwalk was a huge banner bearing Becky's name and several three-foot-high images of her airbrushed, pouting face. The photograph was fashionably severe, and Makedde wasn't sure it suited her. Around the catwalk at least two hundred empty chairs waited for the paparazzi, glitterati and general fashion folk who would soon be arriving. True to form, the gossip columnists had been feverishly speculating upon Becky's dubious fashion credentials, but Makedde tried to keep an open mind.

The dressing-room door could be seen to the right of

the stage, and as she stepped inside, Mak was startled by an instant and intense head-to-toe appraisal. She looked around at seven, beautiful, frowning and unfamiliar faces and thought, *this is going to be fun*. She smiled politely and then glanced at the clothes on the countless racks jammed into the small room.

"Excuse me?" she said to a refreshingly average-looking woman bearing the name tag "Sarah". "I'm Makedde. Do you know which is my section?"

The young girl, who was probably a volunteer dresser, escorted her to a rack bearing a piece of paper marked "Macayly". Even with Makedde's composite card stapled to the rack, they had still managed to get her name wrong.

She went immediately for the size tags in the back of each garment. The standard model size was generally an Australian ten, but some designers made their samples in eights. Makedde had no illusions about her size; she couldn't fit an Aussie size eight if her life depended on it. She bit her lip as she came across a lacy skirt labelled with the dreaded number. Surreptitiously, she attempted to tug the skirt over her hips. The material had no give, the lace didn't look like it would hold and she couldn't get the darn thing further than half-mast.

"This skirt is too small," Makedde admitted self-consciously to the dresser. In a room full of waifs it felt like a confession of first-degree murder.

"We've had trouble with some of the sizes," the dresser said. "We'll switch your first outfit with someone else's." She eyed the other models and pointed to a particularly skinny one. "She's swimming in that slip dress. You'll fill it out much better. Why don't you two swap?"

That was a relief. Normally a stylist would stare at her with disgust and say something like, "Oh dear, you *are* big. Are you having your period?"

Makedde was often intimidated by the size and beauty of other models, and ill-fitting clothes only highlighted her insecurities. Logically, she knew she had no reason to feel this way, but she was acutely aware of every perfect set of lips, every wide pair of eyes, every slim waist and tiny butt around her. Being more voluptuous than every other model in the room could make her feel like a freak if she was having a bad day. In that atmosphere, her flesh seemed sinful beside tiny bodies with skin pulled tightly over bone. It seemed indulgent to have cleavage, or rounded hips. Sure, she was a size ten, in good shape and by no means fat, especially for her height, but it was hard not to feel uneasy when a garment didn't fit. Especially when she was getting paid for an hour's work what most people earn in a week. She supposed that very slim girls might feel the same way when they didn't fill out a bra. It was crazy.

Just as she was about to try the new dress, a familiar face walked in. Loulou, a make-up artist Makedde had worked with several times, exploded through the doors like a fashionable tornado. She carried an enormous make-up case covered in stickers from all over the world, along with several bright shopping bags overflowing with hot rollers, Velcros and hair bands. Her dramatically pencilled eyebrows seemed to perpetually exclaim, "Wow!", her hair was a frizzy bleached eruption and her fingernails danced with blue glitter.

"Makedde!" Loulou cried, spotting her. Loulou gave Makedde a hug that almost knocked the wind out of her. She was a wild one, but a genuine character; she never took anything too seriously, and she seemed to vibrate with enthusiasm even when she stood still. She was an eternal optimist, and was just what Makedde needed.

"Loulou, how are you?"

"Great! How ya goin'? You look divine. I heard you were

in Sydney." Her enthusiasm was catchy, and Makedde found herself instantly wanting to giggle and snort and call people "sweetie".

"How long has it been? Two years?" Mak asked as she stepped into the new slip dress.

Loulou thought for a moment. "Has it been that long? *Sweetie*, you haven't been here all this time, have you?"

"God, no. I was just on a direct booking when I saw you. It was only for a week." She zipped the dress up as far as she could reach and asked, "Does this fit?"

"Divine, sweetie. *Divine*."

"That's good enough for me. Have you been away?"

"Paris. It was *fabulous!*"

"When are you going back?"

At this, her bubbly expression momentarily faltered. "Oh, I don't know . . ."

Paris was a hard market, and Makedde guessed that Loulou was one of the large percentage who hadn't earned enough to pay off her trip.

"Did you work anywhere else while you were over there?" Makedde asked.

"Germany. That was *marvellous*."

Divine. Fabulous. Marvellous. "OK" just wasn't in Loulou's vocabulary. Mak could relate to her attitude to Germany. The catalogues were tedious, but the Deutschmark was worth a bundle. It was a great place to work on one's bank account.

Loulou looked around, smiling. "So what do you think of these clothes?" She pointed to a tiny red dress with spaghetti straps and a plunging neckline. "That'll look great with your cleavage."

Makedde laughed. "Looks like this will be a bra-free zone. I can foresee having a very embarrassing accident in that one."

129

"Let it all hang out, sweetie! The snappers will love you!" Loulou paused, her expression becoming more serious. "Hey, I'm sorry about your friend. I never met her, but everyone is so shocked. Just horrible."

"Yeah." Mak wondered if Loulou could help with the identity of Cat's boyfriend. "Hey, do you know any guys who go by the name of JT?"

Loulou cocked her head to one side. "JT? Nah. There was J.T. Walsh, the actor."

"That's not who I'm thinking of."

"Sorry. I better get started here. I'll talk to you later, sweetie."

"You got it."

The show coordinator, a tall, slim, ex-model type, ushered the girls onto the stage outside the dressing room. The white, polished runway came up around three feet off the floor; just enough to make Makedde nervous about wearing the standard model G-string in some of her shorter frocks.

"Right," the coordinator began, "we want attitude out there today. No smiles. There are four routines, seven outfits each." A couple of models, including Makedde, pulled out little notepads and began to scribble as the woman talked. "First routine begins with four models entering on the beat, then going single and ending with a staggered four." Makedde took down the string of confusing choreography instructions, doodling lines and arrows on her notepad.

She stood there writing, and suddenly had the uneasy sensation that she was being watched. The tiny hairs on the back of her neck stood up and she turned around, scanning the large room. The double doors were swinging slightly, but no one was near them. The other girls were all busy listening or writing and the room was still empty, apart from a couple of preoccupied ladies in fashionable black discussing the stage display.

"The finale routine is a single, centre turn, circle and a peel out," the coordinator went on.

Peel out?

When asked if everything was clear, the models nodded their heads in agreement and the rehearsal began. An impressive stereo system filled the hall with a raucous, alternative dance beat, and the first group of models began their routine. Within moments there was confusion, with girls crashing into each other and barely regaining their balance on spindly high heels. The next group tried to execute the routine with more caution, nervously shuffling past each other. The coordinator was pulling her hair out. After an hour of futility, the routines were shortened and simplified.

All this for one twenty-minute show.

When the rehearsal finally ended, they were ushered back inside the dressing room. Loulou was frantic. They had gone overtime, and she only had forty-five minutes left before the show to make up eight models and create eight elegantly up-swept hairdos. Loulou was flying solo and didn't have the benefit of the store's beauty salon and help from the staff who worked there.

Precisely forty minutes later, after a well-orchestrated operation, Makedde was checking her teeth for lipstick when Becky Ross sashayed into the dressing room, decked out in a plunging cutaway dress. Today her hair was very long and very blonde. Mak suspected extensions. Becky did look fantastic, although perhaps a bit overmade for the cameras. No doubt she had spent hours with her personal make-up and hair artists.

She swanned around backstage, surveyed the painted, preened and up-swept group of models, and said, without blinking an eyelid, "Can we have the hair down? I'd like to see it *long*."

The coordinator went white, and Loulou went even paler. The show was due to begin in five minutes. Hair was hurriedly unpinned and within fifteen minutes the models had been readied for the second time and Becky was posing on stage to signal the start of the show.

Makedde was the first model out and as she strode down the runway bathed in hot lights, she was critically and intimately examined by the invisible crowd. She was nothing short of statuesque and towered over the troupe, a full six feet and three inches in her lofty shoes.

As usual, it was chaos backstage—models, waxed to within an inch of their lives, wearing nothing but flesh-coloured G-strings, were running around with panic-stricken dressers trying to get them into their next outfit on time. Mak had one thirty-second change, and three dressers worked as a tag team to hoist up her black panty-hose and get her zipped, combed and adjusted. At the end of it all, Makedde and the seven other models poured onto the stage in two elegant lines and engaged in that peculiar type of applause, quite unique to fashion shows, where the palms stay glued together and only the fingers clap. The photographers were smiling, having been given a feast of photo opportunities, but the fashion elite were offering only weak praise. Despite the time, effort and expense, Makedde had a sneaking suspicion the whole exercise had been more of a publicity stunt than a fashion success.

Later on, as the crowd was dispersing, Becky Ross could be heard rabbiting on about her designs to a gaggle of television reporters. She was only twenty-one years old, but handled the press like a pro; serving up quick sound bites for the cameras and outrageous page three-style poses for the salivating photographers.

Wary of the tabloid vultures who were prowling for an inside scoop on Catherine, Makedde evaded the crowd by following a waiter through a staff-only door backstage. She passed trays of minuscule ready-to-be-served hors d'oeuvres of goats cheese, wafers and prosciutto, and within five minutes had found her way through the maze of corridors down to the street outside.

21

Patience.

As he waited for his girl to come through the double doors, he hid as best he could his growing excitement. Like a big cat hunting, his movements were considered, slow and unremarkable until the very moment of attack. He imagined her heavily made-up face, her sleek curves and those slender feet, wearing stilettos for his private pleasure. She would make her way home alone and he could take her when the ideal moment presented itself. And there would be an ideal moment. He knew that. The photo in Catherine's wallet was fate, as was the letter he found asking him to display Catherine's body, *his handiwork*, for her to witness at the beach. Now his prize had paraded down the runway in sexy dresses and whore's shoes, *just for him*, and soon he would have her. The waiting would be over.

In time, the other fashion models came through the double doors, chatting and laughing, some nibbling like hamsters on tiny snacks. Makedde wasn't with them. That was good. He wanted her to leave alone.

GET UP TO
4 FREE BOOKS!

You can have the best fiction delivered to your door for less than what you'd pay in a bookstore or online—only $4.25 a book! Sign up for our book clubs today, and we'll send you **FREE* BOOKS** just for trying it out...**with no obligation to buy, ever!**

LEISURE HORROR BOOK CLUB

With more award-winning horror authors than any other publisher, it's easy to see why CNN.com says "Leisure Books has been leading the way in paperback horror novels." Your shipments will include authors such as RICHARD LAYMON, DOUGLAS CLEGG, JACK KETCHUM, MARY ANN MITCHELL, and many more.

LEISURE THRILLER BOOK CLUB

If you love fast-paced page-turners, you won't want to miss any of the books in Leisure's thriller line. Filled with gripping tension and edge-of-your-seat excitement, these titles feature everything from psychological suspense to legal thrillers to police procedurals and more!

As a book club member you also receive the following special benefits:

- **30% OFF all orders through our website & telecenter!**
- **Exclusive access to special discounts!**
- **Convenient home delivery and 10 days to return any books you don't want to keep.**

There is **no minimum number of books to buy**, and you may cancel membership at any time. See back to sign up!

*Please include $2.00 for shipping and handling.

YES! ☐

Sign me up for the Leisure Horror Book Club and send my TWO FREE BOOKS! If I choose to stay in the club, I will pay only $8.50* each month, a savings of $5.48!

YES! ☐

Sign me up for the Leisure Thriller Book Club and send my TWO FREE BOOKS! If I choose to stay in the club, I will pay only $8.50* each month, a savings of $5.48!

NAME: _____

ADDRESS: _____

_____

TELEPHONE: _____

E-MAIL: _____

☐ **I WANT TO PAY BY CREDIT CARD.**

☐ VISA   ☐ MasterCard   ☐ DISCOVER

ACCOUNT #: _____

EXPIRATION DATE: _____

SIGNATURE: _____

Send this card along with $2.00 shipping & handling for each club you wish to join, to:

Horror/Thriller Book Clubs
20 Academy Street
Norwalk, CT 06850-4032

Or fax (must include credit card information!) to: 610.995.9274. You can also sign up online at www.dorchesterpub.com.

*Plus $2.00 for shipping. Offer open to residents of the U.S. and Canada only. Canadian residents please call 1.800.481.9191 for pricing information.

If under 18, a parent or guardian must sign. Terms, prices and conditions subject to change. Subscription subject to acceptance. Dorchester Publishing reserves the right to reject any order or cancel any subscription.

JOIN NOW!

Another twenty minutes passed before the first inkling of doubt crept into his mind. All of the guests and the other models had left, so where was his prize? He peeked through the doors. The starlet was still talking to a couple of reporters near the stage, but everyone else was gone. Where was Makedde? How could she have slipped away?

Biting disappointment seized him, welling up into a violent rage. More waiting? *No!* He didn't want to wait any longer. He demanded satisfaction. He moved away from the doors, blending into racks of imported designer clothing, and forced his rage down, storing and safe-keeping it. He kneeled on the carpet where no one could see and held his pounding head.

Minutes later, the soap starlet emerged with two young men tagging along behind her. She flicked her platinum hair as she spoke. "It was a great success!" she cooed. "They'll love me in L.A. too, I just know it." She wiggled her way towards the elevators, hips moving seductively, her tanned body tottering on tall stilettos.

He would have satisfaction.

Preoccupied, Becky Ross and her small entourage stepped into the elevator, paying scant attention to the man who slipped in the car with them.

22

Later that afternoon, Makedde stretched out on the couch and put her aching feet up. Involuntarily she began to brood, and couldn't help wondering what it would be like to return to Canada. She imagined the whole family would come to see her sister's newborn after the birth, to hug Theresa and congratulate her. "Oh, she's done so well," they would say, and then turn to Makedde and shake their heads. "No children, no husband, no mother, and now not even a best friend. Poor girl." How depressing. Makedde loathed the thought of the attention it would bring, and the constant reminders.

That's why she'd told barely a soul about Stanley.

Stanley was the stranger with the threatening switchblade and the penile weapon, the man who'd violated her life and her trust some eighteen months before. It wasn't so much the shame, but the constant reminders that had led her to keeping it so tightly under wraps. Only her father knew, and the police. And of course Catherine, who'd helped her so much afterwards. She'd held her hand while

Mak had been forced to recall the experience in detail, for the third time, for yet another Vancouver detective. Were the victims of muggings asked so many questions? Such intimate questions? Why had she felt on trial? In the end her case couldn't be proved on its own. If the laws had been different, and separate charges could have been tried together, she knew the outcome would have been very different.

Mak hadn't wanted her family to know. It was better to have secrets than to feel their pity. She hated pity.

But Stanley was in jail now, although not for what he'd done to her.

Auntie Sheila would probably try and set her up with some dentist or accountant again when she got back. It seemed like everyone was trying to get her to settle down. "Why are you always running off by yourself? What do you want to be a shrink for? You're a pretty girl, why don't you find a nice man to take care of you?" They just couldn't understand why she ran the other way when her sister's bridal bouquet was tossed.

The telephone rang, mercifully snapping Makedde out of her melancholia. She hesitated before answering it, prepared for another crank call, but she was relieved to hear Detective Flynn's voice.

"Sorry to bother you, Makedde. Uh . . ." A moment of silence followed, and it occurred to Mak that she liked the way he said her name. "I have been a little concerned," he continued, "I just don't like you getting mixed up in this mess."

It was ridiculously good to hear his voice, and Mak sensed that the impersonal formality that first plagued their communication had vanished. Something about their last meeting had changed things.

"Has Tony been bothering you at all?" he went on.

"Not lately."

The line was silent again. She could hear phones going off in the background.

"Yeah . . ." He paused. "Well, I should go. I just wanted to make sure you're OK."

She suspected that wasn't what he was calling about. "I'm fine," she assured him.

"Good. Bye."

"Bye."

Makedde hung up and crossed her arms, slightly puzzled by their odd, plotless conversation. When the phone rang again, she hoped it was Andy. It was.

"I forgot to ask you," he said. "How's that cut?"

"Oh, it was nothing. A mere flesh wound, as they say."

"How's the flat cleaned up?"

Makedde laughed. "Fine now, thanks. The Lanconide disappeared without a trace and the carbon gradually faded away."

"Lanconide," he said. "You're the first person I've ever known to say Lanconide instead of 'that white powder'. Half the cops don't even know the name for it."

"One of the perks of being my father's daughter."

He laughed. "Um . . . I wanted to ask you . . ." he trailed off, sounding unsure.

She blurted it out before she could stop herself. "Want to get together Friday night?"

"Sure!" he answered, sounding surprised. "Well, actually . . . No. Well. No, that's fine. Yes, that'd be nice."

"You don't sound so sure. It's not a big deal." *Whoops.*

"No, I'd like to. Friday night?"

"OK. Fu Manchu?" she suggested.

"Pardon?"

"Fu Manchu. It's a restaurant. Victoria Street, Darlinghurst. Casual. Good food. Around seven?"

"Great. Shall I pick you up?"

"Yes, I'd like that. See you then." Makedde's heart was pounding by the time she placed the receiver back into its cradle. She felt nervous, silly and excited.

Oh God. What have I done?

23

Becky Ross lived alone in a posh, two-level flat overlooking North Bondi Beach, the opposite end from Makedde Vanderwall's humble lodgings. He watched as Becky wandered around her bedroom, gathering clothes and folding them into a series of large suitcases that were opened on her bed.

She's not going anywhere.

He hid in the darkness of the street, out of sight of prying eyes. Neighbours were tucked inside their homes. Balconies that in the summer brimmed with parties and barbecues now lay barren like abandoned look-out posts.

Becky had not bothered to draw her curtains and was in full view of anyone who cared to look.

He was reaching a new level.

A celebrity.

Fame.

He watched her for a while, enjoying their special style of foreplay. He would try new methods. He could experiment. All the more practice for Makedde.

I'll treat you so right.

140

The engine purred quietly as he drove right up Becky's driveway. He parked the van as close to her door as he could, turned off the lights, and opened the side door. Clutching a bouquet of cheap, blood-red roses, he rang Becky's doorbell. He stepped back to observe her reaction through the brightly lit windows. She didn't seem surprised, but immediately went to a mirror to check her hair and make-up. "Just a minute!" she called out and applied another coat of his favourite glossy red lipstick.

She finally opened the front door and looked at the roses with distaste. She smelled of an expensive, flowery perfume, and she was barefoot, her toenails painted a tacky puce-pink. He would fix them.

Becky didn't notice his leather gloves, or his generic cap. She didn't even look at his face. "Who are these from?"

"MDM Publicity Department. Do you have a pen? I need you to sign this."

"Hang on," she mumbled.

Becky wandered away, disappearing into a room down the hall. He closed the door behind him, holding the knob firmly until it shut with a barely audible *click*. He placed the stack of papers on the sideboard and glanced around the foyer.

Becky Ross had left a pair of stilettos at the door for him. *For him*.

The soap star came back with a pen and bent over the papers. "Hey," she said with confusion, "these are blank—"

Swiftly, he slid the hammer from the back of his pants and raised it over her head. It came down on her skull with a fleshy thud, and buried itself in her luminous blonde hair. With a crunch her face collided with the wooden sideboard and as she moaned and tumbled backwards to the floor, her eyes rolled back in their sockets.

As Becky lay dazed, he slipped the stilettos on her feet, covering her ugly toenails. He picked her up in a fireman's lift and carried her with ease to the back of his open van, dumping her on the floor. With cold precision he shackled her wrists, pulled the blanket over her head, and shut and locked the sliding door. He then returned to the flat, removed the roses and blank papers, and locked the front door. He deposited his props on the passenger seat and took off his gloves before starting the engine. He was pleased with himself. From the time he rang her doorbell, the whole exercise had taken less than two minutes.

24

"Oi! Make that two!" Andy Flynn called across the smoky room.

Jimmy turned on his bar stool, cracking a wide smile at the sight of his partner. "Ah, ya malaka!" Jimmy shouted affectionately and swivelled back to the bartender. "Another Boags Strongarm for my mate, Phil."

In the blink of an eye a second beer was waiting on the dark mahogany bar. Andy settled into his favourite spot, throwing his suit jacket over the neighbouring stool.

"Pos pas?" Jimmy asked.

"I'm all right."

"I thought ya might show."

"This thing's fuckin' killing me," he said.

"I hear ya, mate." They raised their bottles and clinked them together. "Cheers."

A few cops from the Witness Protection Division were playing pool in one corner, and regulars from the Major Crime Squad were downing a few at the other end of the bar. As usual, there wasn't a female in sight, and at that moment, that was exactly how Andy liked it.

He watched Jimmy take long gulps of beer and re-marked, "Ya know, I tried telling Cassandra that beer was designed to be drunk straight from the bottle. But would she listen? Nah."

"So right. Designed that way."

"Exactly. It's the shape of the neck, the pressure as it comes out. Drinking from glasses is sacrilege."

"Sacrilege."

They contemplated that simple, scientific fact for a mo-ment. How was it that women didn't understand?

Then Jimmy asked the wrong question. "You seen her? Cassandra?"

"Not since Tuesday. And I'd rather not talk about it."

"Sure, mate. Birds, eh?" He shook his head. "That Makedde's a babe though. Did I tell you she was in *Sports Illustrated*?"

"No kidding?" Andy was determined to find a copy.

"Yeah. Boy, I'd like a piece of that, ya know what I mean? Pretty fine."

Andy nodded silently. He was almost tempted to confide that he was having dinner with her the following night, but letting that secret out would be a disaster. Dating a key witness was a definite no-no.

Jimmy was still talking. "By the way, got the report on the prints. A few came up nil; probably models. But we came up with one real interesting name."

"Well, you're not going to leave me hangin' are you?" Andy said impatiently.

"No," Jimmy replied, but kept him hanging anyway. He took his time, swigging leisurely on his beer, then licked his lips and went on, "OK, one set comes up with a record. Rick Filles. Photographer. Arrested for sexual assault two years ago."

"What'd he do?"

"Some bird went up to his pad to have her pictures taken and claimed—now get this—that he tied her up wearing nothing but her knickers, took photos of her and touched her up. He swore it was consensual and his lawyer got him a suspended sentence. He got off easy, no pun intended, but now his prints show up in some dead chick's pad. I'd say he's running out of luck."

"I'd like to see those reports."

"Thought ya might."

"We gotta jump on this," Andy said. "I want to know everything this guy has been up to. Every dollar he's made, every parking ticket. If he scratches his arse, I want to know why."

"We'll get on it in the morning."

Andy stared at him.

"Well," Jimmy said again with emphasis, *"we'll get on it in the morning."*

"Where are those reports?"

"Skata. Can I say no to this?"

"Where?" Andy said bluntly.

"In the office."

With Jimmy shaking his head, they grabbed their coats in unison. "Ya know, Kelley paired me with you to mellow you out."

Andy laughed. "Lies. He told me himself that he paired you with me in a last-ditch effort to teach you how to get your shit together."

They gulped down the last of their beer, and wished Phil a good night.

The next morning, Andy was sipping his second scalding black coffee when Jimmy dragged himself into the office. "Good afternoon," Andy said without looking up.

Jimmy came over and leant on his desk as if it were a

crutch. "You sprightly fuckin' malaka. Some of us need sleep, ya know."

Andy held up his coffee. "The lives of innocent women in this city depend on this brew."

"Caffeine has its limits."

"No wonder you never went for the SPG."

"Too sharp for them poustis, mate," Jimmy said, openly disdainful of the ultra-fit, finely-tuned members of the State Protection Group, formerly known as the Tactical Response Team.

"I've got Mahoney quietly doing some checks on this Filles guy. We're gonna set him up," Andy said.

"Good on ya," Jimmy replied sleepily. "Angie stayed up, ya know. She was sitting in that big green chair by the window in the fuckin' dark. Nearly gave me a heart attack. I had my gun out of the holster before I realised who it was. She figured I was rootin' around on her till 4 a.m. Wanted to sniff my collar."

"You should have called her."

"I shoulda gone home. She almost took a frying pan to my head."

"I can talk to her if you want, tell her it was my fault," Andy offered, knowing only too well how easily relationships could fall apart in their occupation.

"Nah. She knows the mate system. She'd never believe you."

25

Maim. Hit. Kick. Palm strike, eye gouge, knee to the face. Get ready Makedde . . .

"Ready and . . . one!"

"Nooooo!" the all-girl warriors cried in harmony, reaching into the air with their right hands, palms up, fingers closed.

". . . two," the instructor continued and they pulled their fingers out like cat's claws, gouging at the eyes of imaginary attackers.

". . . and three!"

In unison each student brought up her left hand to join her right and grabbed the assailant's head, slamming it down, their right knee rising swiftly to smash the face in.

"Grab the coconut off the tree, crack it open on your knee . . ."

Makedde's blood was pumping, sweat beading on her upper lip. The Friday afternoon self-defence class was as good a workout as Jaqui had promised, especially when they brought out the punching bags, but, she had to admit, her mind was on Andrew Flynn.

"Makedde!"

The sound of her own name startled her. She whirled around to face her instructor, Hanna, a tough, heavy-set blonde with a brush cut. Hanna was a black belt in karate who had taught and lectured on self-defence for over ten years.

"Where's your head? You may as well have tried to lick your attacker to death," Hanna scolded, shaking her head disapprovingly.

Through the sweat, Makedde felt herself blush. "Sorry. You're right. I was thinking about something else." *Someone* else. "Let me try again."

In an instant an unwanted but vivid mental picture of Stanley loomed before her. His face was always festering in the shadows of her mind, waiting for any opportunity to remind her that she was far from invincible. She reminded herself that Stanley was now doing time for a series of violent rapes. Knowing that she was safe from him made it a lot easier to use him as a mental punching bag. Great therapy.

"And . . . one!" her instructor began.

"NOOOO!" Makedde yelled and struck Stanley's throat with her palm, gouged at his eerie, pale blue eyes with long fingernails, grabbed his thick head in both hands and with all her might rammed it down into her striking knee. She could almost feel his face bounce off and his body fall to the gym floor. She would kick him in the head now, and stomp all over his . . .

Makedde noticed that the other girls were staring at her.

Hanna was smiling. "Much better. Now for the bag." She handed a large, square punching bag to one of the other students, who looped her arms around the holds on the back and positioned it on the side of her hip.

"OK, Makedde. I want ten hits in as many seconds, each different. And no pussy stuff. Ready and . . . one!"

Makedde could see Stanley grinning as he blocked the exit door, switchblade out, brown hair ruffled, his pants half undone.

"ONE!" Mak screamed, giving Stanley a snap-kick to the balls. "TWO!" a knee strike, "THREE!" a palm strike to the throat, "FOUR!" gouge his eyes, "FIVE!" grab his head and ram it down to a right knee strike, "SIX!" right elbow strike to the head, "SEVEN!" left elbow strike to the head, "EIGHT!" backwards elbow strike, "NINE!" hammer fist to the groin and "TEN!" SQUEEZE THE TESTICLES!

When Mak had completed all ten moves, she stopped screaming, and took a step back to catch her breath. Sweat dripped from her chin to her T-shirt. This time even Hanna was staring. There was a moment of silence, then someone said, "Have you taken self-defence classes before?"

"No," she said, slightly embarrassed. "I'm just a really angry person."

At 5.30 p.m. Makedde arrived back at the flat and threw herself onto the bed, still damp and dressed in her gym sweats. When the phone rang, she let the answering machine pick it up.

"Hi sweetie, it's Loulou," the voice echoed across the room after the beep. "It was great seeing you yesterday. Can you believe this Becky Ross disappearance thing? Rumour has it she eloped with the rugby player, but the police suspect foul play. No kidding! That guy is so foul . . . Oh, I'm rambling again. Call me."

Makedde smiled. Loulou was an incorrigible gossip queen. *Becky Ross's disappearance?* She must have taken off right after the fashion launch. Sounded like another publicity stunt. Perhaps Mak should have checked the papers, there might have been an article on the launch, with humorous reviews about Becky's take on fashion. Mak would call Loulou in the morning. No doubt she'd be itching to find out about her secret date.

He'll be here at seven o'clock, Mak reminded herself for the hundredth time. The thought of his arrival propelled her back onto her tired feet and into the cramped bath. It was shallow and short, and she didn't fit, but she bathed anyway, pouring hot water over herself from an oversized measuring cup, and adding a few drops of fragrant vanilla oil. With her long legs sticking straight up in the air, she shaved from ankle to thigh, careful not to cut herself as she had before. She ran a hand over her legs, and, satisfied they were smooth, began a careful pedicure. She painted her toenails "French Nude" as the shade was called, and kept her toes pointed in the air to dry until her feet started to tingle from lack of circulation. She would be wearing boots so her toes wouldn't be on display, but it made her feel good to pamper herself.

She emerged from the steamy bathroom feeling better than she had in days. It seemed at least some of her worries were swirling down the drain with the bath water. *A date!* She would get over the recent turn of events, and get on. She was sure of it.

As she went to sit down two scrapes on the wooden floor caught her attention. The sofa. Was it out of place? It seemed further from the wall. Had she pushed it across the floor without thinking? She pushed it back and was amazed at how heavy it was. Strange. Perhaps her mind was playing tricks on her. She was, after all, somewhat preoccupied—the cloyed and compelling Detective Andrew Flynn was taking her out. And soon! She did her best to choose an outfit that was both casual and attractive, without appearing as if she was *trying* to look attractive. This was a science unto itself, and it took a while to get it right. Finally she made up her mind, deciding upon her favourite straight black pants and a deep blue fitted jumper that brought out the colour of her eyes.

It was only 6.30 p.m. She forced herself to settle into the chair and read the last few chapters from the dog-eared copy of her true-crime favourite, *Mindhunter*.

At 6.59 p.m. the buzzer announced Andy's arrival.

Makedde leapt out of her chair, sending the book flying. Reading about Robert Hansen, the "game" hunting Alaskan, set her on edge, jumpy at the slightest noise.

She checked herself in the mirror, tugged her sweater down a bit and smoothed her black pants. Her hair didn't look too perfect. Just a bit messy, so she didn't appear to be trying too hard. She grabbed her long coat and a pair of chunky-heeled leather boots, and sat on the floor while she pulled them on. She was sitting by the wardrobe, and, just as she had noticed scratches on the floor beside the sofa, so too were there marks beside the wardrobe. She examined the deep impression of the wardrobe's short wooden legs. The wardrobe legs were at least two inches away from the indents. Perhaps the police had moved things during the search and she hadn't noticed until now.

She stood up, relishing every extra inch her boots afforded her, turned off the lights and locked the door, and forced herself to relax as she descended the stairs. Andy was leaning against a railing outside the front door, wearing Levi's with a white cotton shirt and a well-worn leather jacket. He was also wearing a gorgeous smile.

"Hi."

She did her best to appear cool and unaffected, suppressing a burgeoning thrill deep within her.

He gestured to her outfit, saying, "You look beautiful." The comment threatened to shatter her veneer of detachment. This was sounding like a real date already. "I *am* allowed to say that, aren't I?" he went on, possibly expecting she would bite his head off again.

"Of course. Who doesn't like to be told that? Thank you. You too. Look *good*, I mean. You look good without your suit on."

What? Stop rambling!

"Don't tell my colleagues that or they'll get the wrong impression." Mak laughed. "Actually," he added, "don't tell them anything. I wouldn't hear the end of it if they knew I was here. OK?"

"My lips are sealed."

They maintained an awkward silence on the drive from Bondi to Darlinghurst. She was starting to wonder what she was doing there, and she suspected he might be doing the same.

"Thanks for getting me out of the house," she said, playing down their date. "Like you said, I don't know a lot of people here so it'll be good to hang out with a local."

"Yeah, it's good to get out."

Silence again.

Mak noticed that the Holden Commodore they were in had a sophisticated radio system on the front dash. There was also a big, square flashlight at her feet and when she looked around she noticed a siren light sitting on the back seat.

"Squad car, eh?" she asked, picking up the flashlight and examining it.

"Don't ask," he said seriously. "You can put that in the back if you want."

"I like that this is a squad car," she assured him. "Put the siren on. It'll get us through the traffic a lot quicker."

"Yeah, right."

She gave him a mischievous look. "Come on," she dared.

A teenager in a car ahead of them was in the midst of attempting an illegal U-turn when Andy switched the siren on for a split second. The kid's tyres squealed as he took off down the road. It served as a good ice breaker, and distracted them for a couple of minutes.

Victoria Street was buzzing and after circling the block a few times they finally found a parking spot not too far away. A line of takeaway customers spilled out the front door of Fu Manchu, and they were relieved when they looked through the large window to see that there were a couple of empty tables inside. They grabbed one and sat in uncomfortable silence as the exotic aromas of Asian dishes drifted by them on the way to waiting mouths. The soft sound of Chinese music was barely audible above the hum of the chatty patrons who filled every incense-scented inch of the place.

"So, what do you think?" she asked.

"It's great. How did you find out about it?"

"I like food," she said with a grin.

"That's unusual for a model."

"You bet. Would you like me to order for us?" she offered, gesturing to the menu penned on the wall.

Andy looked momentarily surprised by her suggestion, and perhaps a bit relieved. "Sure."

A waitress approached with a shaved head and Birkenstock sandals, showcasing a butterfly tattoo on the top of her foot.

"We'd like to start with the sang choi bao, then the duck wraps with lots of hoi sin. Salt and pepper cuttlefish and steamed eggplant, too, please." She turned to Andy. "That all right with you?"

He nodded.

"Am I allowed to ask how the case is going?" she said tentatively once the waitress had left.

"Of course. I'm just not allowed to tell you."

She smiled.

"Believe me, it's in good hands and I'll let you know anything that's important."

"I hope so." She'd try him again later, perhaps after a few drinks. Makedde was relieved when the first dish arrived quickly. She thanked their waitress and commented on how great the food looked.

"Uh, yes," Andy replied, eyeing the collage of lettuce and ground meat nervously. "What's it called again?"

"Sang choi bao."

With uncertainty he reached for his water, casually watching her next move.

"I adore this place. Don't you just love Asian food?" she asked, slowly assembling her first mouthful. He followed her lead, placing the mix in the centre of a leaf of lettuce and wrapping it up.

"Yeah. Stir-fry. That sort of thing. Takeaway mostly," he replied, blushing as bits of food slid out of his iceberg lettuce and onto the stainless-steel table.

First date and I've got him embarrassed.

"Do you like it?"

"Yes. It's very tasty . . . when I can get it in my mouth."

"Yeah, they only use the best dog meat and monkey brain mix here. Much better than down the street."

Andy started to choke.

"I'm kidding! I'm kidding!" she quickly backpedalled. "Sorry. I don't know what's gotten into me tonight. It's made with ground pork, spices and onions, I swear."

"Uh-huh."

"Actually, this is the only pork dish I ever eat. The vego version just isn't as good. Generally I have a lot of fruits and vegetables and a bit of fish and chicken," she rambled on. "Some call it semi-vegetarian. I can understand the full vegetarian perspective though; vegetables don't scream as loud when you chop them up."

"Yeah, well," he said vaguely and there was a pregnant pause. "So, what did you do today?" he finally asked.

That was another lively line of conversation. Makedde pictured herself clawing at Stanley's eyes and delivering devastating blows to his private parts. "You really don't want to know," she replied.

Andy looked at her, curious and a little concerned. "What if I really *do* want to know?"

"I played squash with invisible balls," she said under her breath. Now her dinner companion looked confused as well as curious and concerned.

"I just started a self-defence class at the Bondi Community Centre on Friday afternoons. I promise I won't use any of the moves on you, unless it is absolutely necessary."

"Oh . . . good. You can never be too careful. So, have you had a chance to see much of Sydney?"

"Well, it's my second trip here, but I don't get out much at night. As you guessed, I don't know a lot of people."

"I don't get out much either. Work can be a bit all-consuming."

Makedde remembered the argument she'd overheard in his office, and the words slipped out before she could stop them. "Who was that woman in your office the other day? She was beautiful."

She thought she saw a brief flicker of pain in his eyes before he laughed and said, "Oh, Cassandra. She's my ex-wife. Well, almost ex-wife. We're divorcing."

Makedde felt terrible. "Oh, I'm so sorry. I didn't know—"

"That's all right, we've been separated for over a year. The day you saw her she had just come in with more divorce settlement papers. It's no big deal; no kids or anything. Just some property and a car."

"A car?"

"Never mind. Bit of a long story."

The duck wraps arrived and Andy looked relieved that there was something else to talk about aside from Cassandra. Then he looked at the food laid out in front of them—slices of duck fanned out on a large plate, slivers of cucumber and chilli, a dark mushroom-coloured sauce, a mysterious, steaming bamboo basket—and his expression went momentarily blank. Feeling guilty, Mak leant forward and offered him a hand in assembling the meal.

"Here," she said, "let me get it for you."

She gingerly opened the bamboo basket and removed what looked like a flat pancake. She placed the duck, a piece of chilli-coated cucumber and a dab of hoi sin sauce inside it, and wrapped it up. She slid the plate over to Andy, accidentally brushing his hand as she did so. Mak felt like she'd been zapped by an electric current. She looked up and found Andy staring with the same intensity straight back at her.

Makedde broke from his gaze, blushing. "You . . . ah, don't need to use your chopsticks," she managed. "It's better with your hands."

Your hands.

Oh God, she thought, *this is trouble*.

Across the street, hidden in the shadows beneath a broken streetlight, a solitary figure, flushed with violent jealousy and uncontrollable rage, intently watched their intimate dinner.

26

Andy breezed into the office late Saturday morning, coffee in hand, to find Jimmy waiting at his desk with his arms crossed over his protruding belly. With a smirk on his lips he looked like the cat who'd swallowed the canary. He waited until Andy was within close range before he declared, with considerable satisfaction, "So, you're rootin' the pin-up."

Andy spat out a mouthful of coffee. "What?"

"I'm talking to Robertson in the Cross, checking to see if they know this malaka, Rick Filles, and if anything's goin' down, and guess what he says to me?" Jimmy paused, raising an eyebrow. "He says there's not much, except Flynn puttin' the moves on some babe in Victoria Street. And there you are, right in the bloody window with the Vanderwall chick, starin' into each other's eyes like a couple of lovesick teenagers."

"You saw us?"

"Skata, anyone could have seen you. Did you ever stop to notice that the place is a friggin' fish bowl?"

"Shit."

"Was she any good?"

"Hey, I was a perfect gentleman—"

"I bet." Jimmy grinned.

"I dropped her off at home. It's none of your business, anyway."

"You can't let me down, Andy. As of last night, you're a legend. Some of the guys want you to get her autograph. They're bringing in their copies of *Sports Illustrated*."

"You're kidding. You didn't tell anyone, did you?"

"I didn't have to tell anyone! They were watching you! It's risky, but hey, I can't blame you. Hell, I'd jump at the chance. Just don't fuck up this case, Andy. This is a big one for both of us."

Andy shook his head. "Enough said. Now, what have you found out?"

"Well, we're checking through the personals, and there are surprisingly few ads for models. The ones in the employment section are legit, but then there's this one in the section between 'Mistress Chantal', and 'bold, busty, blonde Barbie'. Great little ad. Subtle but effective. Ya know, some of the shit in there is really quite entertaining. I wonder if it's even physically possible to do half the things they claim in those ads—"

Andy cut him off before he got too carried away. "What'd the ad say?"

"I'll show you." Jimmy handed him a folded piece of newspaper. An ad was circled in the same red felt pen that had so tastefully been used to doodle on Makedde's photo. The print read:

MODELS—Photographer requires attractive female models, 16–25 yrs. Good rates.

The reader was urged to call "Rick".

Andy looked up. "You can't be serious. Are we talking the same Rick here?"

Jimmy nodded as he flipped through his notebook and said, "The bills go to a post office box in the Cross for a Mr. Rick Filles."

"Bingo. This is the perfect way in. I'll run it by Kelley and you get Mahoney to call Filles up and arrange a photo session."

"Good idea. Though I don't know if she'd agree."

"She can handle it."

Less than two hours later, Constable Karen Mahoney reported to Andy's desk wearing her well-pressed uniform, hair in a bun and no make-up.

"We have an assignment for you, Constable."

"Great!" she said eagerly, standing with her hands clasped in front of her.

Kelley had given clearance on surprisingly short notice, mostly because it was a small operation that wouldn't require a UC. The only conditions were to keep Mahoney under watch at all times and "not screw it up" as he put it.

Jimmy handed her the newspaper cut-out.

"This Rick Filles character may be luring the women using this article. We want you to check him out and, if necessary, help bring him in."

Her face lit up with excitement but after reading the ad her expression changed.

"Uh . . . you want me to pose as a model for this guy?"

"You'll be wired, and we'll have people watching you at all times."

"Watching—"

"To ensure your safety," Andy said. "We have to see if this guy is our man, and if he is, you'll be the one to save all the women out there who are in danger right now."

This statement seemed to have the desired impact.

"Yes, sir."

"Jimmy will fill you in. I want you on this right away."

"I won't have to get . . . *nude* or anything, will I?"

"You can't afford to make this guy suspicious; we don't want him tipped off. But your safety is our number one priority. Use your own judgment."

She seemed to ponder it for a while. "What about Tony Thomas?"

"Hunt, Reed and Sampson will take care of that," Jimmy said. "This is more important. We need you." Andy saw him put an arm around her as they disappeared down the hall.

At last, Andy had time to think. For one blissful moment the office was empty. It was a slow Saturday, and even Inspector Kelley had gone home. He pulled his phone over and dialled Makedde's number. It rang a few times before she answered with a cautious-sounding, "Hello?"

He was alarmed by her tone. "It's Andy. Everything all right?"

There was a pause. "Yeah. Just some strange calls."

"What kind of strange calls?" he asked, suppressing a strong urge to jump in the squad car and drive round to the flat.

"Oh, I'm sure it's nothing. Hang-ups. I think so many models have stayed here that people are calling and expecting someone else to answer."

Andy hoped that was the reason. It sounded plausible, but it still made him uneasy. "Tony been bothering you?"

"No, actually." She paused. "Thanks for dinner last night, by the way. It was nice to get out."

"My pleasure. But, maybe next time I'll choose the restaurant." He hoped there would be a next time.

"I'm sorry about the food, I know it was a bit tricky—"

"No, I loved the food. It's just that the place is . . ." He stopped himself, deciding it was pointless to let her know the entire police force had watched them dine.

"I understand. It's not your style. What kind of food do you like?"

He wanted to see her again. He wanted to watch over her, make sure she was all right. She was so different from Cassandra. "I'll show you tonight . . . if you'll let me," he said.

"Uh . . . sure," she replied.

Maybe he had sounded too eager. "Or not," he added.

"No, I'd love to."

"Same time?"

"See you then."

He hung up the phone and realised he was no longer alone.

"Uh-huh," Jimmy said with his eyebrows raised.

"Not a word," Andy warned him. "Not a word—"

"Anyway, as I was saying, this is a real important case and it would be a *real* shame if one of us fucked it up somehow, like by getting personally involved or—"

"Jimmy!"

He fell silent.

"Thank you," Andy said emphatically. "Has Kelley spoken to you about the added help?" They needed more research assistants to cover all the similar sex case histories in their records.

"No. He hasn't said a word to me about anything."

That didn't surprise him. It was common knowledge that Andy was Inspector Kelley's favourite. When Inspector Kelley had arranged to have Andy flown to Quantico to study with the FBI's Behavioural Science Unit, Jimmy was not given a chance to go along. Nor did the new unit in Canberra invite him down. Andy suspected his partner preferred it that way. It took the pressure off him, so that Andy was the one expected to perform miracles.

The inspector's favouritism had allowed Andy a rare opportunity to study investigative profiling with the FBI's elite serial crime unit. They were recognised as the best in the world. Andy knew this case was his opportunity to prove that the confidence in him was well-founded, and it was a burden he felt privileged to bear.

"If we can't get more manpower, we'll have to make do with what we've got. As usual."

And that meant longer hours for everyone.

27

Mak was curled up against the arm of the lounge in a foetal position when the intercom buzzed.

"Hello?"

"It's me. Andy."

"Hi. Come on up."

In a second he was at the door, and when he walked up to her and smiled, she felt some of the tension dissipate.

It's all in my head.

"Hello," he said, carefully watching her eyes. "Are you all right? Any more calls?"

Mak looked away. "A couple," she admitted. It was more than a couple. The furniture was freaking her out, too. Things seemed to be changing position on a daily basis.

"How many calls?"

She tried to think. "Eight, maybe ten today."

He frowned. Two deep creases formed between his eyebrows and his lower lip stuck out a little. "I don't like the sound of that. That's not just wrong numbers."

She sat down on the couch, and he followed her lead, sitting at the opposite end, just far enough away to avoid invading her space. She thought him polite, but wished he would hold her instead.

"Are you hungry?" he asked. "We don't have to go out if you don't want to—"

"No, I want to. But can we just sit for a moment first?"

"Of course. Anything you want. Have you been able to talk to anyone about this? A counsellor? A person in your position might need—"

"I don't need to see a psychologist," she said, cutting him off. "I've got nothing against seeing one, obviously. After all, I want to be one eventually. But really, I don't need to. Not now." She knew she wasn't being logical. All the warning signs were there.

"I wasn't inferring that you *needed* one, only that it might be—"

"No," she insisted, a little too loudly.

Andy was looking at her, his deep green eyes revealing his concern. She hadn't seen anyone look at her with such caring for a long time.

"Tell me about Catherine. Were you very close?"

"She was a good friend . . ." She trailed off, uncertain that she could handle that particular conversation.

"It's OK if you need to talk about it," he prompted her.

She knew that if she started, she wouldn't be able to stop. Finally she decided that she didn't care. "She'd lived near my family since she was little. Both her parents died when she was very young, and these awful foster parents took her in. She used to come over to our house a lot. I guess I kind of mothered her because she was a lot younger. Or maybe I was more like a big sister. Over time we grew apart, but when she started modelling a few years ago we became best buddies again. We both started quite young; fourteen, fifteen years old. I knew what it was like to be thrown into it like that, so I showed her the ropes.

But it wasn't always me helping her out. She was there for me when I needed her."

Makedde recalled the attack by Stanley, and remembered the gruelling police investigation, and how Catherine had turned down an overseas assignment to stay with her and support her. But Stanley was in jail now and it was pointless to dwell on the past. It was none of anyone's business, and she certainly wasn't about to burden this kind man with it, who was nearly a stranger after all, and who was politely allowing her to ramble on. "Anyway, Catherine was really supportive," she said vaguely, "and I really miss her."

"And now you feel you have to help her because she helped you. That's understandable, but there's nothing any of us can do for Catherine now. We can only catch her killer and live our lives."

Andy was right, and Makedde was determined to do just that—catch Catherine's killer.

He seemed to read her thoughts. "I know you want to help, but I'm not going to let you get involved in this case any further than you already have. We've got it under control—"

"Really? Then where is this psycho? Sit him in front of me so I can watch him suffer the way she did! Show me—"

"Makedde. Sometimes there can be no *true* justice," he said, putting a warm, comforting arm around her. "Some things can never be made right."

It's true; Catherine's murder. Mum's death. Nothing can make it right.

Tears rolled down Makedde's cheeks as Andy held her. She moved towards him and their lips brushed. At this, he pulled her tightly to him, his arms firm and muscular against her trembling body. Those soft lips came close to hers again. She watched them through teary eyes; watched them until they were upon her, softly kissing, lips parting, sweet-tasting, so gentle. She felt the weight of him, pressing her into the couch, his mouth more firmly now against hers. They moved together with passionate eagerness; fingers, lips, bodies, melting into one.

She couldn't help herself, and clearly, neither could he.

28

He watched her window from a park bench across the street, barely aware of the rain slowly soaking him to the skin. Beyond those closed blinds her warm, sensuous, candle-lit world lay seemingly untouchable. He could never be part of her life. Not in that way.

But everything was prepared. His patience would be rewarded. She would be his finest possession yet.

I'll wait until the candles go out.

At 3 a.m. the door of her building opened. A tall man paused, looking back up the stairs. Though it was dark, he could tell it was the man she had dined with. The detective. He wanted to slice his throat from ear to ear. Show Makedde how much she meant to him. Show her how he wouldn't tolerate competition.

He watched as the detective stood at the door, then turned and started back up the stairs, letting the door close behind him.

Furious, he leapt from the bench, clenching his fists tightly. He spotted a sickly pigeon resting quietly on the grass. In one quick movement, he snatched it up, twisting its small neck until the bird convulsed in fatal paroxysms. He dropped it to the ground, his latex gloves smeared with blood.

His patience was running out.

29

Just before 11 a.m. the following morning, Detective Flynn's mobile phone rang out sharply in the quiet room. Although the flat was small, he had difficulty finding his pants. He stumbled around half asleep.

They had barely slept a wink.

Makedde was dead to the world and he wanted to answer the phone before it woke her. Andy got down on all fours, squinted under the bed and found his dark blue suit pants wrapped around a bed leg with the squealing phone hanging out of the pocket.

Makedde stirred and mumbled something incoherent.

As Andy's fingertip touched the phone, the ringing stopped. He put it back down, his eyes resting on Makedde's soft curves. The doona was pushed down past her knees and a single sheet clung to her naked body. She would be cold. Gently he pulled the doona over her.

"Andy . . ." she murmured without opening her eyes. She turned, and he found himself inches from her face. Some make-up, now smudged, clung to her long elegant lashes. Full lips parted slightly with her deep breathing.

There was space beside Makedde on the bed. He slowly bent backwards, as if to limbo under some invisible bar, and supporting himself with the bed post, managed to slide under the doona without disturbing his sleeping beauty. As soon as he made himself comfortable, the phone started ringing again. He snatched it up off the floor, and irritably whispered, "Hello?"

"Perfect gentleman, huh?" Jimmy asked, sounding impressed.

"What is it, Jimmy?"

"Hate to bother you, Casanova, but we have another one."

Cupping a hand over his mouth, Andy whispered, "Are you saying what I think you're saying?"

"You won't believe this one. Becky Ross, the soapie star. They just found her in some bushes in Centennial Park. What a mess."

"Jesus." He was responsible for another lost life because he wasn't smart enough to put the pieces together. Here he was, getting it on with a beautiful girl while someone else was being murdered. And not just *any* beautiful girl, but a key witness.

"You're in bed with her, aren't you?"

"Shhhh," Andy whispered.

"You dog. Want me to pick you up?"

"No. I'll be down there in twenty minutes."

"Bring the panties."

"Piss off."

Andy switched off the phone and savoured one last moment beside Makedde's warm, slumbering body. "I have to go," he whispered in her ear. "I'll call you." Reluctantly, he prised himself from her bed, stepping over empty containers of Thai takeaway and noting that his clothes, which had found their way into all the corners of the room, were horribly wrinkled. He would have to dash home before Kelley saw him.

Tearing off a portion of a Thai menu announcing "free home delivery", he scrawled Makedde a note:

Had to go. I'll call you.—A

He eased himself back into the real world, feeling uneasy about what he'd done, and wondering how Makedde would feel when she woke up alone.

Centennial Park had been thrown into chaos—uniformed police were in the process of cordoning off large areas and blocking many of the roads and pathways and Sunday strollers looked confused as Andy drove slowly through, his siren squawking at odd moments. It was a beautiful clear day, and the public had come out in droves to enjoy a sunny family picnic or a bike ride through the park. They wouldn't have dreamt they would be taking their children to a major crime scene.

Andy flashed his badge at one of the uniformed officers and was directed towards an area of dense bushes down the road past the park's popular restaurant, an area made conspicuous by the blue-chequered police tape which stood out ominously against the trees. As he got out of his car Constable Hunt walked briskly up to him and blurted, "Look out, she's ripe."

Andy shut the car door and pulled a pair of latex gloves from the inside pocket of the navy suit he had quickly grabbed from home. "Are we sure about the ID?" he asked Hunt.

"It's her. Becky Ross. No question about it. I've seen her in all the papers and on television. See for yourself."

A cluster of people was assembled near the bushes, and some others stood further away, including a trim, elderly man holding a large German Shepherd by a lead. He spoke with animated gestures while Constable Reed took notes. No doubt he was the poor bastard who had discovered the body. Andy saw Jimmy and the forensic pathologist, Sue Rainford, who was crouched near the bushes. He approached them, and was still a few feet away when the sharp stench of decomposition assailed his senses.

The victim was on her back, legs spread-eagled in a degrading and unnatural pose. She was naked, except for one expensive-looking, blood-stained stiletto shoe. She had been grotesquely mutilated—disfigured almost beyond recognition.

Andy exchanged glances with his partner.

"Pos pas? Nice of you to join us," Jimmy said under his breath. "Looks like our guy watches the soaps. Should we add that to your profile?"

Sue Rainford was on her knees examining the body. She was a quiet, unflappable woman in her late forties, shaped like an exaggerated pear, with short brown hair and glasses. "Victim is a female, Caucasian, aged in her late twenties. Deceased several days," she said matter-of-factly into a microrecorder as she made an in situ examination. "The body is in a supine position, with the hips maximally abducted. No gross deformity of the limbs. Extensive blood loss is evident on the body, but not in the surrounding area. The victim was probably moved to this location post-mortem."

Becky's platinum hair spilled over the grass, matted and tangled with deep red gore, and her eyes, once sparkling with ambition, stared with rheumy lifelessness at the sky. Her wrists and ankles were raw and caked with congealed blood and maggots and other insects were crawling over her blistered body, dutifully going about their morbid business.

"She can't have been done before Thursday," Jimmy commented. "She had some kinda launch."

The pathologist continued recording her notes. "No apparent ligature marks around the neck. Lacerations evident around both wrists. The nipples have been completely excised. There is an extensive vertical incision from the lower torso to the pubic region." When Sue stood up, her face looked unusually pale. She glanced at Andy and he could see fear behind her glasses for the first time in years of working together. "Gentlemen, there is considerably more blood evident in these wounds. I suspect the killer made a number of these incisions while the victim was still alive, and possibly conscious."

"More than—" Jimmy began.

"Much more than the others. The first victims we found had largely post-mortem mutilation, but it appears he is now keeping them alive while he . . ." She didn't need to explain further. "I'll know more when I get her on the table."

"Jesus, the press are going to have a field day with this."

No sooner had the words been spoken, than the deep rumble of helicopter blades whipped the air far above their heads. They looked up to find the barrel of a news camera bearing down on them.

"Skata! How'd they know? Get them the hell out of here!" Jimmy yelled, frantically waving his arms in the air. "Fuckin' malakas! They're ruining the crime scene!"

The helicopter kept a distance above them and yet the trees shook and leaves fell as if they were in a wind storm.

"We should contact the immediate family right away and let them know what's happened before they watch it on the news," Andy shouted above the noise of the helicopter. He was worried.

Their killer was evolving.

30

The clock was flashing 11.59 a.m. when Makedde finally woke. It felt odd to rise at such a decadent hour, and she found herself sitting bolt-upright, panicking that she may be late for an appointment. As her mind cleared she remembered she had no appointments, and then with a creeping sense of dread she remembered what had happened the night before.

Andy?

She was alone in bed, and suddenly, unreasonably, she felt betrayed. She'd had more experience with unreliable men than she cared to remember, and she hoped she hadn't become involved with yet another. She noticed a section of torn paper sitting at the foot of the bed and her heart raced when she saw the writing on it. Reading it, she cracked a wide smile. She rose, wandered around the flat and found the plastic takeaway containers stacked by the kitchen sink, and her clothes, which would have been strewn everywhere, sitting in a civilised heap on a chair. None of the bathroom towels were wet—Andy must have been in a hurry, but had made a quick effort to clean up the flat regardless.

Very classy.

As Makedde was running a shower, the phone rang.

Andy!

She streaked across the room, snatching the phone up by the third ring.

"Hello."

Click.

She frowned, put the phone down and gazed out the large window. The blinds were not fully closed. Perhaps Andy had opened them before he left. Covering herself with her hands, she moved from the window, her stomach queasy. Once in the bathroom, she locked the door and stood before the mirror staring down her frightened image. In a moment joy had turned into fear. Beyond the locked door the phone rang again. After several rings, the answering machine picked it up. "Hello? . . . Sorry, it's just a machine," her voice replayed, "leave a message and I'll call you back."

"It's Andy. Are you there?"

Clutching a towel, she ran back into the front room and grabbed the phone. "Hi," she said, breathless. "How are you?"

"Good."

"Me too."

"Sorry, I was called in. Um . . . Something came up." He sounded uncertain. "I might be finished a bit late—"

"I'd love you to come over again, if you want to."

He paused. "OK. I'll call when I'm about to leave."

"What's going on?" she asked.

"I can't really say at the moment but I should be able to tell you a bit later."

"Something to do with the case?"

"Yes."

"Come on," she pressed.

He hesitated. "You know that lead about that photographer? The guy who put the ad in the paper? Well, we're checking him out today. I'll tell you all about it when I see you."

It was one o'clock by the time Makedde left the Bondi flat. It was a gloriously sunny day and Bondi Beach was crowded with people enjoying the first bit of decent weather all week. The cafés overflowed with exuberant customers and the waves were peppered with surfers. The sky was clear blue and the wind brisk as Makedde strolled past the shops, chomping on a nori roll and sipping a bottle of water.

She slipped into a newsagent and spied the paper containing the advertisement Andy had mentioned. Flipping past sections of employment opportunities and used cars, she found an ad for models to call "Rick", nestled between a promise of sexual adventure with "Sex-change Sue", and an ad for "new, exotic" ladies at a massage parlour. *Could this be the guy?* she wondered. Catherine would never go for that kind of line. How did he get to her?

A sun-kissed surfer in a T-shirt and boardshorts was paying for a thick copy of the Sunday paper and Mak got in line behind him. He smelled of the sea, his blonde hair still salty and damp.

"What's it like out there today, mate?" the man behind the counter asked him.

"Few wicked left-handers. Terrigal's been flat all week compared with this."

Terrigal.

"No kidding," the man said, giving him his change. "I

was up there for the Food and Wine Festival and the waves were pretty good."

Makedde caught the surfer's arm and he spun around to look at her with startled green eyes. He had freckles across his nose, neon pink zinc across his lips and a smile as wide as the Luna Park funny face.

"Sorry to bother you," she said, smiling back sweetly. "I heard you say Terrigal."

"Terrigal Beach, yeah."

"Where is that exactly?"

"Ah, not far. A couple of hours' drive north," he told her. "Hey, you American?"

"Canadian. Thanks—"

"You out here with anyone?"

"Yes. Oh, and I'm parked illegally, I'd better go. Thanks again." She tossed her payment on the counter and left before he could get another word in. With the newspaper folded under one arm, she continued down the street at a less leisurely pace.

JT Terrigal
Beach Resort
16
14

The scrawl had been nearly illegible and written at a sharp angle but it was making more sense now. She'd have to tell Andy about it when she saw him. Perhaps the numbers would make sense to him. An extension? A room number? On her way home, a book in the window display of a shop in Hall Street caught her interest. It was titled *Birthdays—A Personality Profile*, and although Mak was usually sceptical of the daily horoscopes, she couldn't resist.

She went inside and flipped it open to her birthday.

Skimming over assets like *charming* and *attractive*, a warning that she could be stubborn and the usual reference to her being born on Groucho Marx's birthday, she came to a paragraph that disturbed her. *Those born on this day have a thing about violence*, it read. *Being disturbed by it, or tending to indulge in it. Violence is attracted to this person. They must learn to be less obsessed . . .*

She slammed the book closed, making a loud noise that was rewarded by some strange looks from the other customers. *Violence? Attracted to me?* She slid the book back on the shelf, forcing the thought from her mind. She wandered back onto the street, into the crowd of surfers, hip locals and romantic couples.

As soon as Makedde entered the flat she grabbed the phone and dialled 013 for directory assistance, asking for "Terrigal Beach Resort". Bingo.

Catherine was to meet the man she called JT at Terrigal Beach Resort. The only mystery was what sixteen and fourteen stood for. It wasn't the tail end of the hotel's phone number. Makedde took a guess and phoned the resort.

"Terrigal Beach Resort. How may I help you?" a woman asked in a perky voice.

"Could I have room sixteen-fourteen please?"

"I'll just put you through." The phone rang several times, then the woman came back on the line. "I'm sorry, you must be mistaken. Room sixteen-fourteen is unoccupied at the moment. Which guest were you trying to reach?"

"Um." *What next?* "I have a message here to call my friend JT in room sixteen-fourteen. I've been away though, so I'm not sure how old the message is. When was he staying there?"

"I'm sorry, but we can't give out information about our

guests," the woman said firmly. "But if you'll give me your name, I'll check to see if there are any messages for you here. Otherwise you can give me the surname of the guest you are trying to reach and I'll see if they are presently registered with us."

Damn.

"That's all right. I'll call back later."

Well, at least the mysterious scrawl was no longer so mysterious. Catherine had been planning a romantic weekend with her lover boy. But just who was he? Surely the police could access the hotel records and find out whose name the room had been reserved under.

Andy wasn't due for a few hours, and Makedde couldn't wait to tell him about her find. But first, she needed to indulge her curiosity. She tore the ad from the paper, and examined it again as she dialled the number. Her call was picked up after three rings.

"Hello, is this Rick?" she asked in her best breathless Marilyn.

"What's your name, doll?"

"Debbie. I saw your ad."

"You American?"

Sure, why not? "Yes, I'm from L.A."

"How old are you?" Rick's voice had a nicotine growl. He sounded like he was at least forty.

"Uh, I'm twenty-three."

"What's your bust size, Debbie?"

"I'm a forty double D. Gosh, I hope I'm not too big."

"No such thing, babe. And your waist size?"

"Well, that's the funny thing, Rick. I only have a twenty-three-inch waist. I feel a bit self-conscious that I'm so top-heavy, but a photographer in L.A. wanted me to model some lingerie once, and he seemed really happy with the photos."

"You a blonde?"

"Oh, yes," she breathed.

"Natural?"

"Pardon?"

"A *real* blonde? All over?"

Yuck. "Oh, yes. All over."

They arranged a Wednesday night photo session and he gave her his studio address in Kings Cross. She giggled girlishly and asked if there was anything special she should bring.

"Stilettos. Knickers. I have some costumes here, too."

I'll bet you do. "OK, see you then," she said as seriously as she could manage.

She hung up and burst into hysterical laughter. Rick must be tickled pink to have a ditzy, top-heavy, blonde Californian coming to his studio. He'll sure be disappointed when he gets stood up. "A forty double D with a twenty-three-inch waist!" she screamed, wiping a tear from the corner of her eye.

He had specifically asked her to wear stilettos, but then any glamour photographer probably would ask the same thing. She questioned whether a clever killer would be so direct. In Makedde's experience, it was the ones who weren't so obvious that were the real danger.

31

Detective Flynn stood at the front of the room, the anxious faces of his task force watching him intently, ready to take notes. He ached to get back to Makedde, and pictured her lying in bed, covers pulled back to reveal naked curves. He had managed to remove himself from the demands of the investigation for one enchanted evening, but he was back at the sharp end now, and he had a large team of men and women depending on his every word.

"First of all, I'd like to thank all of you for your dedication to this case, especially on a Sunday afternoon," Andy began. "As you know, we have a fourth victim, actress Becky Ross. The autopsy just completed indicates that the time of her death was sometime late Thursday night or early Friday morning. Now, I will say it once more just to be sure that I'm making myself crystal clear. It is *vitally* important that we not allow any leaks about this case. If anything gets out, each of you will be in deep shit, got me? OK, enough of that.

"I've prepared a more in-depth profile of our killer. There are copies for each of you." He handed out the stapled photocopies and they passed them around. "Now remember, this is a general profile to be used as a tool in the investigation. Our killer is categorised as an 'anger excitation offender'." He looked up and caught the eye of some of his team. "That means he's sadistic. He may not have started out showing such tendencies, but he's certainly moving in that direction now—the latest murder confirms this. He is keeping his victims alive while he mutilates them.

"This type of offender will often use a con or a disarming line to lower the victim's guard and gain confidence. During the attack he may say things like, 'Call me Master', or 'Lord' or something like that."

Hunt barely managed to suppress a chuckle.

"Shut up and take notes, Hunt," Andy snapped. "Or you'll be the one assigned to check every sexual assault file for the past five years."

Hunt shut up.

"He may ask his victim, 'Does it hurt?' He may ask her to beg and he may humiliate and call her names to satisfy his needs." He watched Hunt's face, daring him to comment. "He may take photographs or videotape during the attack. He may inflict wounds, as we have seen, to the parts of the body which have sexual significance to him; breasts, feet, vagina, anus, and so on. He has an obvious fetish for feet and toes, and in this latest killing he removed the nipples of the victim. In an early stage of his deviancy he may have simply bitten or cut them in some way.

"Now, past sexual assault cases may give us more leads. Obviously, those in which the offender is currently serving time need not be included. This guy is very careful, but he may not have always been. He may have learnt some tips from other crims in prison or he may have his own little library on forensic procedure. The offender is likely to enjoy using sexual bondage apparatus and torture devices.

He may keep trophies or a diary. He brings an assault kit with him containing weapons, sexual props and bindings. He may stalk his victims or plan the attacks in advance. Such attacks may last from four to as much as twenty-four hours before the victim's death or release. Forensics agrees with this conclusion in the case of all four of our recovered victims."

"Psycho," Jimmy muttered under his breath.

"I was just getting to that part. We are possibly dealing with a violent psychopath with a high IQ, which means he could be very charming and very convincing. All of his victims have been white and we believe he is also white. He is methodical and reasonably mature. I estimate he is in his mid-twenties to late thirties and lives in the Sydney area. He has a private place to commit these crimes and hold his victims captive. This celebrity angle gives us a whole new perspective—he's reading the papers, reading about himself, and he's liking it. He reckons he's famous now. It's a fluke that the body wasn't found earlier. He's still not leaving them in hard to find places. He's not that concerned about their discovery.

"OK, that's it from me for now. Get to work on your assigned duties, and *communicate*. I want each of you to know what everyone else is up to at all times. For those of you working with Jimmy on this Rick Filles lead, he wants to say a few words."

Jimmy stood up, grinning. "You're a hard act to follow." He moved to the front of the room, one thumb hooked in his belt loop under his spare tyre. "OK, Mahoney goes in at five o'clock. She'll have the wire in her, uh . . . bra."

Andy turned his back from his team and rolled his eyes. Jimmy had a way of sounding like he had no authority even when he was helping run a major investigation.

"Everything goes as we discussed," Jimmy continued.

"We'll be in the van across the street. Mahoney's hoping to find incriminating photos, weapons or bondage devices for forensics to test. If anything gets hairy, we haul her out of there pronto. Look you guys . . . and girls, we got a good lead here, so let's nail him!"

Everyone cheered and rose from their seats.

"You have a way with words, Jimmy," Andy remarked as they filed past him to leave.

It was late when Andy arrived at Makedde's door, straight from work once again. He looked tired and stressed, but was happy to see her. Makedde had a lot she wanted to talk to him about, but she felt she needed to clarify a few things first.

"Andy—"

"Yes?" He leant over and kissed her unexpectedly. When they parted lips she felt a little light-headed.

"I think that last night—"

"Was wonderful," he interjected.

"Well, yes," she continued, "but I think things moved along a bit fast. I don't normally—"

"Me neither."

She looked up, sceptical. "Really?"

Andy stared straight into her eyes and said, "I don't think either of us were expecting things to turn out this way. But I, for one, am glad that they have, regardless of the risks."

Everything was too fast, too uncertain. Makedde didn't know what to say. "Just realise that I don't jump into things with both feet,"—*Yes, I do*—"and last night was different for me," she blurted.

"Understood. Say no more."

She smiled, relieved at having made herself clear. *Clear about what? Am I just trying to tell him I'm not that easy . . . usually?*

Mak led him to the couch and they sat together. She wanted to change the subject. "OK. I've got something to share with you. You know the note that Catherine wrote, about JT and Terrigal and all that? Well, I figured out that she was going to meet her lover, who she calls JT, in room sixteen-fourteen at the Terrigal Beach Resort."

Andy didn't say a word.

"If you check the hotel records, you'll probably find out who Catherine was having an affair with before she was murdered." Makedde emphasised the word "murdered", sensing that Andy was unimpressed with her information, again. "OK, what's up?" she finally asked when he didn't respond.

"Well . . ." Andy looked sheepish. "We know that a man was staying there, but he denies any relationship with Miss Gerber, and we're inclined to believe him."

Mak felt her face flush with anger.

"You needn't have gone to all that trouble. Please let us handle the investigation."

How could he have not told her? She took a deep breath. "This man, does he have a first name of JT?"

"No."

"OK, does he have the initials of JT?"

"Yes, actually he does, but that's all I can tell you, OK? I shouldn't be discussing this with you. Can we not talk about work, please?"

She shook her head, rage building. He wasn't getting off that easy. "How long have you known about this guy?"

"Not long. Just calm down."

"Calm down? Jesus! You think I'm obsessed with this affair she was having, don't you?"

Andy put his hands on hers and she shook them off angrily. "I think you lack objectivity here," he told her gently. "We don't have any right to intrude on this man's life just because a girl scrawled some note that *might* point to a room he was going to stay in."

"Wait," she said with sudden insight. "*Was* going to? He cancelled the reservation?"

Andy looked slightly puzzled.

"You do realise what that means, don't you? Catherine was killed on a Wednesday and discovered on Friday. If the room booking was cancelled before my ID on Saturday morning, then whoever reserved the room must have already known that she was dead, and wouldn't be showing up. That means they had something to do with her death."

"Whoa! Slow down there Miss Marple." He flashed her another one of those irritating looks of underestimation. "*If* this man cancelled his hotel reservation, it could be for any reason at all. And he says he's never even met Catherine Gerber. There's nothing to tie her to him."

"Yes there is." Makedde proudly slipped the ring off her thumb. "Check the inscription."

Andy took the thick diamond ring in his hand, frowning, and turned it over and read the inscription. His eyes widened. "Where did you get this?"

"It was in Catherine's jewellery box. I found it when I packed up her stuff."

"Why didn't you tell me? This is evidence!"

"I didn't tell you because you were being an arsehole. Sort of like you're being now."

Andy stood up from the couch. She could see him change when his temper rose. The sensitive man had vanished, and one big walking ego had taken his place. "I can't tell you about the case. You know that. I'm not supposed to tell you anything, and I'm not even supposed to be here. So if you're pissed off that I didn't tell you about where the note led to, tough."

Makedde crossed her arms and legs. Her muscles tensed. She watched him pace back and forth.

"This could be considered tampering with evidence. This is a fucking murder investigation for Christ's sake, and you're withholding potential evidence!"

"You guys had your chance," Makedde declared, her tone steady. "I told you everything I knew about the affair. You searched her flat top to bottom. You must have found the ring and didn't think anything of it. That's not my fault. And after the way you reacted the last time I came to you with information, you can bet I wasn't eager to come to you about this."

Andy continued to pace the room. He slipped the ring in his pocket and anxiously ran a hand through his hair.

"OK, maybe I should have told you about this guy, but I couldn't, you know?" he said. "We didn't have anything on him but her scrawl, and even that was vague."

"Well, the ring's not vague."

"The ring may change things. Look, there are things I can't tell you," he said.

"I know."

Andy stopped pacing and came over to her on the couch. He squatted down, and gently rested his hands on her knees. Makedde was closed off, her arms tightly crossed, eyes deceptively dry.

"This is my job on the line. The more I tell you the deeper I get." He reached over, and with a single fingertip, gently traced an imaginary line down her cheek. "I'm in deep enough already," he said.

"Andy, what about . . ."

In an instant his mouth was upon hers. They embraced one another eagerly, kissing long and hard. He pushed her back onto the couch, and she slid her hand over his shirt,

187

down the small of his back to feel the firm strength of his buttocks.

"God, you're frustrating," she murmured.

Andy gently trailed his tongue down her neck.

"Do a Sean Connery for me," she whispered.

At first he seemed surprised by her request, then he smiled. "The name is Bond, James Bond," he said in a perfect, mellow Scotch accent.

Meow.

"More," she said, wrapping her legs around him.

"You're a sight for sore eyes, Miss Money Penny—"

"More!"

"Um . . . One Vodka Martini, shaken, not stirred."

She kissed him again. "Oh James . . ." she said, giggling.

Hours later they lay naked and exhausted on crumpled sheets. The room was dark, save for the tiny flicker of a candle near the bed.

"Hummaganna," Andy mumbled unexpectedly.

Makedde opened her eyes. "What?"

"Hmmff." He shifted and flinched. "Go away. Hmmff." His eyes were still closed.

"Go away. Hmmff. Cassandra," he continued to mumble. "I want the car, dammit," he suddenly blurted more clearly. "Bitch—"

Makedde jabbed him hard in the ribs and he stopped. She didn't have the heart to let him sleeptalk himself into saying something he'd regret. "Mmm," he murmured, barely opening his tired eyes. He rolled the other way and they stayed quiet for a while, but she wasn't quite ready to drift. As her mind wandered, curiosity drew her irresistibly to seek answers.

"I hope you don't mind my asking," she queried softly, rolling over to spoon his body. "But you told me about

Rick Filles and his photo studio in the Cross. What was it like?" Andy rolled onto his back and tilted his face to her, his eyes still closed. "I'm sure you can at least tell me about that. Can't you?" she prodded.

"Sure," he mumbled, half awake. "Wait." His eyes snapped open. "How did you know his studio was in the Cross? I didn't tell you that."

"Didn't you?" She let out a little laugh, thinking of the ridiculous measurements she'd quoted. "Let me tell you, that man sounded like a real sleaze."

"*Sounded* like? You didn't talk to him, did you?" He was suddenly very awake.

"Just for a moment. I wanted to hear his ploy. It was harmless."

"Fucking hell!" He sat up and slammed his fist down violently, shaking the bed. While Makedde lay stunned, Andy closed his eyes and shook his head, making an effort to calm himself. He took several deep, deliberate breaths, and she imagined him counting to ten. Anger management.

"What do you think you're doing?" Andy asked her, sounding a little more controlled. "You're impossible. You can't do stuff like that!"

"I didn't leave my number or anything," she protested, deciding to sit up in bed as well. "I said I was Debbie; a six-foot, blonde, double-D cup lingerie model."

His gaze made a detour to her breasts as she sat up. "Well, I think Debbie would've had a more enthusiastic response than the lady we sent in," he said dryly.

"What happened?"

Andy took her hands in his, peering at her sternly under furrowed brows. "You have to promise me you'll stop this. I'll tell you whatever you want to know, so long as you promise to stop chatting to suspects and putting yourself in danger."

She batted her mascara-smudged eyelashes. "I promise. So, why do you suspect this guy?"

"Well, we have to pursue all possibilities, and Rick is just one of them. The first two known victims were in the sex trade and may have answered the sort of ad that he placed."

"You can't possibly be suggesting that Catherine would answer an advertisement like that?"

"No. I doubt that," Andy agreed. "But despite popular fiction, serial killers aren't robots. Sometimes they change tactics. Your friend may have been a victim of opportunity that doesn't fit with the other crimes."

"So you sent an officer to pose as a model for this guy?"

"Well, we *tried*. Constable Mahoney, the one who drove you home the first night. She was a bit nervous I think—"

"Wait a second . . . you sent Karen in?"

"Well, yes . . ."

Makedde tried to imagine the look on Karen's face when the photographer asked her to stick out her chest and suck on a Chupa-Chup. "Isn't that like sending a nun to Hugh Hefner?"

In the dim light, Makedde could see that Andy's cheeks had gone red. "As it turns out . . . yes. She's the right age, and a good cop, but she just couldn't pull it off. She was too embarrassed to be believable."

"What happened?"

"After shooting one roll of film, he sent her home. She didn't find anything suspicious in his flat, no bondage gear, nothing. Just stacks of porn, and a bit of lingerie."

"Well, being a sleazebag doesn't mean you're a killer, otherwise you'd have to arrest half the photographers in Milan," Makedde said.

"That bad?"

She rolled her eyes. "You have *no* idea. That kind of

photographer doesn't load his camera until the clothes come off. This Filles guy probably didn't even take any photos of Karen."

"They do that?"

"Oh, yeah. They wouldn't want to waste their precious film." She paused. "Let's not go there. Any priors or motive?" Andy stared at her. "What now?" she asked impatiently.

"Sometimes you sound just like a cop. Was this the dinner conversation at your house, or what?"

Makedde laughed. Her father had tried to keep his ongoing cases out of the dinner conversation, but, much to the chagrin of her mother, he couldn't seem to help himself. It was pretty much all he had to talk about, and Makedde supposed that she didn't help matters by egging him on. Her mother and her younger sister, Theresa, would sit in silent disapproval, leaving the table as soon as possible. But her father's stories never put Mak off her food.

"Just answer the question, Detective," she said, pushing Andy back onto the bed and pinning him down.

"Yes, he has priors." Andy paused. "I really don't like these crank calls you're getting."

"I'm sure it's nothing." Mak straddled his naked hips and leant over him.

He tried to maintain his serious tone. "I don't like the way you keep getting yourself involved in this."

"Don't worry about me. Just find the guy."

"Easier said than done—on both accounts."

"Any other leads, Mr. Detective?" she asked, running a finger down his chest. She wanted to pin him down and keep him there. She wanted to take control. Makedde had forgotten how great it was to feel sexy, and she felt like a girl with a new toy.

"A couple . . ." He couldn't keep his eyes from her breasts. "We're still keeping Tony Thomas under pres-

191

sure. A lot of dead ends—oh, will you stop that? That tickles!"

She laughed and rolled off him.

Andy faced her, the humour gone from his eyes. "This guy, whoever he is, is a seriously sadistic bastard."

"All the more reason to make sure he's stopped right away," she said. "What if you tried setting this Rick guy up with another model?"

He got her drift. "No, no. Makedde, get this stuff out of your head! You promised me you'd back off if I told you what we were doing."

"But I could do a much better job—"

Andy gently covered her mouth with his hand, cutting her off mid-sentence. "Promise me, *promise me*, you won't get involved. Let me handle this."

She slowly nodded her head, and he removed his hand.

"Sorry," he said. "You just can't put yourself in danger like that. We've got an entire task force working on this. We'll catch him. I would never forgive myself if something happened to you."

"Well, as long as you and your police pals take care of things, I won't need to. But don't blame me if I have to arrest someone—"

"What?"

Makedde smiled to let him know she was kidding.

"Impossible," he muttered and tried to roll on top of her, but she flipped him onto his back and straddled him again, pinning his arms back. He grinned at her, visibly aroused by her assertiveness. "You are uncooperative, aren't you?" he teased. The grin was wiped off his face when she reached under the bed and produced his handcuffs.

"What the—"

In seconds she succeeded in manacling his wrists. She snapped them on hard like a cop, and he winced at the brief pain. "I hope you have the keys," she said. His eyes were wide. She'd been dying for the right moment, and now she had the big, strong detective naked and at her mercy, her favourite fantasy realised. Well, almost. Sean Connery in *Dr. No* was her favourite, but this was a close second.

His mouth hung open in shock, a look she found titillating from such close quarters. She kept his bound arms pinned above his head, stretching his shoulders back. His underarm hair was soft and dark, and she inhaled his scent before devouring his vulnerable body with kisses and playful bites. His nipples went hard, and she played with them with her tongue while he writhed.

He cleared his throat. "So, ah, you like to—"

"You talk too much, Detective," she said, cutting him off with a firm hand over his mouth.

He didn't protest.

32

Detective Flynn floated into the office on Monday morning, blithely unprepared for what was in store for him. He could taste Makedde on his lips, and his thoughts were still leisurely reclining with her in her bed. She had surprised him; she possessed a fiery sense of adventure but also a hidden vulnerability. Contradictory, that was the word for her. He was also excited about the new lead, thanks to the ring Makedde had found. It seemed that Mr. Tiney Jr. had lied to them. He *did* know Catherine. Andy looked forward to sitting that rich prick down in the interview room and putting the ring on the table in front of him. There'd be some frantic backtracking then.

It took a few moments for Andy to register the tense silence that pervaded the office. He wandered through, his usual steaming brew in one hand, and his pace slowed as he picked up on the foreboding atmosphere. His colleagues were looking up from their desks as he passed, their faces communicating unspoken pity. Something was very wrong. By the time Andy reached his desk, his mood had started to sour.

Jimmy rushed over. "Kelley wants to see you right away. I don't know who told him . . ."

Andy walked towards Inspector Kelley's office in a surreal daze, Jimmy's words fading like a distant echo in his head. He knocked lightly on his mentor's door, and a dispassionate, "Come in," was the only response. The Detective Inspector was looking out the window, and he didn't turn to greet him. Even by Kelley's reserved standards, this reception was unusually cool. The hot seat was pulled back from the desk, waiting.

Andy started to speak but Inspector Kelley cut him off. "Sit down, Flynn." The chair creaked loudly as Andy sat. "You have something you want to talk to me about?"

"No sir," Andy replied, momentarily puzzled. "Well yes, I have some new information about James Tiney Jr., but Jimmy told me you had something you—"

"I *really* think you have something you want to explain to me. And it better be damn good, Flynn."

"Well, sir . . . if it's about the headline on the soap star, it couldn't be helped. We all knew it wouldn't take the press long to pick up on it—"

He was cut off again. "You've become involved with a witness. You've compromised this investigation," Kelley said to the window with chilling detachment. "I can't tell you how disappointed I am."

Andy looked at the back of Kelley's head, wishing he could somehow reverse his mistake. How could he be so stupid to risk everything over a girl? "I'm sorry, sir. It was bad judgment on my part . . ."

"I'm taking you off the case."

Andy was stunned. "But sir—" he began feebly.

"The decision has been made. I've saved your arse before, but that was different. I can't sweep this under the carpet. We, and by that I mean you, are under a lot of scrutiny in this investigation."

A year earlier, Andy had beat a suspected paedophile to a pulp in a blind rage. He had since found better ways to deal with his temper, at least some of the time. Kelley covered up the incident, probably because he secretly agreed with the justice of it, but sleeping with a witness was just plain sloppy. Andy knew that nothing he could say would change a thing, not once Kelley made up his mind. He had officially screwed up the biggest investigation of his career.

Andy stared hard at Inspector Kelley's beautiful old, carved oak desk. It was part of a distant world he would never reach, a future pulled out from under his feet.

Kelley turned his eyes to his fallen protégé for one last moment. That look lasted no more than two seconds, but its imprint lingered. "You have some vacation time coming, Flynn. Take it. I'll put you on something else when I think you're ready."

Andy felt a sour lump in his throat. "But sir, if I can just explain—"

"Your gun."

They were two words Andy never thought he would hear. He rose from his seat and pulled back his suit jacket to remove his Glock nine millimetre. He slowly placed it on the desktop. He knew he should have been grateful that he hadn't been directly suspended, or had his badge taken away, but being taken off the case seemed like punishment enough.

With a disappointed wave of his hand Kelley gestured for him to leave, and continued to stare at the passing cars outside the building.

Andy left without another word.

33

JT sat behind his immaculate desk and unwrapped his lunch—smoked salmon with capers, horseradish and iceberg lettuce on rye. They'd got it right this time. Perhaps his complaints had convinced them to fire the incompetent staff.

It was shaping up to be a good day. It had been over a week since Catherine's murder and the police still had no idea. That note she'd scrawled was a close call, though. How could he have been so stupid as to use the company account to book the room? Sure, it was a tax write-off, but it was also lazy on his part. He would have to be more careful in the future. But even with all that, the police didn't have any damning evidence. He was confident they had believed his story. Perhaps the ring would never be found. That thought made him smile as he bit into his sandwich.

Invading his quiet moment, his secretary's voice crackled over the intercom. "There's a call for you on line two, Mr. Tiney—"

"Rose, for God's sake, I'm eating my lunch!" Little bits

of bread and horseradish flew from his mouth. "Take a message!"

"Sorry, sir. The man says it's important. It's a Mr. Hand."

JT sat up straight, put the sandwich down and nervously wiped the corners of his mouth. "Yes, Rose. Thanks, I'll take the call."

"Hello?"

"This is Mr. Hand," Luther's gruff voice came through the line. "I have good news. The lover-cop is taking a vacation."

"A vacation?"

"Yeah, and a gift has been delivered to the lady, which should have the desired result."

A tingle ran down JT's spine. Perhaps Luther was worth the expense after all. "Good. Good work. Do I need to know more?"

"It's all taken care of."

JT didn't want to know the details. He didn't want to be sullied any further with the whole sordid affair, he just wanted results, and it seemed that he was finally getting them.

"Thank you," he said.

The phone went dead.

34

Makedde held the envelope cautiously between two fingers, sensing something malicious before even opening it—the way only her first name was typed in block letters on the front, the way it had been hand delivered, waiting menacingly for her under the door. She could see that it contained a photo . . . no, a laser copy of a photo. She pulled the piece of paper out slowly, holding the corner in pinched fingers. It looked familiar. It was a slightly grainy copy of a photo from her modelling composite card, but it was somehow different . . .

Her eyes widened.

It was a photo of Makedde, *dead*.

She was wearing a bikini, or at least she should have been. It was hard to tell if there were any clothes at all in this version of the photograph. Her flesh was torn with streaks of blood and gore. Her pupils had been scratched out, rendered as little more than grey, lifeless globes.

Makedde dropped the photo and it fluttered to and fro in the air as it fell to the floor. She gripped her churning stomach and held her throat tightly as dry heaves of revulsion overwhelmed her. The typed message burned into her eyes. She turned and tried to blink it away, but it remained. Black, bold ink on red flesh:

YOU ARE NEXT

Makedde called Andy's mobile number, her hands sweating. The phone rang at least ten times before an eerily robotic voice told her, "This call is being transferred to another line. Please hold." *Where the hell is he?* His message kicked in, "This is Detective Flynn. I'm not available at the moment. Please leave a message and I'll return your call."

"Ah, it's me," she said vaguely. "It's Monday, um . . ." she looked at her watch, "four o'clock. Call me. It's urgent." She hoped she wouldn't get him in trouble by leaving the message. He had told her not to, because it was a work pager, but surely he'd understand when he found out what had happened.

With the photo staring up at her, the threat to her safety seemed suddenly undeniably concrete. She was no longer convinced that the break-in had been unrelated and she began to wonder again about the furniture. *Had it really moved?*

She called her agency in a panic, but Charles clearly didn't understand the urgency. "You want to move *now?*" he asked distractedly.

"Yes, it has to be right away. Do you have any other flats available?" She knew how hard it was to find furnished accommodations, but she had to try.

"Hmm. It depends on how many girls you want to share with. I think there'll be a vacancy in the Potts Point one next week." They frequently had up to six travelling models staying in one agency-owned flat at a time.

"Next week? I really need to move now."

"What's the problem?"

She couldn't tell him. She didn't want to tell him. She didn't want to tell anyone except Andy. "Never mind, I just . . . Could you get me a place to stay as soon as possible?"

"It's not that easy, but I'll see what I can do."

She couldn't afford a hotel. Once she got hold of Andy, perhaps he could help her find a new place. Maybe she could even stay with him for a while. That wasn't such an unpleasant thought.

She paced the room, waiting for the phone to ring.

I'll be fine. I can protect myself.

Grab the coconut off the tree, crack it open on your knee . . .

Impatient, she called Andy, but got his pager again. *He'll call back soon*, she told herself. Just kick back and relax. Read the paper, watch television. He'll call any minute and then you can get out of here. She pulled the protective plastic off her neighbour's rolled newspaper. They never collected their mail, so she assumed they were on vacation. *Wise idea*. She unrolled the paper and laid it across the bed. The front-page headline was chilling.

SOAP STAR MURDERED

Television star Becky Ross, who went missing after the launch of her own fashion label on Thursday, was found murdered in Centennial Park yesterday. Sources believe she is the fourth victim of the "Stiletto Killer" . . .

Horrified, she dropped the paper, then kicked it off the bed, as if the truth would disappear if only she didn't read about it.

. . . fourth victim of the "Stiletto Killer" . . .

. . . went missing after the launch of her own fashion label . . .

How could that be? Dead? Just days ago, Mak was modelling her clothes, sharing the catwalk with her. And now she was dead. So that's what Andy was called away for. Why didn't he tell her?

The phone rang, and she snapped it up. "Andy—"

"Makedde, it's Charles. I may have something for you, but you can only stay there for three weeks—"

"Oh my God! Thank you!"

"Are you all right?"

"Yes, I'm fine. Oh, that's great news. When can I move in?"

"There's one available in Bronte, it belongs to one of our models, Deni. She's in Europe. She could use the rent money."

Fantastic.

Within fifteen minutes she was out the door and out of breath, dragging her bulging suitcases into a taxi and leaving the horrible newspaper behind.

35

He listened at her door.

Silence.

Luther knew she wasn't there. Nor was she likely to return soon. A girl wouldn't return to the flat after a shock like that. Not even a brave girl like Makedde.

Luther had watched her hurried departure with mixed emotions. Suitcases in tow, wearing a baseball cap and sunglasses, she had left in a taxi. He had thought she was headed for the airport, which would no doubt make his client very happy. But Luther had felt disappointed seeing her slipping away. She intrigued him. Never before had he so enjoyed watching someone's every move. She brought out his homicidal side, but the whole city was searching for a murderer. It wasn't a good time to kill.

She would have been a recreational hit, an indulgence. It had been several years since his last one. Unpaid. Spontaneous. A pleasure. The last one had been pretty, but not a model like Makedde. But he'd lost his chance to take her. Or so he'd thought. As it turned out, she wasn't heading for the airport at all. Just some little place near Bronte. She was still within his grasp.

He smiled.

Even though he knew it was pointless, Luther decided he should make his client happy by searching the flat one last time. If he hadn't found the ring before, it almost certainly wasn't there. But he had his own reasons for wanting to go inside. He would have to make it quick—Makedde might have called the police, despite her affair with the suspended detective.

With callused hands he jemmied the door, as he had done on numerous occasions previously. It was a clean and simple process—the lock had no T bolt, it was just the standard type that should really only be used on internal doors. Safety obviously wasn't much of a priority for Makedde's modelling agency.

The flat was barren. The week before, Makedde had packed Catherine's things into bags and cardboard boxes and had addressed them to Canada. Luther had searched them all. Now with the boxes gone and her own belongings removed as well, the space looked very empty. She had left in a hurry. The bed was dishevelled, there were unwashed dishes in the sink, a newspaper lay crumpled on the floor. It wasn't the way a well-mannered girl like Makedde would normally leave her accommodations. She must have been very scared.

He opened the wardrobe doors and found a few metal hangers and a lone sock. He noticed that she had shifted the wardrobe back to its original position. On Friday he had been searching underneath it when he heard her coming up the stairs. He'd hidden in the kitchen alcove, behind the dividing counter, sitting cross-legged on the floor. He had remained quiet and still, his patience serving him well, ready to silence her if need be. She was lucky, and instead she lay on her bed for a while, then showered. He had even caught a tantalising glimpse of her naked body when she emerged from the bathroom.

She was too beautiful.

Flawless.

That's when the urge hit him.

Makedde had dressed and made herself up. She'd even read a book for a while, only a few feet away from him, and all the while, he imagined the way she'd look with his hands around her pretty throat. Then her date arrived downstairs, just when he was ready to make his move. Perhaps it was for the best.

He checked through the rubbish bin and found nothing of interest, only food scraps and meaningless crumpled pamphlets and papers. In the bathroom he found that she'd forgotten her toothbrush and in the medicine cabinet there was a lone Tylenol pill and a packet of tampons. She'd left the bath towels, some of them used. Finally, he sifted through the newspaper and magazines left scattered on the floor near the bed. Under the paper he found what he was looking for. His gift was right there. A smart girl like Makedde would have taken it with her, he thought, as proof that she was in danger. But it seemed she was in too much of a hurry to leave.

Silly girl. Now no one will believe you.

Having served its purpose, he pocketed his tasty little happy snap, and left the place as he found it.

36

On Tuesday morning, Makedde woke disoriented and distressed. From the moment she opened her eyes she was plagued with a deep, gnawing dread that she couldn't quite put a name to. She blinked and rubbed her eyes before leaning over to check her watch beside the bed. It was 8 a.m.

Another one. Another murder.

Had it been a dream?

She'd left more messages for Andy, which he hadn't returned. It was hard for her to be angry at him, though. If Becky Ross had just been murdered, that would naturally take top priority. The police would be scrambling. She thought she might call the police station about the photo, if she felt desperate.

Makedde didn't want to admit to herself that she might have overreacted. Any weirdo who read the papers and happened to know where Catherine had lived could have slipped her that note. Was it really a doctored photo of *her*? Was that really what she'd thought she'd seen? Maybe it was a joke. Maybe she was imagining things, the way she had imagined that the furniture had moved by itself. A paranoid, overactive imagination was a sure sign of stress.

It was good to move anyway. Hopefully she'd be back in Canada before Deni got home, and compared to the Bondi flat Deni's place was pure luxury. The view was superb, overlooking Bronte Beach, and there was a quaint porch and a small backyard. It had one large bedroom and a guest room, a separate kitchen, and an adult-sized bathroom; one where she didn't have to sit on the toilet seat to wash her hands. The walls were soothing apricot, the floors polished wood. The furniture was a bit thin on the ground, but what was there was expensive and tasteful. There were two telephones and an answering machine she was welcome to use. There was even a laundry. *Heaven*.

The one drawback was the distance from public transport. She would need a car. On her many travels Makedde had generally relied on taxis, buses and occasionally trains, and even though she had an international licence, she'd had minimal experience driving on the "wrong side of the road", as she thought of it. She thumbed through the Yellow Pages and found a local outfit—aptly titled Lowe-Rent—and booked a date with a five-year-old Daihatsu Charade.

After one bus ride, half an hour of walking, countless directions from strangers and one advance from a wino, she eventually found the William Street rental offices, paid her deposit and was shown to her car. She slid into the driver's seat nervous but excited. Like a pianist about to perform a recital, she cracked her knuckles, flexed her hands, and curled her fingers around the wheel.

I can do this. I have control of my life. New flat. New car. New me.

She pulled out of the carpark, driving past a larger-than-life illustration of a smiling koala exclaiming, "For the best deals, think Lowe-Rent!"

Think left.

She turned onto William Street and followed the manic stream of bumper-to-bumper machines and found herself in no time at all successfully driving on the left-hand side of the road.

See? I'm fine. No weirdo is going to scare me off.

Acclimatising herself to the joys of Sydney CBD motorsport, she took the car down William to College Street before heading back towards Bronte. She was crossing a six-lane intersection when she heard the loud honking of horns.

Is that for me?

"Oi! You're on the wrong side of the road!"

Tyres screeched as she came to an embarrassing halt in the middle of the intersection. An angry orchestra of noisy horns filled the air. The lights changed. Cars started towards her, still beeping. She started to reverse, but the traffic going in the other direction blocked her route.

"Damn tourist!" someone shouted.

Some cars drove slowly, faces gawking out the windows. They stared at her the same way they would a mangled car wreck. Finally, she saw her chance and gunned it up the street as fast as she could. No longer under fierce scrutiny, her instinct was to pull over and abandon the car at the first opportunity. But she kept on, and before long she was out of the worst of the traffic and was nearing Bronte. Her new abode had about everything except a garage. She drove around and around and finally found a parking spot some four blocks away. The price of living near the beach she supposed.

When she got inside, the answering machine was flashing. She hoped it was Andy, wanting to take her out somewhere. She would let him drive. Then perhaps they could pick up where they'd left off on Sunday night.

Eagerly, she replayed the messages.

"Hello sweetie! It's Loulou. You are impossible to reach! Where did you move to? Let's get together. Call me."

Makedde waited eagerly to hear Andy's voice on the next recording, but the messages ended.

She frowned.

It's a weekday; he's busy. He'll call later.

Maybe he'd gone off her? Had she been too assertive?

Nah. He loved it.

Flipping open her day-book, Makedde dialled Loulou's number and after three rings it was picked up.

"Hi Loulou, it's Makedde."

"Makedde! How ya goin' sweetie?" She sounded excited. But then, she always sounded excited. "I still can't believe that Becky Ross is dead, she had such a bright future ahead of her."

"I know, it's horrible," Mak replied.

"Didjahavagoodweegend?" Loulou asked.

"Pardon?"

"Did-you-have-a-good-weekend?" she slowly enunciated, as if Makedde were deaf.

"Sorry, yes. I did."

"Were-you-on-the-phone-the-whole-time?"

"Knock it off," Makedde laughed. "I'm not deaf, I just prefer English, and no, I wasn't on the line the whole time."

"Because every time I called, the phone was busy."

Makedde's mind went back to the long hours Andy and her had spent, not wanting to be disturbed.

"Oh, we took the phone off the hook. I mean . . . I. I took the phone off the hook." *Oops.*

"Oh, really? Who's the lucky guy? Is he a hunk?"

"Loulou, I can't really talk about it. But, yes, I had a great weekend." *Really great.* "Anyway, I was calling to see if you wanted to get together for a little retail therapy? I haven't been shopping for a while."

"Baby, what an idea. You know I *love* shopping!"

"Tomorrow? We could have lunch in Paddington," Mak suggested, "then hit the boutiques."

"Shop till we drop! Sounds *divine*. Bring your portfolio, I didn't get a chance to see it at the show."

"Sure."

"Where are you living now?"

"Bronte. It's a real nice place that belongs to another girl from Book. Do you know a model named Deni?"

"Total bitch," she said flippantly. "Just kidding. Never heard of her. Bronte's not too far from me. My car's in the shop till tomorrow afternoon. Can you pick me up?"

Those were the last words Makedde wanted to hear.

"I do have a rental car, but it's—"

"Perfect! Pick me up at noon. See you then sweetie."

Into the dial tone, Makedde said, "OK, sweetie."

Makedde finally gave up her waiting game and called Central Homicide. She couldn't find the photo that had so disturbed her, so she didn't think she should mention it to whomever answered, but nevertheless, she thought she might have better luck tracking down the elusive Detective Flynn.

A female officer answered. "Central Homicide."

"Is Detective Flynn there, please?"

"Sorry, he's not available. I'll put you through to Detective Cassimatis if you like."

Damn. Makedde hesitated. Andy would be mad, but that was tough luck. She was getting mad herself.

"Detective Cassimatis."

"Hi. I'm trying to reach Detective Flynn."

"He's not available," Jimmy said. "Is there something I can help you with, Miss . . ."

"This is Makedde Vanderwall. You're Jimmy, right? His partner?"

"Oh . . ." There was a long pause. "Makedde. Have you seen him today?"

"No. I've been trying to get hold of him for a couple of days."

Another pause. "Well, like I said, he's not available. Is there anything else?"

She was taken aback by his rudeness. "Uh . . . no."

He hung up.

37

He sat on the park bench outside the Bondi block of flats, wringing his hands and staring forlornly at her darkened window. There had been no movement, no sign of her for the past four hours. No one of interest had entered or left the building. No statuesque, beautiful blonde. No *Makedde*. He had spent hours staking out her flat between his shifts at work, and still there was no sign of her.

Had he lost her because of his stupid job?

Once upon a time, it had thrilled him to attend his work. But now he had other things on his mind. More important things. His job was getting in the way. He needed his hours free to pursue that which rightly belonged to him. But he couldn't quit work. What would his mother say? Could he keep it from her?

He slid his hand into his jacket pocket for comfort. The scalpel felt hard and reassuring through the nylon fabric. Night had descended, and he was ready; but she was nowhere to be found. His prize was gone. He was so angry. Angry and disappointed. He was to cure her of her sins. It was meant to be. She was the special one. How could he let her slip away?

He patted his pocket. He'd scour the streets, comb the city, explore every avenue and lane, leave no stone unturned.

We'll find her. Don't worry, we'll find her.

38

At noon on Wednesday, Makedde honked her horn outside Loulou's block of flats. She waited in the car, deep in thought. On the seat beside her was a copy of Weekly News, a gossip tabloid. A poster of the front cover had been up in the window of a newsstand when she walked by, emblazoned with the headline SOAP STAR SLAIN. In the article there were a lot of quotes from mysterious "sources" and a mention of the fact that statuesque model, Makedde Vanderwall, discovered her dead friend Catherine Gerber only one week before Becky was killed . . .

Makedde imagined Catherine's killer buying a stack of copies and tacking them to his wall to join other headlines like, *MODEL SLAIN* and *BODY DISCOVERED WEARING STILETTO*. She was thankful that her picture was not included in the article. Her thoughts were broken when a whirl of bright fuchsia caught her attention. Loulou was bounding towards the car, all smiles in a hot pink mini-dress and platforms. Her purse was lime-green with little gold flowers, her fingernails painted glittery lime-green to match, and her blonde hair back-combed into a gravity-defying mushroom-shaped cloud. She resembled a spinning radish topped with yellow straw. Somehow, she managed to make even Vivienne Westwood look conservative.

Loulou bounced onto the passenger seat, picking up the magazine as she did. "God, she's everywhere. Poor thing. Hey," she said, looking around, "this car ain't so bad for cheapo rental."

"Perhaps. But the driver is."

"The driver?" Loulou looked puzzled. "Oh, yeah, wrong side of the road. How are you finding it?"

"Do you want to drive?"

"No. I'm sure you'll be fine. Come on, let's go."

"It was worth a try," Makedde mumbled as she pulled away from the curb.

They ate at a groovy little café on Oxford Street, where Loulou's fashion sense seemed to fit in perfectly. Loulou must have been hungry, because she barely said a word through the entire meal, but once she'd polished off her spaghetti primavera, she wasted no more time.

"So, tell me about this hunk of yours."

Mak almost choked on a piece of steamed broccoli. "Hunk? Well, he's . . ." *He is a hunk.* "I . . ." she started again. *I think I'm falling for him. Or was . . .*

"Good God girl, get it out! What are you babbling about?"

Makedde smiled. "Yes, well, I'm sort of seeing someone. I think. But that's all I can tell you."

"Who is he, James Bond?"

"Very funny, Loulou."

"He's not some snapper, is he?"

"No, he's not a photographer. I just can't say who he is right now. And besides, I'm not sure if it's going anywhere."

She wasn't going to let up that easy. "Super-M? Oh, God, he's not your booker?"

"Charles? No, no. He's not my type at all. Actually, I don't think I'm his. I'm pretty sure he's gay. And no, this guy's not some supermodel. He's not even in the biz."

"Oh, that's right, *Charles* is your booker. Yeah, he's still with Paulo. So, your hunk's not in the biz," she pressed. "A politician?"

"Loulou! Knock it off, please."

"All right, all right." She sat sulking for a moment, scratching at a grease stain on the tablecloth. "Can I see your book?"

"Sure. That I can do." Mak hauled the heavy portfolio out of her bag and plonked it on the table between their empty plates.

"Nice head-shot. Who did the make-up?" Loulou asked with a wink.

"Mmmm, can't remember. It was taken in Vancouver a month or two ago. I don't think you'd know them anyway."

"I wouldn't be too sure," Loulou countered, flipping through a few pages. She stopped at a photo halfway through the book. "Wow! Where did you shoot that? Those shoes are *divine*."

"Thanks. Miami. Those shoes were so uncomfortable. The heels must have been eight inches high. It's almost two years old. I took some time off, you see . . ."

"Time off? Why on earth did you take time off? You're in your prime, sweetie. You can take as much time off as you want when you're dead."

My mother was sick, and Stanley was on trial. "Oh, I . . . I just felt like I needed a break."

"Any photos of your hunk in here?" Loulou went on, oblivious to the fact that she had touched on a nerve. "I won't tell anyone, I promise."

Makedde laughed. "No. Can we please not talk about him?"

"Men. I had a guy stay over last week, and when I woke up, he was just staring at me with his mouth open. My eyebrows had come off on the pillow! He freaked!"

Makedde let out a ridiculous squealing laugh, loud enough for several of the other patrons to look up.

"Time for a little retail therapy?" Loulou asked, getting up from the table.

"Yes! Please. I thought you'd never ask."

Umpteen credit card swipes and several hours later, they returned to the rental car and shoe-horned themselves in with their spoils of the hunt. It had taken Makedde almost an hour to prise Loulou out of The Look make-up shop— there had been a tug-o-war with a mob of gleeful sales assistants, and, needless to say, the shelves looked very clean when they had eventually left.

"Got everything you wanted, sweetie?"

Makedde looked at her hand-sized shopping bag containing a single lipstick, and said, "Yeah. I won't ask if you have, because I'm not letting you back into that store."

"Next time, sweetie."

"Next time."

Makedde got behind the wheel, and as she went to pop her new lipstick into her shoulder bag, she froze.

"What's wrong?" Loulou asked.

"My book! Oh God! My portfolio! It's not here! I must have left it . . ." Makedde flung open the car door and ran full-tilt for three blocks until she reached the café. An older couple was eating at the table at which Makedde and Loulou had earlier sat.

"Excuse me," she panted. "Have you seen a black portfolio here, with some model pictures in it?"

The lady slowly turned to her partner, and then back to Makedde. "Sorry, dear, no."

"Are you *sure*?"

They shrugged their shoulders as Makedde made for the nearest waiter. He didn't look familiar.

"Excuse me, have you seen a model's portfolio here? I think I left it at that table," she pointed, "around 12.30 p.m. It's very important."

The young man smiled at her. Makedde hoped it was because he knew where it was.

"You're a model, huh? You're a very beautiful lady. So tall—"

"Please, have you seen it?" she asked again.

"Sorry, no."

Her portfolio contained the original photographs of the best of her many years of work. The photographers and their negatives were scattered all over the globe, and the magazine covers and editorials were probably out of print now.

"Maybe I can help you," the waiter offered, moving closer to Makedde.

"Did you see the book? Can you tell me who sat at that table after we did?"

"No. I just began my shift."

"Then no, you can't." Makedde glanced around the café. "Look, can I leave a number with you in case it turns up?"

The waiter's eyes lit up. "Of course," he said with a smirk.

She scribbled her agent's phone number along with the name "Miss Vanderwall". No doubt he would think she was coming on to him. "Just in case the portfolio turns up, OK?" she said again, trying to make herself clear.

Angry at being so careless, she turned and walked stiffly back to the car, digging her fingernails into her palms.

Loulou was waiting in the passenger seat, listening to the radio. "What happened, sweetie?" she yelled above the music.

Makedde got in and switched off the radio with a little too much force. The dial came off in her hand.

"Not there, huh?" Loulou asked.

"Not there," she confirmed, and silently drove Loulou home.

Makedde walked in the front door frowning, and threw her bag on the floor. "Shit-shit-shit-shit-*shit*! How could I do that?" she said out loud. "You stupid, stupid girl!"

Only once in ten years had Makedde forgotten her portfolio. She was fifteen years old, in Milan for the first time, and had been calling her agent from a public phone booth. She got straight onto a tram and was clattering down the Corso Venczia before she realised she didn't have it with her. Thankfully, when she got off and ran back, it was still sitting where she'd left it. Since then she had been vigilant.

Until today.

Reluctantly, she called Charles. "You *what?*" he yelled down the line. "How could you lose it? How long have you been modelling?"

"I should know better, yes."

It was one of the first rules of modelling—protect your portfolio at all costs. Never put it in check-in luggage when you fly. Never give it to a friend to take somewhere. Never, *ever* lose it. No portfolio, no work.

Charles was still berating her, "Let's hope whoever has it, returns it, and soon. I've got clients I want you to see. Come in tomorrow morning. We'll see what laser copies we can scrape up for the moment."

Not an encouraging thought.

39

"Fucking, goddamn, greedy women!" Andy Flynn shouted as he tossed his head angrily, his alcohol-numbed brain causing the room to sway and roll. "Fuck 'em!" he yelled for no one to hear. He pounded his right fist straight into the wall. The plaster was unforgiving, as were the half-healed cuts along his knuckles. They split open again, but he barely felt a thing.

How could Cassandra have taken his stereo? That bitch only ever listened to crappy country music stations anyway. What did she need his hi-fi system for? She'd stripped him of everything that mattered—the Honda, the house, and now his music. She had sure laid out the welcome mat, just what Andy needed after being kicked off the most important case of his career. "Vultures!" he screamed, and threw his empty beer bottle against the wall. It shattered into hundreds of tiny shards, littering the old Persian rug.

"Fuck it!" he bellowed and opened a fresh beer with his bleeding hand. Andy thought about what it would be like; what a complete relief it would be to deal with Cassandra properly. She and that simpering lawyer of hers needed to be taught a lesson; avarice was such a natural state for the two of them, they deserved to be hauled kicking and screaming into the real world. His head swam, and he decided maybe he should lie down, but he hit the couch too hard and missed the cushion, thumping his head into the armrest, splashing both himself and the couch with beer. He tried to focus on the half-empty bottle in his hand. How long had he been drinking? A day at least, probably two. Was it day or night? The curtains were closed and he couldn't tell. Did it even matter? He didn't have to go to work.

Kelley hates me. Took my gun away. I fucked up . . . and why? Because of another damn woman. Fuckin' manipulating whores, all of them.

His black mood was all-encompassing and he began to dwell on the blonde temptress, the one who had gotten him into this mess in the first place. She'd become an addiction, and now he was paying for it. His head started to ache, and his first thought was to reach for the Jack Daniels. He wouldn't need a glass, it would go down just fine straight from the bottle. He reached out for it, confused that his hand wasn't paying attention and knocked it over.

"Shit," he managed to slur in protest.

40

By early evening, Makedde still hadn't heard from Andy Flynn. She had questions that demanded answers, but no one, it seemed, was willing to provide them. If the police weren't going to do anything worthwhile, then she would have to take matters into her own hands.

A photo session with Rick Filles was about as appealing as a date with Norman Bates, but as the hours uneventfully crept closer to their nine o'clock appointment, it seemed like her only hope. What if he was the one? What if she could expose him? Rick hadn't acted suspiciously with Constable Mahoney, but that didn't prove anything. She wasn't his type. But Debbie would be.

If Rick was Catherine's killer, and the one who sent Makedde that revolting, mutilated photo, showing up at his studio surely would catch him off guard. He might give something away. But he might also act unpredictably, or worse, dangerously. Precautions had to be taken. Her appointment was only three hours away. She had to work fast, and she knew exactly who to call.

"Hi Loulou. How are you?"

"Darling! Have you found your portfolio?"

"I'm afraid not. Sorry if I was in a bit of a mood when I drove you home."

"Not at all. I totally understand."

"I wanted to ask you your dress size."

"Dress size? Twelve . . . mostly."

Makedde smiled. *Close enough.* "I was wondering if you could do me a favour . . ."

Just before nine o'clock, Makedde arrived at a dark, decrepit and graffitied block of flats in a side lane off Bayswater Road in Kings Cross. Most of the streetlights had been smashed and the footpaths were eerily deserted; it was as if some disease had swept through, wiping everyone out, leaving the infected streets unfit for human feet. The only sign of life was the flickering light of a television set in a flat on the third floor of the building. Someone was safely tucked away, watching a gameshow. Mak could hear the applause.

Why am I playing this game?

She wondered if Rick Filles was a modern-day Harvey Glatman—the hard-core, bondage-obsessed serial killer who, posing as a photographer, terrorised the Hollywood modelling world in the fifties. A shiver ran up her spine at the thought, and she froze. But that was the point of this expedition, wasn't it? To be smart enough to suss him out and expose him before he had the chance to harm more women.

Just one hour, that's all. You can do this.

With some trepidation, Makedde knocked on the door and it creaked open unaided to reveal a darkened stairwell. She stepped inside and fumbled for a light switch. There was none. All she could make out was the dim outline of the stairway leading up.

I'm doing this for you, Catherine.

She was relieved to find a round, white timer switch on the far wall on the first-floor landing. Pressing it, the stairwell was flooded with light from a single fluorescent tube. A handwritten sign told her the studio was on the fourth floor. She looked around. No elevator. She sighed. Four flights of stairs in stilettos. Things were looking worse by the minute. Dolled up in a blood-red bustier and a short black miniskirt, Makedde knew she looked like a cross between a Vargas pin-up girl and a gift-wrapped Barbie doll. It wasn't a look she went for often.

She bent forward and cupped her hands under her breasts, heaving them upwards. It had the magical effect of turning her already generous bosom into Debbie's outrageous, Jayne Mansfield-like proportions. The bustier was cut low, revealing two perfect, gravity-defying semi-moons of dangerous cleavage. He'd probably notice that she'd exaggerated a bit on the phone, but she was sure he wouldn't be disappointed.

Reaching his studio door, she once again cursed the Australian government for not legalising pepper spray for civilians. Her fashion arsenal would have to do—hair spray, a hat pin and the trusty paring knife.

Play the role. Nothing to fear. It's just a movie.

I wish I knew how the script ended . . .

Rick Filles answered his door as soon as she knocked. His eyes were the first things she noticed. They were disturbing, misshapen, and far too small for his face. She had never seen such tiny, ill-proportioned eyes. Beady and bloodshot, they shone like hot marbles.

"Hi, I'm Debbie," she said in a breathy voice, adding a soft giggle for effect. His eyes went straight to her breasts. It was a relief. Hopefully he hadn't noticed her fear. He led her inside, all the while unashamedly ogling her cleavage.

"Wow. What a great studio. Do you, like, do a lot of photos?" She was careful to bob her head from side to side when she finished the sentence.

"Shit yeah. What's your poison, doll?"

"Poison?"

"Drink?"

"Oh, whatever you're having."

As he wandered over to the kitchenette, she discreetly surveyed the studio. She made her way over to a glowing light-table and scanned the slides. Soft porn. Girls in heels on sports cars. Nudies. Nothing spectacular, certainly nothing original. He had probably left them there for show. But there was an interesting stack of folders on the floor underneath. Perhaps that was where more damning photographs hid.

On one side of the room a rack of frilly lingerie waited. Standard stuff. Pink teddies. Red garters. Crotchless panties. They could wait all they wanted, she sure as hell wasn't going to put them on. To her left an inconspicuous doorway aroused her interest.

Rick returned with some clear liquid in shot glasses and set them down on the light-table. Makedde kept her bag firmly on her shoulder, hoping the makeshift weapons it held wouldn't be needed. "Do you have any photographs I can look at?" she asked.

"Sure, doll." He pointed at the slides.

"Any others? I'm just trying to get ideas."

"Nah. The rest are . . ." he hesitated, "with a client."

Yeah right. "Too bad. Do you have some outfits?"

"Over here." He gestured to the rack of frilly half-there underwear.

"Do you have anything else? Something a bit . . ." She winked.

"What do you have in mind?"

225

"Anything . . . kinky?" she suggested, and flashed him a smile. She sipped gingerly at her drink and almost gagged. It tasted like lighter fluid. His eyes lit up like an adolescent boy witnessing his first centrefold. Any minute she expected to see drool forming in the corners of his mouth. Without warning he slipped an arm around her waist and pulled her towards the mysterious room. "A kinky one, eh? You've come to the right place, babe."

His hand felt hot and sticky through Loulou's tight top. His face was close to her neck. Makedde tilted her head away, trying to avoid the foul breath drifting up her nostrils. *What is that smell?* She tried holding her breath. Every instinct told her to fight. Elbow strike to the throat and run! Fast! But she couldn't. She had come too far. He released his grip to open the door, and she quickly snuck a glance at her watch. It was only 9.30 p.m. She had half an hour to go. She had to stall him.

A slimy grin creased his face. He held the knob in his hand, his eyes burning like the windows of a furnace. Painstakingly he opened the door, inch by inch revealing the contents of his special room—a startling array of leather, latex and chains hanging from walls and hangers. Her eyes rested on a painful-looking metal contraption with leather straps.

Bloody hell, what's that?

He looked to her for approval. "Ooh," she exclaimed. *Oh shit.*

On one wall a set of chains and cuffs dangled expectantly. She found it hard to picture someone voluntarily allowing themselves to be tied up there; she recalled the marks on Catherine's wrists. How much had she struggled? Was it leather or metal that had so effectively restrained her, cutting into her tender skin?

The chains were just the entrée. There were leather

whips, some with painful-looking red tassels. There were spiky looking clubs and innumerable phallic devices. Candles. Needles.

She had to show the police this.

"I bet you'd look great in one of those," she said, pointing to one of the outfits.

"Nah, not for me. I like to dominate."

And what do you do when you dominate? "Have you ever tried one on?"

"Not those outfits, no."

"Neither have I. I'll try one on, if you do," she suggested.

He studied her for far too long, devilish eyes measuring her up. Could he sense her fear? She mentally prepared herself to fend off an attack.

His reply surprised her. "OK."

"You first."

"No, I insist. You first."

"No, please, *you* first."

A twisted parody of politeness.

Rick Filles was serious about the proposal. He wouldn't back down, and Makedde couldn't back out. "Wait here. Let me pick one and surprise you," she whispered. Mak shut the door behind her and flipped a light switch. An overhead lamp came on, spreading a dim, cherry glow.

"I'm waiting," she heard him say through the door. His voice made her shiver.

Her mind got away with her and panic threatened to take over. She had a sudden flash of Stanley bursting through the door and pinning her to the floor, kneeling on her biceps with all his weight with his switchblade shiny and sharp pressed against her cheek. She pushed the thoughts aside, reminding herself again that Stanley was in jail, and the man she faced now was much shorter and weaker, and she was far better prepared.

TARA MOSS

She chose a black leather bodice and peeled off Loulou's red bustier, stuffing it in her purse. The bodice was tight, with a plunging neckline decorated with gleaming metal studs. She struggled into it, the merciless corsetry forcing her waist into absurd dimensions.

"Your turn," she managed to say as she grabbed a pair of latex hot pants sporting curious metal rings, and passed them to him.

He hesitated, his eyes narrowing to slits.

This is not good.

She slowly ran a finger along the swell of her breast. It worked. His eyes widened and followed her finger. "Come on, baby, try it on for me," she whispered. "Please?"

Rick walked into the room and partly shut the door, one beady eye still keeping watch over his prey. He turned from her for a moment and she saw her chance. Lunging forward, she slammed the door shut and swung a chair beneath the knob.

"Hey!" he yelled. "You bitch! Open this up!"

There was no time to waste. She ran towards the stack of folders sitting under the light-table and frantically searched them. *Damn!* Just forms and papers.

"Bitch!" he yelled again, and she could hear the chair creak dangerously, about to break.

She had no time. Shoes in one hand, she took the steps two by two, the sound of his shouts fading as she reached the street. She started to run, then out of the shadows came a neon blur.

"Sweetie! What happened?" Loulou exclaimed.

"Quick!" Mak said, breathless and still running. Loulou took her cue and followed. "We've got to get out of here!"

They ran for blocks before they reached Loulou's car, fresh out of the repair shop. Bored drug-addicts and street-walkers watched them pass with disinterest. Loulou

228

started the engine. "What happened? Wasn't I supposed to barge in and act like some jealous lover or something?"

Makedde felt sick. "Things got a little out of hand," she admitted.

"I can see that. Did you get what you wanted?"

"Well . . . yes and no," Mak said. "He's got some weird shit goin' on, but I didn't find anything directly linking him to Cat."

"Where's my red boob-top?"

"In the bag."

"Where'd you get the leather thing?"

"The S&M dungeon from hell. You can have it. I won't be wanting any souvenirs."

"Groovy," Loulou said, admiring the studs before they sped off.

41

He lay on top of the bedsheets, eyes closed, curtains drawn. He wanted to rest, to clear his mind, but he couldn't. There were sounds coming through the wall, depraved noises disturbing his quiet. He picked up some cotton balls and stuffed them in his ears, succeeding in blocking out only a fraction of the din. In the dim room, he squinted at the photograph tacked to the wall.

My girl.

Makedde.

She was perfect; long, slim, elegant legs barely concealed beneath a short leather dress. Deliciously high heels forced her slender feet to arch, calves flexed.

Whore.

It antagonised him that the photograph wasn't clear enough. He couldn't see the tiny, blonde hairs on her thighs. He couldn't see the small, bluish veins of her feet, pumping sweet blood back towards her heart.

She'd left the photo there for him. She wanted him to cure her. She'd even led him to her new flat, where she lived alone.

Don't worry, I'm coming for you soon.

But the noises wouldn't stop, they were breaking into his thoughts. They became louder. He could hear them right through the walls; groans like animals, the bed squeaking.

Mother!

He covered his head with the pillow. He was a child again, just a little boy; his pillow a teddy bear, covering his ears to that terrible racket. He was back in that house, trying desperately to block out the sounds, stuffing his school clothes under the door.

Mother! Mother, stop it!

Days and nights it had persisted. For years it wouldn't stop; sinful debauchery, and the smell. The loathsome odour of lust and profligacy had filled the house, filled his young nose.

Mother!

Only *he* stopped it. He cleansed her in the white-hot flames of hellfire, burning away her sin, the house a pillar of bright heat. He had watched it from down the street, watched the flames lick the sky.

Now he tried to ignore the persistent noises coming through the wall. He pretended it wasn't happening again. After all these years, it *couldn't* be happening again.

Mother can't be a whore now. I cured her.

Makedde wanted his special punishment too and he would take great pleasure in giving her what she needed, once the time was right. He'd watch her until then; follow her through the streets, watch her in her new lodgings and above all exercise patience.

It was meant to be.

But first, preparations had to be made.

42

On Thursday afternoon, Makedde walked towards Book agency feeling stupid, but glad to be alive. She still hadn't shaken off the previous night's horrors. How long would it have taken Rick Filles to escape his little romper room? She didn't even want to know. She never wanted to face those beady eyes again. She longed to tell Andy about her find but he still wasn't returning her calls. And Jimmy, what a prick! She didn't want to talk to him again.

She strolled into Book agency with a casual wave to the receptionist, forcing herself to walk tall and smile. Charles was busy on the phone with someone, as usual. Mak glanced around the room, admiring the composite cards on the walls; Christy's impossible cheekbones, Ester's awe-inspiring lips. It was enough to make any mere mortal feel like a mutt. Book had a lot of top editorial models, but perhaps Mak would have been better off at the other big agency in town. They represented Elle, Rachel and Jae Jae, among others, and they were more established.

To her surprise she spotted her portfolio on top of some

papers on the booking table. "Oh my God!" she screamed with relief. "My book!"

Skye smiled. "We got it this morning. You're awfully lucky."

"Who found it?"

"I don't know. It was on the doorstep when we opened."

Makedde felt as if a ten-tonne weight had been lifted from her shoulders. She couldn't have imagined tracking down all her vital magazine clippings from Paris to Vancouver and then trying to locate all the photographers. She quickly flipped through it to check that everything was intact. Halfway through the book, she came to a blank page. A photo was missing.

"Damn. There's a shot missing."

"Are you sure?" Skye asked.

"Yes. Every page was filled before. Look," she said, holding it open, "there's an empty one."

Makedde wondered why anyone would want to steal just one photo. Bikini shot? Something sexy that a young guy might want to keep as a memento?

Memento.

She remembered Loulou. *Those shoes are divine.*

With horror she realised which photo was missing. Mak flipped through the book one more time to check. Yes, it was the photo from Miami with the high, stiletto shoes.

"Skye, I really need to know who returned this book."

She looked at Makedde, puzzled. "Well, there wasn't any note."

"Could anyone have seen them? The building janitor? The receptionist, anyone?"

"She told me it was just there when she arrived."

"What time does the building open?"

"Eight, I think. Now, don't panic. It's just a photo. You have enough other shots to balance your book."

No, Makedde thought on her way out the door, *it's more than that*.

Makedde called the cleaning company just before they closed. As the Book agency receptionist understood it, the cleaners had someone come in every Thursday from five to eight in the morning to vacuum the halls and stairwells and clean the toilets. They would have been there when her portfolio was left. She had to know who this person was, and what they'd seen.

An older woman answered the phone.

"This is Detective Mahoney calling from Central Homicide," Makedde said. "I'm investigating a complaint about some stolen property in a building your company cleans. Can you tell me which of your employees was working in the High Tower building in the city this morning?"

"That would be me," she said apprehensively.

Makedde tried to sound as professional as possible. "And your name, ma'am?"

"Mrs. Tulla Walker."

"Mrs. Walker, I would like to ask you some questions about this morning."

"Yes. I'll help in any way I can," she replied eagerly.

"That's much appreciated. What time did you arrive at the High Tower building this morning?"

"Five."

"Did you notice any packages at the door of the building, or inside the building?"

She took a moment to answer. "Yes . . . I did. I saw a parcel addressed to the model agency upstairs. I brought it right up and left it at their door. I promise."

"And where did you find this parcel?"

"Leaning against the front door."

"Inside the building?"

"No. Outside."

"Did you notice any forwarding address or note attached to the parcel?"

"I don't think so." She paused. "No note. I think it had a single address . . . just to Book Model Agency. I didn't notice anything else."

Damn. "Thank you for your time, Mrs. Walker."

"I swear I didn't take it! I left it at the agency's door. I swear!"

Makedde felt a twinge of guilt at the woman's panic.

"I believe you, ma'am. You're not under suspicion," she assured her. "Thank you for your time."

Feeling a bit sheepish, she hung up the phone.

43

Night fell, chill, dark and windy. The trees bent, bushes rustled. Every preparation had been made. There was nothing left to do but wait. Minutes ticked by. Hours. The leaves whispered in the darkness.

Her car pulled up around ten. It looked shiny and freshly polished, glinting glossy red in the street light. She parked in her driveway and he watched as she cut the engine and went around to the boot. She was alone.

High heels.

He smiled.

He was well camouflaged within the bushes, and watched her gather up an armload of groceries, shut the boot and walk up to the house. Her hair was swept into a neat bun. She wore a dark business suit with a skirt that rode above the knee. Sheer nylon stockings shimmered as she walked.

He would give her the surprise of her life.

He removed a pair of latex gloves from his pocket and put them on. When he heard the front door unlock as she entered her house, he made his way swiftly to the sliding balcony door at the side, quietly letting himself in. Hours earlier, it had taken mere seconds to release the lock. The house had no alarm.

It felt exhilarating to be inside with her so close, the waiting nearly over. He heard her walk down the hall towards the kitchen just beyond him, and place the groceries down on the kitchen table. She turned and started to leave the room, and for a moment he thought she would come right into the dining room where he stood. His grip tensed on the hammer. But no, she was going the other way, into the living room.

The stereo came on.

He smiled again.

She played with the radio dial for a few seconds, settling on a she-done-me-wrong country tune before walking back to the kitchen. Silently, he placed his bag on the floor near his feet. He stepped into the open doorway. She was bent over the grocery bags on the table. She had taken off her suit jacket and was wearing a thin, silky blouse. Her beautiful dark hair had been freed from the bun. He moved towards her undetected; she was still preoccupied with her purchases. He could smell her intoxicating, expensive perfume.

He raised the hammer.

At the very last instant she sensed something and turned. "What—"

The hammer came down with a deft thud upon the crown of her skull. The sensation of impact was an incredible release. The thrill of it spiralled down like a current through his muscles and back up to his head, making his temples throb with pleasure. The blow sent her sprawling backwards onto the linoleum and her head hit the cupboard with a crash.

He bent over her.

"You wore my favourite shoes," he whispered appreciatively. "Thanks for making this easy for me."

She was nearly unconscious. She didn't try to fight; just moaned incoherently. He knew she wouldn't resist him. She had a petite body. It was easy to drag her up the carpeted staircase. He felt so strong, so powerful. He pulled her to the bedroom and lifted her onto the bed. He removed the twine from his back pocket and with expert hands rolled her on to her stomach and tied her wrists and ankles together. He then turned her over to face him. Her legs were forced under her, the blue skirt pulled up over her thighs to reveal lacy panties. Her sheer stockings had ripped, leaving a long spidery ladder up the inside of her thigh. The skin showing through was the colour of ivory. Her eyes were dull, rolling in her head, but she was breathing.

He left her for a moment and fetched his duffel bag from downstairs. Entering the bedroom again a moment later, he saw that she was becoming more lucid, her moans becoming words. But she wasn't screaming.

In a wavering voice she asked, "What do you want?"

He placed the bag on the floor by the foot of the bed and reached down to it. He unzipped the bag and removed the knife.

She screamed.

He couldn't have that, not in this neighbourhood. He forced his hand over her small mouth, smearing red lipstick across her cheek and muffling her cries. The lovely sharpened blade mesmerised him. Such peculiar beauty in that perfect moment. He felt her struggle under his body.

Finally he answered her.

An hour later he emerged from the bedroom, removed his gloves, carefully deposited them in a sealable plastic evidence bag and put on a fresh pair. He would make a quick tour of the house before he left. He entered the study and examined the large, leather-lined desk. Overpriced antique. There were real estate brochures stacked on top, an English dictionary, travel books. He spotted a labelled folder sitting to one side.

Divorce.

He carefully opened the folder and flipped through the pages. The lawyer's fees were high, but she'd got her money's worth. There were property appraisals and forms, and a letter written in legalese regarding a property in Lane Cove. He read it twice and pocketed it.

Satisfied that he had all he wanted, he grabbed his duffel bag and left.

44

James Tiney Jr. wasn't going to stand for it. They didn't have anything on him. How could they drag him down here? By the time he was finished with them, the police would be very sorry they had treated him in this manner.

"How dare you!" he protested. "I'm a respected member of the medical fraternity and of this community." He pointed his finger threateningly at the heavyset, woggy-looking detective. "My father is very good friends with your police commissioner, and I am quite certain that he would object to such treatment, particularly as it makes me look like I'm involved in this terrible killing. I have a public image to defend. I won't stand for this!"

"Hold on there, old son. We've only brought you in to help us with our inquires." The detective placed his meaty palms on the tabletop and leant over, his belly straining over the edge. "Mr. Tiney, we questioned you specifically about your booking at the Terrigal Beach Resort, why you cancelled it, and if you knew Miss Gerber. You told us you'd never met her, and you were planning on staying in that room alone."

JT wiped his brow with a clean cotton handkerchief. "That's correct."

"I think you've been telling us porkies."

JT slammed a fist down on the table. He hoped it made him look adamantine. "That's it! What's your name? I'll have your badge!"

The detective crossed his arms calmly. "My name, for the fourth time, is Detective Senior Constable Jimmy Cassimatis. Frankly, I don't give a shit if you complain to your daddy, whoever he is. I'm here to solve a murder, and you aren't leaving this room until you've told me the truth."

JT was speechless.

"How old are you?" Jimmy asked.

"What?"

"How—old—are—you?"

JT patted his forehead with his hanky. "I'm forty-six."

The detective chuckled quietly, making his belly jiggle beneath his strained white shirt. "I was curious, 'cause you know, I haven't used that 'I'll tell my daddy' thing since I was ten. But hey, whatever."

JT was stunned into silence by the detective's disrespect.

"As I understand it," Jimmy went on, "you've got a wife and two kids. You've got a public image. Fine. I think you also had a mistress. I think you were going to meet her in that hotel and I want to know why you cancelled that booking."

"I wanted to get away for the weekend and relax by myself," he said. "That's not illegal, is it? I cancelled the booking because something else came up. Some business I needed to attend to. Financial stuff. You wouldn't understand."

"Uh-huh." Jimmy leant over the table again. "I spoke to your wife. She thought you were going to Melbourne for a weekend business meeting." The detective turned his chair around backwards and sat opposite, straddling it, his arms folded across the back.

"You . . . you . . ." JT stuttered. "You spoke to Pat?" His wife's name trickled out like unwanted spittle. "What-what-what did you tell her?"

Jimmy softened. "Relax, pal. I didn't tell her you were fucking a luscious nineteen-year-old fashion model. I just wanted to know where she thought you were." He leant in on his chair and smiled. "Hey, she was hot. She was young. She was asking for it. It's understandable. So, you were fucking her. Big deal. You didn't want your wife to know. That's understandable, too. But you've been lying to me and now I want the truth."

They had him. They knew that he was involved with Catherine. They knew he had lied. What if his wife found out the truth? What if his father found out? He would lose his position in the company. He would lose his pay cheque. He would lose everything.

"I told you before. I don't know what you're talking about. I never even met the g-g-gir—"

"Before you attempt to finish that sentence . . ." Jimmy stopped him, and pulled something from his pocket. He placed it on the tabletop.

JT's jaw dropped open.

My ring.

"Care to revise your statement?"

45

Friday morning marked the start of a crisp, clear day. The winter sun rose quietly in the sky, casting golden rays across the cool sands of Bondi Beach. The early surf-lifesaving crew rode the morning's unimpressive waves on long-boards, and a couple of dedicated power-walkers shuffled along from one end of the beach to the other.

Makedde was halfway through her run and felt like taking a breather before heading back along the beautiful coastal path to her place at Bronte. She stopped at a park bench near her old building at South Bondi, and try as she might to exercise away all thoughts of the past few days, she couldn't help dwelling on her missing portfolio photo and her incommunicado detective.

She wondered whether she should call the police and talk to someone in a different branch. Maybe they would be more open-minded. She needed to tell them about Rick Filles, and the missing portfolio shot, and the mutilated photo that some sicko had left her. She had to find out where the investigation was heading.

If you hadn't slept with him you'd be able to call him right now and find out what's going on.

She rotated her shoulders and stretched her hamstrings, shaking off her rhetorical questions. Her body had complained at her early rise, but now with her blood pumping, she felt invigorated. She sat down on the bench and turned to look at the Bondi flat window. She thought about the candle-lit evenings she and Andy had spent just a week ago. Her hands gripped the back of the wooden bench, and she winced as a tiny splinter dug into her palm.

Makedde examined the small, painful sliver embedded in her hand and with long fingernails, carefully pulled it out. She noticed the prickly edges of freshly scratched graffiti on the bench. Someone had carved something into the wood with a knife.

Her eyes widened as she read the three short letters:
MAK

"No," she insisted, "you don't understand. I *have* to talk to him right now."

"I'm sorry, Detective Flynn is not available at the moment. What is this in regards to?"

Mak tried to remain calm. "The Stiletto Murders."

"I'll transfer you to Detective Cassimatis. Please hold."

Oh no. Not him again.

"Cassimatis."

"It's Makedde. I'm still trying to locate Detective Flynn. Can you tell me where he is?"

"Oh." He sounded surprised. "Makedde. I've been trying to reach you. Where are you? I guess you've seen the paper."

"What paper?"

The line was silent for a moment. "Have you been with Andy for the last few days?"

"No. I said I hadn't seen him. That's why I'm calling. What's in the paper?"

"I think you've already caused him enough trouble."

"What are you talking about? What's going on?"

"It isn't doing him any good to take off like this."

"He's gone away? Where?"

Jimmy was silent for a moment. "He hasn't contacted you at all?"

"No! That's what I said. What's going on?"

"Did he tell you he was going through a divorce?"

"Yeah."

"Where are you?" he asked.

"I moved. I'm in Bronte."

"Don't go anywhere. I'd like to ask you some questions. What's the address?"

Mak gave it to him without hesitation, and he told her he would be there in minutes. She ran outside and scanned the street for a newspaper. Down the block there was one hanging out of the mail box. *Sorry*, she thought as she snatched it up. There was a photo of Cassandra's beautiful face and below it, a report:

DETECTIVE'S WIFE KILLED BY SYDNEY RIPPER

Last night Sydney police discovered the body of Mrs. Cassandra Flynn, wife of Homicide Detective Andrew Flynn, in her Woollahra home. Her murder is believed to be connected to that of four other young women brutally slain in Sydney since June 26 this year. Each victim was found wearing a single stiletto shoe. Detective Flynn's whereabouts are unknown and the police urge anyone to come forward who may have any relevant information.

TARA MOSS

Makedde dropped the paper in disbelief.

Jimmy Cassimatis was built like a teddy bear; short and round, with a midsection that in his thirties was already well on its way to resembling a barrel. His arms were covered in the same thick down of black hair that poked up over his collar. He had an informal manner that reminded Makedde of a boy she knew in school who never really grew up.

Having surveyed her digs he now stood in front of her, attempting to be professional. "Miss Vanderwall, I got some questions for you." She suspected he could make iambic pentameter sound like slang. She waited for his next sentence, but for a while the detective was silent, slowly pacing the floor. She decided to break the ice.

"You're Andy's partner. Wouldn't he tell you where he was going?"

"You're his chick. Wouldn't he tell you where he was going?"

Chick. Very classy.

"A chick is a farm animal, Detective. The *Herald* seemed to insinuate that Andy was a suspect. Is he?"

"Andy told me you were a shrink. I don't like shrinks," he barked back.

"I'm not a shrink. I'm *studying* to become a shrink—I mean a psychologist. Is he a suspect or not?"

"Well, as long as he's missing, he looks guilty as hell. I, for one, ain't convinced he did it. But it doesn't look good. That woman was a handful."

Mak remembered the rage that had seeped out of Andy's pores after the argument she'd overheard. "It's unusual that she was found in her home. The other victims were dumped in parks and secluded areas. Do you think it's the same killer?"

"I'm the one who's supposed to be asking the questions here," Jimmy snapped.

"Ask away," she said.

"Do you know where Andy is?"

"Like I told you, no."

"Has he contacted you at all since Monday?"

"No!" This would take forever if he kept asking the same questions. "What happened on Monday?"

Jimmy stopped his pacing. "He was kicked off the case because he became involved with a witness."

"Really?" Mak choked on her guilt. "How did that happen? How did they find out?"

"They just did." Jimmy looked upset. "What did Andy tell you about his wife?"

"He said they were divorcing and he'd just been served the papers. He said there were no kids. He didn't like to talk about the whole thing, really. When we went out he drove a squad car, so I figured there may have been some sort of dispute over their possessions. His wife has the car?"

"Two," Jimmy said. "She has two perfectly good cars." This thought seemed to anger him. "Did you ever see him irritated about the divorce, or at his wife?"

"He didn't sound like he wanted to kill her over it, if that's what you're getting at." She had to ask the big question, the one she hoped she knew the answer to. "Does Andy have an alibi for the previous murders?" She held her breath, waiting for his reply.

"Yes. Catherine and Becky, anyway."

She exhaled. "So, the only reason that he could possibly be under suspicion is because of his relationship with the victim and his subsequent disappearance?"

"Not quite."

"What else is there?"

"I can't tell you."

"What *can* you tell me? Is he innocent? Is he a killer? Did he kill his wife in a rage and then stage it to look like the others? If he shows up at my door should I run for my life? What?"

Jimmy didn't respond. He wasn't even looking her in the eye.

"I know you must hate me for getting your partner in trouble," she offered, "but believe me, it was never my intention. This situation has caused me a lot of pain, too."

His hands were laced tightly behind his back, his face stern. Makedde suspected he was the type to repress his emotions. He would probably have a heart attack by the time he was forty. When he finally spoke, she was surprised by what came out of his mouth. "Were you really in *Sports Illustrated?*"

She laughed. "Uh . . . yes. A couple of years ago. What's that got to do with anything?"

He didn't respond, but she noticed his tough exterior melt just a bit. "Come on, Jimmy. We both like Andy. We're both confused by what's happening. Let's help each other out." She smiled at him. "Are there any reasons to suspect Andy apart from his relationship with the victim? Fingerprints at the scene?"

"You don't want to know—"

"Like hell I don't want to know!" It angered her that he still wasn't taking her seriously. "I practically fell on top of victim number three, who happens to have been my best friend, I've been ransacked, sent threatening mail and attacked by some psycho with a sex dungeon, so if you honestly believe I'm going to get squeamish on you—"

"What was that about a dungeon?"

"Rick Filles. Andy told me you were investigating him. Well, I've got a real juicy tale to tell about his nocturnal activities. That guy is seriously twisted. But first, I need you to tell me what else ties Andy to the murder. Please—"

"You didn't happen to go to his place and lock him in his little room, did you?"

"Well, actually—"

"So that *was* you! Andy said you were the meddling type, but I never thought . . ." The phrase stung a bit. Makedde preferred to think of herself as curious and resourceful, not meddling. "We hauled him in for questioning not long ago," Jimmy continued, "and he accused us of setting him up with a sexy undercover cop who trapped him in that room of his. There's no way that was Mahoney."

Makedde felt her face go red.

"He's still being investigated over some assaults, but he's been cleared of the Stiletto Murders." Jimmy became contemplative. "Andy's in deep, deep skata," he said, frowning. "You know he's run into problems with his temper in the past."

She remembered the look of rage she'd seen on his face. "Come on, what's happening?" she pressed. "If he has an alibi for the others, it can't be that bad. They can't seriously think—"

"They think he might've done a copycat," Jimmy said, cutting her off. "Used his knowledge of the crimes to stage it the same. He had motive and, well . . . his fingerprints and blood were found on the kitchen knife used in the murder."

46

"Jimmy, you look bloody awful," Phil said, sliding a beer across to him.

"Then I look better than I feel." Jimmy sighed and slumped forward on his stool, letting his belly hold him up against the bar. The place seemed empty without his partner around.

"Wanna talk about it?"

"Nah."

"Go on mate, what's up?" said another sympathetic voice, but it wasn't the bartender this time, it was the young man on the next stool.

"Ed, right?" Jimmy had seen him around. He was a regular who worked at the morgue.

"Yeah. Geez, yer good with names. So what's getting you down tonight, mate?"

Jimmy took a long swig of his beer and wiped his mouth with his sleeve. "Can't really talk about it. It's that fuckin' case I'm working on."

"The Stiletto Murders?"

Jimmy nodded.

"Yeah, everyone's talking. Is it true your partner killed his wife?"

Bloody papers. Now everyone thinks they're a friggin' detective. "No mate. I don't think he did."

"But he disappeared, right? Isn't he the main suspect?"

"I'd rather not think about it if ya don't mind."

The young man shook his head. "I understand. Must be tough when you think you know someone and it turns out you don't know them at all. Geez, he looked normal enough to me. How could he do that to his own wife? Bloody sickening."

Jimmy didn't respond. He felt anxious about the case and he couldn't relax while this idiot rambled on. Maybe he should get home to his wife early for a change.

"Mind you," Ed continued uninvited, "I heard that woman was a real greedy bitch. She was taking him for everything, right? And you gotta hand it to the guy, setting it up to look like the Stiletto Murderer was clever. I guess he made too many mistakes, though."

Jimmy got up to leave. He had no desire to discuss his partner with some guy who had already found Andy guilty based on uninformed barroom gossip.

"I'd better get going."

"I hope it's nothing I said," the young man offered feebly.

"Nah, goodnight."

But something Ed said *had* jogged Jimmy's memory, only he wouldn't realise what it was until later that night.

47

Sitting cross-legged on the couch in the Bronte flat, Makedde stared into space, wondering whether a woman could know if she were sleeping with a killer. Plenty of other women had been fooled. History reeked of incredible stories of betrayal and misplaced trust. Bundy's girlfriends. Kemper's mother. Makedde's father had talked about some woman in the twenties . . . Frau Kirchen? No, Frau *Kurten*, in Germany. It was one of the worst case studies he had read about. Frau Kurten had been unaware of the seventy-nine assaults, rapes and murders her husband had committed. They had been married for ten years when he was arrested. Peter Sutcliffe also had a wife, as did Jerome Brudos and countless other violent killers. Hell, even Stanley had a pregnant girlfriend. How could Makedde honestly believe that she knew Andy Flynn after a few lusty encounters?

A dull pain drew her attention to the fact that she was digging her nails into the palms of her hands. Her whole body was tense and hunched over, her breathing shallow, her teeth clenched. She uncurled her fingers and made a concentrated effort to relax.

Jimmy's words still echoed in her head. He had explained that Andy was blood type AB, a blood group found in only three percent of the population while Cassandra was type O, a blood group found in forty-six percent. Cassandra's blood was all over everything; the bed, the sheets, walls, floors, and the knife left at the scene. Had the AB type killer been injured in the struggle, or had the killer attacked Andy before killing his wife?

Andy's knife was missing from its sharpening scabbard in the kitchen drawer. His fingerprints were on it. His blood. Size ten shoe prints, the same size as Andy's, were tracked through the blood that had pooled beneath Cassandra's body and through the house they had once shared.

Makedde was still wide awake at midnight. Under her pillow lay the paring knife. On the bedside chest of drawers a can of hairspray sat beside a lighter. The telephone speed-dial was set for 000 and she had Jimmy's mobile number. What more could she do at this hour? Sitting on the bed, surrounded by her little arsenal, Makedde started reading *Without Conscience; The Disturbing World of the Psychopaths Among Us*. It was a bestseller written by one of the professors at her university in British Columbia. Appropriate, if not comforting reading.

Luther lumbered towards the Bronte flat, unseen and unheard. A man of his confronting appearance preferred to operate by night. It was better when his prey didn't see him approaching, when the fear came quickly, his victims caught off guard. He went around the back of the building, his huge feet sinking silently into the damp lawn of the neighbour's property.

Your back door man.

James Tiney Jr. would be happy to be rid of this meddling beauty who had caused him so much trouble. He was upset that the cops had found his ring. The police were all over him, and his wife had found out about the affair. It wasn't Luther's fault, but still, he was happy to remove one thorn from his client's side, free of charge. It was a win-win situation; it was something Luther would enjoy, and all the while JT would have an airtight alibi and this murder would wipe him off the suspect list. He had given JT clear instructions. "Deal with the police tonight. Deal with your family tonight. Don't spend one minute alone." He hadn't told him why, just that it was important. JT would thank him later.

The street was quiet at this hour. There were some vehicles parked up the street that he hadn't noticed before, but none were anywhere near her place. If they had been her visitors they would most probably have parked closer. No, he was sure she was alone. Having Makedde all to himself would be such a pleasure. Luther could almost taste the sweet conquest.

He would do it as the Stiletto Killer.

Struck.

Tied up.

Cut.

Thoroughly enjoyed and possessed. Just like the cop's wife. Flynn would be extra guilty over that little detail. The thought made Luther smile. He stopped at the edge of Mak's backyard and listened before pulling a knitted ski mask over his head. He would be quite a sight, well over six feet tall, sporting a black commando-style jumpsuit, gloves and a ski mask. He carried a tyre iron, gag, handcuffs and a very sharp six-inch skinning knife. He would use them in the correct order. With memories of Makedde's naked body enticing him, he started from his spot. He would come closer, until he could see her alone through the window, then he would make his move.

He heard a noise.

Something rustled in the bushes behind him.

He crouched down and tried to pinpoint the source, pulling the skinning knife from its sheath in one swift, precise movement. But save for the soft patter of falling leaves, the bushes were still again.

Quiet.

It was probably a bird, a possum maybe.

He started again towards the porch steps.

There was another noise.

Luther whirled at the sound and caught a blur of movement as something flew towards him. Although nowhere near his size, a creature struck him off balance, sending him sprawling across the wet ground. Luther's knife fell from his grasp. He shoved the attacker away with great force, and as it flew back he saw that it was a man, fairhaired and small, with his teeth bared in silent aggression. His eyes were wild, limbs flailing as he sailed backwards.

Luther groped across the damp grass, searching futilely for his knife. The man was coming again, with the reflection of a sharp blade catching the light as it swung in his hand. Luther roared with fury, kicking out and connecting with his attacker's groin. The thin blade sliced through the air, nicking Luther's ear, then the tip tore through his jumpsuit and into his muscular shoulder. He cried out, more in anger than pain and leapt to his feet.

There was movement within the house and the porch light flicked on to partially illuminate the backyard. He saw his foe scurrying away. The man's size certainly didn't match his strength. Luther had to get out of there. With all the noise, the cops would be on their way any moment. It wasn't worth the risk. Something warm oozed from his left ear, and when he raised a hand to wipe it he saw a slick of blood across his glove.

Fuck!

JT had some explaining to do.

48

What was that noise?

Something had woken her again. Sounds by her front door . . . footsteps? She had heard yelling near her back door, but when she had gone to the porch there was no one there. What time was that? What time was it now? She reached under her pillow, grabbed the paring knife and held it upright in one hand like an impatient dinner guest. A fist pounded on her front door. Someone was speaking in an urgent whisper.

"Makedde? Are you up?" a familiar voice said.

Makedde sprung from her bed, knife in hand, and her book slid off the bed and landed on the floor with a thud. She was wide awake now.

He spoke again. "I saw your light on. I know it's late . . ."

Her clock read 1.30 a.m. "Damn right it's late, Andy," she replied, trying to sound tough as she moved towards the door. *Late in more ways than one.* She checked that it was deadlocked and the security chain was pulled across.

"I really need to talk to you," he said meekly.

Her fingers tightened around the knife. "What do you

want to talk to me about? Hey . . . How did you know I lived here?" she challenged, her mouth inches from the door.

"Makedde, I didn't do it. I read about it in the paper this morning—"

"Great. Then why don't you walk yourself down to the nearest police station and call me in the morning."

"I've already been to the police . . . Can we do this without the door in the way, please?"

"You've been to the police, have you?" she said sceptically. "Have you talked to Jimmy?"

"Yes."

"When?"

"This evening. I know he came to talk to you today. That's how I knew you were here."

Oh, thanks, Jimmy. "Did he tell you you're a suspect?"

There was a long pause. For a moment she wondered if he was still there. Then he said, "I knew I was a suspect before I walked in there—"

"And how did you know that?"

"Maybe I should go—"

"No, wait." She hesitated. "Where have you been?"

"Lane Cove. It's a long story. Can I come in now? I'm feeling a bit ridiculous talking to you through your door."

"Hang on." She cautiously opened the door a couple of inches, the chain pulled tight.

Their eyes met. It was Andy; the same man she had made love to, the man she had thought she could trust. His hair was lank, uncombed, his face unshaven. She thought she smelled the faint odour of alcohol.

"Andy," she said, "please understand my position. You took off without so much as a good-bye, and now that you're a murder suspect, you show up unannounced at my door at 1.30 in the morning."

"I should have called, but I need to talk to you now. I didn't do it. You have to believe me."

"Why don't you ever call before you show up? Do you promise you talked to the police? They know you're back?"

"I promise."

"And you spoke with Jimmy tonight?"

"Yes," he insisted, leaning into the gap in the door and looking into her eyes.

"So if I call him right now, he'll back up your story?"

He pulled back. "It's 1.30 a.m."

"He's a cop, isn't he? Aren't you guys on call twenty-four hours a day? I'd say this is pretty important," she said, watching his eyes, studying him for a sign that he was nervous about having his location known. He didn't flinch.

"I shouldn't even be here, but if it will make you feel better, call him." He cast his eyes downward. "I'd better leave. I shouldn't have come tonight."

With that, he turned and walked away. Makedde just watched him through the door, her knife flush against the frame. He walked to the street, then turned and said, "I'm sorry you became involved in this."

"I'm sorry about your wife," she replied, and she was. She wanted to believe he was innocent; that was the problem. Her emotional involvement might impair her judgment.

Perhaps it already had.

The telephone rang at 8 a.m. wrenching Makedde out of a deep sleep. Her body felt heavy, as if it had sunk halfway into the mattress, and she was experiencing what felt uncannily like a hangover. But she hadn't touched a drop.

"Hello?" she said weakly.

The voice sounded distant. "Mak, it's your father."

"Dad! How are you? I'm sorry I haven't called."

"How are *you*?"

"Uh, I'm fine . . ."

"Uh-huh." Something in his voice seemed to indicate that he knew all was not well. The line was silent for moment. "Theresa is doing well," he said. "It won't be long now. Sure wish your mother could have seen it." She heard him take a deep breath. Sometimes she forgot how strong he was, how well he had coped with Jane's death.

"Do you know a Detective Flynn down at Central Branch?"

Oh no. Here it comes.

It didn't really surprise her that her father knew about Andy. Obviously he was keeping tabs on her, again. Predictable. He probably had contacts in every city in Australia, and anywhere else she might plan on travelling to.

Leslie Vanderwall went on when she didn't respond. "I'm pretty sure you two have been introduced. He's a tall guy. Dark hair. Works in Homicide."

"Yes, I think I know the one. Hmmm. Really cute? Nice arse?"

Looks great handcuffed to a bed . . .

"Makedde!"

"Dad, you know I hate it when you snoop. When did you start checking up on me?"

"When? I think you were eleven years old and sleeping over at a friend's house. Or so you said." He paused. "This guy you've become involved with is a suspect in the murder of his wife, Mak. This is serious."

"Dad—"

"He has a bad reputation, too. A temper."

"That's bullshit. You made that up. He may be a bit volatile, but he is very well respec—"

"Listen to me for once! You've got yourself into a mess over there and you should come home," her father implored.

"I have things I need to tie up first. Trust me. I can't leave now."

"You have to!"

"I can't. I won't."

"You really are your mother's daughter. Stubborn as all hell."

"I'll be home in a few more weeks, and then it won't matter. I'm too wrapped up in this—"

"Can't you see that's the problem? You've put yourself in danger again."

That stung. If he brought up the whole nightmare with Stanley, she would hang up on him. She wished she'd never even told him she'd been attacked, but she knew one of his cop friends would have blurted it out anyway.

"Hey, I don't *put* myself in danger, OK? And I'm fine here. Besides, I don't even see Andy anymore."

"Really." He didn't sound convinced. "Well, you may not put yourself in danger, but you certainly don't seem to jump out of the frying pan when things heat up."

"I'll see you in a few weeks," she said bluntly. "I'll be back before the first contraction, I promise."

She started to put the phone down but he spoke again. "Don't shut me out!"

"I'm not," she said, but did exactly that.

Late that afternoon, as dark clouds rolled in from the south, Makedde wandered down to Bronte Park for a brisk walk. She needed a bit of exercise and the fresh coastal breeze to fill her lungs, and hopefully shed some light on the myriad of unanswered questions. She had stayed home all day, too preoccupied and self-conscious to integrate into any populated scene. Fighting with her father had made things so much worse. She hated ending a conversation with him on such a sour note.

She walked back and forth through the park and the damp sand on the beach, contemplating what Jimmy had told her. Andy had an alibi for the other murders. Unfortunately he didn't have one for the murder of his wife. What Jimmy had told her about Rick Filles didn't surprise her in the slightest. Apparently he'd preyed on young, impressionable girls as young as thirteen. She hoped they hadn't been abused in that disgusting little room of his, with those horrible contraptions.

The skies opened up as she walked, and although it wasn't cold by Canadian standards, there was certainly a Sydney winter chill in the air. Makedde pulled the hood of her jacket up over her head, and listened to the rain's pitter-patter on the vinyl. She was alone in the park, except for a romantic couple nuzzling each other under one of the wooden picnic shelters, wrapped tightly in a huge woolly blanket. It was the happiest thing she'd seen all day, but a strange, unexpected sadness came over her at the sight of it. She was deep in thought when the sound of a passing car caught her attention. It was a late model red sportscar, freshly polished. Something about it set off a distant warning bell.

A strong wind whistled through the trees at the edges of the park and she buried her chin into her collar. It was getting dark. Time to head back. Makedde walked with her head down, mulling things over.

One word echoed repeatedly in her mind . . . *guilty*.

49

"James Tiney Jr. please," Luther snarled into the phone, feeling odd having to hold the receiver to his right ear instead of his left. He stared at his reflection in a small shaving mirror, examining the bandage covering his left ear. A spot of blood was leaking through it.

"Who may I ask is calling?" queried the receptionist.

"Tell him it's Mr. Hand, and it's important."

"Oh, I see. One moment please."

Luther didn't feel patient. Not at all. JT hadn't been straight with him. He had some serious explaining to do.

After a few moments, JT's irritating voice came on the line. "Yes. What's going on?"

"I'm only going to ask you this once," Luther stated firmly. "Who else do you have working this assignment?"

"What—"

"Don't make me ask you again."

"N-n-no . . . no one else. Why? What's happened?"

"I'm dropping the job."

"You what?!"

"You're not being straight with me. And here I was

263

about to do you a big favour," Luther hissed angrily. "You screwed up."

"What are you talking about? Why did I need an alibi last night? I fought with my wife all night because of you. I'm going through hell here because you didn't find the ring, and you're giving *me* grief!"

"You know what I'm talking about. There's too much heat now. Consider us even."

"B-b-but . . . but what about the payments I made?" JT sounded pathetic, stuttering like a spoilt child who wasn't getting what he wanted. "You didn't do the job! She's still in town. The police got the ring and now I'm fucked! You can't do this to me. What about the money I gave you?"

"Consider it payment for my ear."

"What? Hey, I want my money back!"

"Have a whinge to Consumer Affairs."

Luther hung up the phone, ignoring JT's snivelling protests. Controlling his irritation with deep breathing, he pulled the mirror closer. Blood soaked the new bandage. If the cops found part of his ear at the scene, they could match it. He couldn't afford to be questioned about anything. Maybe it was a good time to head north again. He could use the sunshine.

50

There was a surprise waiting for Makedde when she got home. A man was sitting on her stairs, staring at her. One dim light over the front door cast a faint glow across a cheek, the other side of his face was in darkness. He was smiling.

Andy Flynn looked haggard. It was as if he had just stepped out of a tumble-dryer. How long had he been waiting in the cold wind? She wasn't disarmed by the innocent look of defeat on his face.

"Makedde, I was hoping you'd come home soon. I really need to talk to you," he said. "I just need you to know that I didn't do it," he continued. "I could never do something like that."

"I don't think it's a good idea that we meet like this," she managed to say. *Don't get him angry.* "Maybe we could—"

"No." He cut her off aggressively. "Please . . . I *need* to talk, just for a moment."

"Why don't we get a coffee then, and talk about it— there's a place just around the corner. We can get out of this wind." He didn't respond for a moment. She had to get them out of the empty street. She had to get them in public. "Come on, it's not far."

Minutes later they were seated at a table in a Bronte café that she had passed on her walk home. It overlooked the now darkened beach through a huge pane of glass. The waves were crashing angrily on the shore. A storm was brewing, but the rain had temporarily ceased. Makedde rubbed her hands to warm up.

"OK," she said, "why don't we start at the beginning. One minute we can't keep our hands off each other, the next minute you won't return my calls."

Andy sat there for a moment, silent and hunched.

But then, like a helium balloon that begins to drop and pucker after too many hours, the aggression seemed to leak out of him. He was slowly collapsing in front of her.

"You have a really terrible habit of turning up unannounced. You do realise that, don't you?"

He offered her a weak, "Sorry." Then he seemed to come back from somewhere. He chose his words with care, "I fear I . . . may have put you in danger."

It was not the kind of reply she was expecting.

"You've put me in danger?" she asked the messed up part in his hair.

"Inadvertently," he added without looking up.

"Inadvertently? Like your wife, you mean?"

He tilted his head. His eyes were sad and weary. "Yes."

"Forgive me if I don't take that well, considering what happened to her."

The waitress placed their drinks gently on the table and quickly disappeared. Makedde watched as Andy cupped his hands around his black coffee and closed his eyes. Perhaps there was no reason to fear him at all. It was time to find out.

"I'm not a murderer," he declared. "I didn't kill any of

those poor women, and I certainly didn't kill my own wife. But I believe that whoever did knows how far I am willing to go to catch him, and he's trying to get me out of the way."

"You mean the killer tried to frame you?"

"Yes. Cassandra was just a tool for him, a way of getting to me. That's why you may be in danger . . . If he knows about us he may try to use you next."

Was it that simple? A set-up?

"Do you have any reason to believe that he's after me?"

"Only what you told Jimmy. We can't know for sure, but it got me thinking."

"They aren't going to do anything to protect me though, are they?"

"No. They can't. Even if they wanted to, there isn't enough evidence to justify the manpower."

No surprise there. *Why didn't I save the mutilated photo?* "So let me just clarify something here. You had nothing to do with the death of your wife? You were framed?"

"I swear."

"And where were you when she was killed?"

"I was alone, drunk and miserable in a house at Lane Cove where I went the moment I was suspended Monday morning." His eyes pleaded for trust.

"But you can't prove it."

"No."

Uh-huh. "What were you doing at Lane Cove?"

"I had to get away. It's a little investment property. We had a tenant in it at one point."

Mak was still sceptical. "So, if it was your place then why didn't the police just contact you there? They were searching for you, you know."

"It was Cassandra's place actually, and it's still in her name. She was going to transfer the title to me as part of the divorce settlement. She got the Woollahra house, which is worth more. I couldn't stand the thought of living in it, so Lane Cove was fine."

"And the kitchen knife?" she asked, continuing her interrogation.

"Stolen."

"The blood?"

He offered her his right hand, and flexed the thumb out as if he were asking for a lift. "See that cut?" Her eyes rested on a thin gash. "It's thanks to your lecture on the benefits of fresh fruit and veggies."

She remembered their first date and her silly comment. She doubted it would have had any effect on his eating habits. "When?"

"Saturday. It's the only explanation I can think of."

The only excuse you can think of?

"And that was the last time you used the knife?"

"Yes. I left it in the sink. I was with you after that. When I left for Lane Cove on Monday I didn't take a lot of stuff with me. I had no idea how long I'd stay. I just needed to cool off. Escape. I don't know if the knife was gone by then. All I know is it wasn't there yesterday. It was lying beside Cassandra's body."

"Something I still don't get; if you don't live at the Woollahra house with Cassandra, and you had to pack some stuff to go to the Lane Cove house, where are you living?"

"I've been staying at the Holt Hotel. It's a crappy little place in the Cross. That's why I never wanted to take you there. With this case, I haven't had the time to properly move."

"Is Jimmy still heading the investigation?" she asked.

"The Stiletto Murders, yes, but they've got someone else handling Cassandra's death. Jimmy thinks I'm innocent, to my face at least, but there are a lot of people who think I used my knowledge of the crimes to do a copycat. For all I know, some jumped-up little prick is dedicating every spare moment of his time to finding a hole in my alibis for the other deaths, too."

"What are you going to do?"

"I don't really know, to be honest. I don't know how, but I've got to catch this guy. It's the only way I can prove my innocence. They have a new lead on Catherine's case but they won't tell me anything about it. I have officially been off the case since Monday. Even Jimmy won't let on." He sighed. "I don't know what they think I'd do. Even if I could find this guy right now and beat a confession out of him, it wouldn't mean diddly-squat."

It sounded like something he'd tried before. "Did Jimmy give you the impression it was a good lead?"

"Not necessarily. Just something new. If it was solid enough they would be all over it, and they aren't."

"They're all over you."

"Exactly."

They smiled together for the first time in what seemed like an eternity.

"You look tired. You must have had a hell of a week," she offered.

"You could say that. I'm really sorry I didn't call you. I have no excuse, but the longer I stayed out there, the more I didn't want to talk to anyone."

"Least of all, a woman," she added, pointedly.

"I guess so," he admitted.

His manner was so strange. It was like someone had knocked the wind out of his sails. She wanted to say that she understood, but she would be lying. Things could never be the same again. She looked down and saw that her cup was empty. She needed to get home and think about what he had said, without him around to influence her.

"It's late. I should get to bed."

"I'll walk you to your door—if that's all right."

"Sure."

The night was stormy and electric as they walked back, dark clouds moving over them, heavy with rain.

"Thanks for hearing me out," he said, when they reached her door.

She stepped away from him and wished him a good-night. He seemed to sense her caution, and respect it. It was good to have talked with him, to have heard his side.

But on which side lay the truth?

51

Cold rain fell heavily upon him; branches bent and strained in the wind, bowing as he passed silently through the streets. Black-clad, he moved with well-practised feline stealth. His mother's cat, Spade, who he had studied for so many years, moved with a similar agile grace.

Makedde's car was easy to find—the words "Lowe-Rent" were printed in tacky blue lettering on a sticker on the rear windscreen. It was parallel-parked tightly between two older looking cars a block away from her Bronte flat.

He considered himself a careful planner and there was no doubt that this new scheme would work. All he needed to do was be patient, and he could be very patient when he wanted to be. This time there would be no meddling oaf to surprise him and ruin his moment. Whoever the competition had been, he was sure the man wouldn't return.

He stopped a few feet from the car and glanced up and down the quiet street, listening, assessing. Nothing. Only wind, rain, and rustling trees. Everything had to be perfect, just like last time. No mistakes.

He was truly proud of the creativity he had expressed

with his last girls. They had been so weak in the end, whimpering, begging. Soft skin stained with tears and blood. Beautiful. Makedde would be the ultimate. Fate brought them together, fate that was written in the features of her face. She would be an important possession; the tenth shoe, a symbolic number.

The police made him laugh. Five? They were so inept, so deluded.

Number ten.

She can't be rushed.

Satisfied he was alone, he removed a small flashlight and a pair of pliers from his bag. Holding both in one hand, he laid himself flat on the wet asphalt and shuffled under the front of the car, ignoring the steady rain soaking his legs. He switched the flashlight on. He was under the engine block. With a trained eye, he quickly found the starter motor wires and disconnected them. He then neatly tucked them up out of sight.

Flashlight switched off, he wriggled out from under the car. It had taken less than sixty seconds. *Very good.* His clothes were gritty and soaked. The street was still empty. He felt buoyant as he walked back to his van. He would wait for his prize in the wee hours of the morning, right through the day if necessary. Wait in the shadows until the moment was perfect.

And it *would* be perfect . . . soon.

52

At 8 a.m. the next morning Makedde dialled Jimmy's number. She wanted to find out about the new lead Andy had mentioned, but she also wanted to discuss a hunch she had about the car she kept seeing. A clue had come to her in her dreams. She was sure of it. Andy was following her. But why? Why didn't he mention it? He had complained about Cassandra having the Honda, and now he had it back. How far had he gone to get it? Had he followed her all day, and then waited at her front door? And there was something else. He claimed the cut on his right thumb had been caused by chopping fruit with the knife that was later used to kill his wife.

But Andy was right-handed.

She walked out onto the porch and watched the Bronte waves. Makedde planned on leaving in two weeks, at the very latest. Her family would never forgive her if she wasn't home for the birth of her sister's first baby. She had promised herself that she wouldn't leave until Catherine's killer had been found. She would hate to go home with her tail between her legs, a failure. No, she would stay just two weeks longer, then she would be satisfied that she had done all she could.

The phone rang. Automatically, she ripped it out of its cradle, "Jimmy—"

"Hi, Makedde, this is Suzy from Book."

Suzy? "Sorry, I was expecting someone else."

"How soon can you get into the city?"

"Uh . . . Twenty minutes if I cab it. Why?"

"A girl has phoned in sick. They're waiting for someone right now for an *ELLE* fashion shoot. Four hours. Half-day editorial rate."

"Great." *ELLE* would make excellent tear-sheets to add to her portfolio. Suzy gave her the address and Makedde called a taxi as soon as she hung up. Suzy? There were so many bookers, and she didn't remember half of their names. Suzy was probably the one with the red, curly hair. Within minutes, the taxi had arrived and with her portfolio and make-up shoved in a bag slung over one shoulder, Makedde barrelled down the stairs and headed for what would be her last job in Sydney.

Andy Flynn could have sworn his colleagues moved away from him when he stepped into the elevator. The two constables to his left turned their backs when he got in, and the Chinese-Australian girl from forensics who was stuck on the other side of him looked very uncomfortable being caught in the same car. She averted her eyes and practically jumped when Andy made a tiny movement.

Welcome to reality. The men and women who made up the force that he was part of, or *had* been part of, were now treating him like a leper. Guilty until proven innocent. Didn't they know he had an alibi for the murders of those women? But his alibi for the other crimes wasn't enough. They probably thought he killed his wife and staged it to look like the others. None of them seemed to have much trouble swallowing the idea, either. Those who didn't know better tended to treat cops who specialised in serial killings with suspicion. Studying with the FBI had raised him in the ranks, but it had alienated him too.

The old elevator rattled its way up to his floor at an interminable pace. When he finally stepped out he thought he heard the other passengers exhale with relief. Andy didn't want trouble. He only came because he needed to know the test results. No one had returned his calls, not even Jimmy, and he was tired of being dicked around.

Examining his footwear was ridiculous, and Andy had told them as much. He maintained he was framed, and if that were true, the tests would prove nothing. He had old boots he hadn't worn in years, anyone could have taken a pair along with a knife. They could have tracked them through his wife's blood and returned them to the pile. It would have been easy.

Andy walked into the Homicide office and saw that Jimmy wasn't around and most of the detectives were out. Inspector Kelley was there though, and looked surprised to see him.

"Uh, Flynn. What are you doing here? You know the footwear tests have been delayed."

"Oh, great," Andy said with an irritated frown.

"Something's come up," Kelley said, sounding a little more sympathetic. "We're no longer focusing our investigation on the weapon and shoe prints in your wife's murder."

"Are you trying to say that I'm no longer a suspect?"

Kelley's face hardened. "I'm not saying anything at this point. What are you doing here?"

"I just wanted to find out about the tests. Don't worry, I'm not planning on sticking around."

"I hope this situation is sorted out soon," Kelley said,

then disappeared down the hallway. It seemed Kelley didn't quite know how to treat a persona non grata. No one did.

Andy started to leave, but stopped when he spotted Jimmy coming out of the elevator. His long-time partner did a double take, then signalled a distracted hello to Andy and walked right past him to answer a ringing phone on his desk. Andy watched as Jimmy mumbled into his phone. The secrecy was driving him crazy.

"Skata! What do you mean you lost him!" Jimmy suddenly screamed into the earpiece. His olive skin turned beet and veins started popping out on his neck. "How's that possible?" The sentence was punctuated by his fist hitting the desk. Jimmy slammed the receiver down. Someone's ears would be ringing.

"Oi, Jimmy. What was that about? Lost who?"

"Oh, skata! This is a mess!" he whispered. "I never believed you could do it, mate. So, I kept my eye out for someone who might have it in for you. Someone who would want to frame you, like you'd said. There was this guy at the bar," he went on, "Ed Brown. We just put him under surveillance and he's pulled a fast one." Jimmy rubbed his face with shaking hands. "Oh fuck, we lost him . . ."

Andy was barely able to take in the rest of what Jimmy was saying. He felt ill. They had found the Stiletto Killer and then they had lost him.

It got worse. "He made a call before he took off," Jimmy said. "We had the tracer on. It was to Makedde."

Andy didn't have to say a word—his expression said it all. He was back on the case, whether their Inspector liked it or not.

"Kelley'll have my head for this. Oh, fuck it." Jimmy

reached down to a steel security drawer and pulled out a gun. He handed it to Andy without hesitation. "We're looking for a '76 VW van. Blue. I'll fill you in while we drive."

53

The phone call came only half an hour after Makedde had flopped on the bed, exhausted from her four-hour modelling job that had lasted well over seven. She'd spent the day in wispy little asymmetrical dresses and smudged eyeliner, hanging off gritty window ledges in a disused Surry Hills warehouse. All in the name of *ELLE's* new fashion outlook. It had been a relief to close her eye-shadow-greased lids when she got home, but soon the phone beside the bed had rung, robbing her of that moment of peace.

"Hello?"

"Makedde?" a man's voice politely inquired. "This is Book Model Agency."

Yet another one whose voice she didn't recognise.

"Makedde, I'm sorry it's such short notice but we need you at a casting in the city in thirty minutes."

Thirty minutes!

"It's very important that you get there on time. It's for a pantyhose commercial, so show your legs. Heels would be best. Make sure your feet look good."

She didn't bother to complain. She was used to last-minute appointments, which often meant cancelling other plans.

"When is it shooting?"

"Uh, next week."

"What does it pay?"

"Thirty thousand."

Wow. That was exceptional. An average commercial would generally pay ten or fifteen thousand to a no-name model like her. That sort of money would cover text books and tuition, and then some.

Makedde took down the address and thanked the booker. She was grateful that her legs and feet were already smooth, moisturised and unmarked, and she had her portfolio again, too, although it was still incomplete. All she had to do was change into something appropriate and get there on time.

Nineteen minutes later Makedde was in a panic.

Not now!

She turned the ignition of her rental car again, but there was nothing. She gripped the key hard, inserting it with deliberation, turning it . . .

Nothing. Dead.

I don't have time for this!

She hopped out of the driver's seat and popped the bonnet. Mak squinted at the greasy tangle of wires and steel, eyes running over the hoses and metal curves, but she couldn't see the problem. She was inexperienced with a car's inner workings, and the low light certainly wasn't helping. She ran around to the boot to check for a flashlight, but there wasn't one.

She had gotten ready as quickly as physically possible, choosing a brief dress and high shoes to show her long legs to full effect. She had barely taken the time to fix the make-up from her morning photo shoot, and yet still, here she was, no closer to arriving at the appointment on time. Damn agency. Disorganised. Or maybe the client was the one to blame? It wouldn't be the first time. Either way, it seemed that Charles was too busy to deal with her these days. She was being fobbed off to any old booker. Maybe she should have changed agencies after all.

A pale blue van passed by, then backed up alongside Makedde, and a young ginger-haired man leant out of the driver's-side window. There was something vaguely familiar about him.

"You need any help?" he asked casually in a soft, friendly voice.

"Oh, I'm fine, really, thanks," she said.

He looked down at the open bonnet. "Are you *sure* you don't need some help?"

What do I do?

Ed Brown waited patiently as Makedde made up her mind.

54

The unmarked police Commodore tore down the William Street, its siren wailing with an urgency largely ignored by the rush hour traffic. They were quickly stalled by a mass of waiting vehicles; men and women returning from work with no idea that blocking the road could result in another violent murder. Andy leant out the passenger window and screamed, "Move it! Get out of the fucking way!" His outburst had little effect apart from frightening a young mother whose car was jammed up beside them. The sleeping infant in the back seat didn't stir.

"Hang on," Jimmy said, turning the wheel hard to the right and sending them over the median strip. They accelerated up the right-hand side of William Street, the siren screaming out its loud, flashing warning to the cars speeding up from the opposite direction. Once they passed a set of traffic lights Jimmy took them across the divider again with a thud and a squeal of tyres.

Andy sat with both feet hard up against the footwell and one hand clenched tightly around the grab handle above the door. "Tell me about this Ed Brown guy. Who the hell is he?" he asked is partner.

"A morgue attendant. A regular at our bar. You'd recognise him if you saw him, Andy. He was the attendant the day Makedde came in to identify Catherine Gerber." Jimmy's eyes never once left the road. "I think the malaka must have seen you two together after that, and he got jealous. Cassandra was his way of getting you out of the picture. He chatted me up at the bar a few days ago, real casual-like." He stopped talking for a moment to honk and curse at some drivers who weren't getting out of the way. "He asked me about you. He knew about Cassandra and he knew you'd disappeared. He said he thought you'd killed your wife. I didn't agree, but there was something unsettling about the guy. He was just so insistent to talk about you and the case. Were you suspended? Were you the main suspect? All that."

"What did you do?"

"I didn't think much of it till I was heading home. But it got me thinking about the morgue, and that the sharp instrument the killer used might have been a scalpel. I didn't have a lot of other leads, so I checked his background. He lit a few fires in his teens, minor offences, but it got me thinking about the 'homicidal triad'—you know, all that stuff you were crowing about when you came back from the States—extended bedwetting, cruelty to animals, arson. I got Colin to ask around at the morgue, see if anyone noticed anything suspicious. Colin gets back to me yesterday, says some autopsy tools had gone missing. Turns out Ed Brown was fired on Thursday."

"Same day Cassandra was killed."

"Exactly. I reckon the guy's using these tools on the victims. So we put him under surveillance, and now this. He's a slippery bastard. I don't know how he knew we were on to him, but he figured it out pretty quick."

The traffic wouldn't move out of their way fast enough.

Makedde, hang on.

55

Makedde was clearly anxious. That was good. Her guard would be down as she tried to hurry to that nonexistent pantyhose casting, with thirty thousand dollars at stake. He could see her flushed complexion and quickening breath. Her breasts heaved in and out, causing the buttonholes on her cardigan to stretch slightly open and shut. Her dress fell to mid-thigh, and she was swaying just a bit on her high, black stilettos. Her unconscious movement strained the thin heel when she rocked back, tensing her knees.

She doesn't recognise me. No one ever does.

He knew he didn't have much time left to get out of the city. The police, stupid though they were, would be on his tail. He wasn't going to go down without his special prize.

"No really," she told him, "I'll be all right."

Perhaps she was better prepared than he thought. Obviously the money wasn't enough. She would take more convincing. She was probably more jaded than the others, and smarter.

He smiled at her, gentle and friendly. "Really, it would be no trouble." He tried the clincher. "My wife had a Charade before we married. Exactly the same model, a '93. Always gave her trouble, too."

The corners of her mouth turned up slightly, and she looked again at the rental. "Do you know how to fix them?" she finally asked.

Ed stepped out of his van smiling and carefully slid the hammer down the back of his pants. "Oh, yes. I'm a mechanic actually," he lied.

"Really?" She seemed relieved. "What's your name, anyway?"

"Ed," he told her. "Ed Brown."

"Nice to meet you. I'm Makedde. I'm afraid I'm in a bit of a rush."

He came right up next to her. She was tall beside him, with those shoes. The shoes she wore for him. "Are you sure you wouldn't rather just get a ride? It'd be quicker."

She ignored his suggestion. "Can you see what's wrong? I know it's a bit dark."

He looked up and down the street. It was empty.

He leant into the engine bay, tugged at an HT lead, lifted the dipstick. "Oh, there it is. See this?" he beckoned.

She leant forward over the engine.

The hammer moved swiftly and Makedde fell forward.

With strength and practised dexterity he propped her up and carried her to the van. He crawled in with her and slid the door closed behind him, and in a matter of seconds had ripped off her cardigan and shackled her wrists.

No time.

He could hear a siren wailing in the distance. He had no time to secure the gag, but what did it matter? She was out cold, and where they were going, no one would hear her. He took one last moment to enjoy the sight of her, helpless in that skimpy black dress.

My prize.

56

Andy had been calling Makedde every five minutes from his mobile since they had left the station; but she wasn't answering. He hoped that Ed would be too wrapped up in trying to save his own skin to abduct her. Maybe she was working. Out for a run.

The churning in his guts told him otherwise.

A tanned, long-haired surfer stood and gawked as the squad car came to a skidding halt in front of the Bronte building. Andy leapt out of the passenger seat and ran to the front door, with Jimmy not far behind. He thought he heard the faint sound of sirens wailing in the distance; backup on its way.

He hammered on the door. "Makedde!"

No answer.

"I'll go round the back." Andy ran across the lawn and up the porch steps two by two. He looked for her through the window. "No sign of anyone. Let's do the back door," he called out.

Jimmy appeared in seconds. They counted to three and kicked the door in together.

There was no one in the main room . . . the kitchen . . . the bathroom. In the bedroom tracksuit pants and a sweatshirt had been flung into one corner. A couple of drawers were open, and a makeup case was spread out on the bedside chest of drawers. She must have been in a hurry. They hadn't missed her by much.

Sirens cut out on the street outside. Jimmy let the officers in the front door and briefed them on what was happening, while Andy searched frantically for a clue as to where Makedde had gone.

"There's a team ready to go in to Ed Brown's flat," Jimmy said. "We're working on dispatching a search helicopter to spot the VW. What next?"

Andy could sense the abrupt change in attitude. He was one of them again. They believed him.

57

Screams. Hellish screams stretched out into space and snapped like an elastic band pulled too far. They sounded distant, removed; but through the nausea and confusion, Makedde knew it was her own mind creating the terrifying sound. Unconsciousness floated towards her, an endless void beckoning her away from the pain, and she had to struggle with all her will to break free from its temptation. She was on her back, wrists shackled together and secured to something. Hard steel jarred against her back as she was flung up and down. Sluggishly, she tried to take in her surroundings, but there was noise and movement, and not enough light.

Her left ear felt sticky where it was rubbing against her upper arm. Her arms were stretched so far above her head that her shoulders cried out with pain at every bump. She couldn't move or relax them. The thumps and swerves pulled her back and forth. Through one squinting eye she saw that she was lying on the floor of an old van.

She remembered the red-haired man.

He was going to help her with her car.

Tilting her head back, she tried to make out what was holding her wrists—it appeared to be heavy metal cuffs, chained to the wall.

The van swerved.

Makedde's legs swung back and forth, her stilettos rolling loose along the floor. She was aware of an odd smell, not unlike disinfectant, that drifted up from the blanket she was lying on, the walls, from everywhere. It filled her nostrils and entered her lungs, forcing out a sneeze. And there was something else . . . tea-tree oil? Distantly familiar.

The face of her mother Jane flashed into Makedde's mind. Smiling as she gently rubbed tea-tree oil into Makedde's tiny wrist, soothing the little scrape she'd earned falling off her skates.

Another flash . . . Catherine. Dead. Wrapped in a shroud of cloth. That smell, tea-tree oil, and the underlying odour . . . decaying flesh.

Makedde could smell death in the van where she lay.

Through half open eyes she could see the back of the driver's head through a part in the curtains. She had met him in her nightmares these past two weeks. He killed young women just like Makedde, and now he was going to kill her.

58

Just over an hour after the phone call, Andy Flynn stood outside the decrepit, three-storey block of flats in Redfern that Ed Brown had shared with his disabled mother all his adult life. Dead weeds and grass poked out between the bricks. Electrician's tape held together a few window panes. The entire structure seemed to lean slightly to one side; the side that held flat number eighteen.

An APB was out. Every patrol cop, every hospital, every point of departure alerted. A search helicopter had just been scrambled. Ed Brown was on the run. They had finally put a face to the Stiletto Killer.

But Andy knew it wasn't enough.

If he had been on the case, would it have come to this? If he had continued to keep his eye on Makedde, would this have happened? Would he be standing outside the killer's flat hours too late?

Makedde's flat had turned up nothing. Book Model Agency confirmed that she was not on any known assignment or audition since she had finished a shoot for *ELLE* magazine earlier that day. She couldn't be considered missing for another twenty-three hours, but no one knew where she was.

"The place is already crawling with D's," Jimmy said, interrupting Andy's train of thought. Andy recognised a few of the detectives milling about; Hunt, Reed and Sampson had just arrived. They still looked like a bunch of rookies.

Jimmy stuck close to Andy as they entered the building and climbed the stairs to the third floor. Ed's mother was a paraplegic. There was no lift. They immediately spotted Mrs. Brown in the busy third-floor hallway. She was sandwiched into an old, standard-size wheelchair, huge rolls of flesh spilling out in all directions. She waved her white, flabby arms about and yelled at an unfortunate young officer who was attempting unsuccessfully to calm her down. She looked unusually haggard for someone Andy had been told was under fifty. She had painted herself in heavy make-up that settled roughly in the creases of her worn face. Andy took in the garish red lips and fingernails, and the revealing top that barely held heavy, stretch-marked breasts. A blanket partially covered the fleshy stumps of amputated legs. She wasn't wearing pants.

Mrs Brown didn't appear embarrassed at her state of semi-dress, nor did she seem particularly saddened or frightened at the chain of events; just angry. In an irritatingly high-pitched voice she cursed loudly, making outrageous threats. A pot-bellied man with a sparsely furnished head of white hair and a nose like a rotting tomato gripped her shoulder protectively. He was the building's superintendent; a married man by the name of George Fowler who was in his late sixties. Flynn guessed that George may have taken his building duties to a new level with Mrs. Brown, and he wondered what hold such an overbearing and unattractive woman would have over a married man. Viagra gone wrong, perhaps.

Andy and his partner left them to make their way to the doorway of flat eighteen and Ed's mother began yelling again. "He didn't do nothin'!"

A crime-scene officer wearing latex gloves and carrying camera equipment ducked under the chequered police tape. Andy and Jimmy followed. Flat eighteen was a foul-smelling two bedroom suite with a small bathroom and split kitchen/living room. The pungent odour of smoke and hops oozed from the walls and furniture. Andy counted five full ashtrays in the one room alone. The place was a mess. Stacks of dusty newspapers and magazines sat on every surface in the living room. There were scattered bottles and even an open lipstick which had left a red stain across the carpet. A tower of secondhand books rose up to meet Andy's eye; dog-eared romance novels and pulp fiction. Two threadbare couches looked to be rotting.

In an instant Andy could picture Ed's life—years of bringing home the groceries for mum; frozen dinners, beer and prescriptions. Bathing her, changing her, turning her over in bed. The only privacy in his room with the door closed.

Sitting with abject disinterest, a black cat watched them pass. Its intense yellow eyes shone in the dim room. Jimmy noticed the cat and gestured mockingly towards it. "Hello little Lucifer . . ." The cat hissed at him and narrowly missed him with a vicious swipe.

Andy noticed three large tubs overflowing with empty beer and liquor bottles. VB appeared to be a favourite, with any form of vodka a close second. He wondered if Cassandra's house could possibly have smelled as bad after his drunken days there. "Good to know they recycle," he muttered as they passed.

"Skata! She looks familiar," Jimmy said, pointing to a large picture frame. It held an old black-and-white photograph of a young woman, and even with the heavy make-up and outdated hairstyle, the resemblance was unmistakable.

Makedde.

Mrs. Brown had once been beautiful—blonde hair, light eyes, perfect nose. Any vague doubts that Ed hadn't abducted Makedde instantly vanished. Andy could see it all. Dahmer had a thing about his dad.

Ed Brown had a thing about his mother.

The floor of Ed's bedroom was raised six inches. Had Ed chosen the room for that reason? It was obvious that his mother would not have been able to enter her son's room without assistance. In stark contrast to the rest of the flat, Ed's room was obsessively clean and neat. There was a desk with a lamp, an empty wastepaper basket, a single bed and a set of shelves on one wall. There were no rumpled clothes, no loose papers, nothing out of place. You could bounce a coin on the bed.

The smell of smoke was barely noticeable. Instead, the room reeked of strange odours that irritated Andy's nose. The crime-scene photographer set up his equipment and began taking photos under the bed. The covers were pulled back and a series of bright flashes illuminated the neatly spaced collection of shoes.

Nine single high-heeled shoes. Stilettos.

Nine.

Andy recognised a couple of them—the red, scaly, fake snakeskin shoe that matched Roxanne Sherman's; the shiny black one with the thin ankle strap that had belonged to Catherine Gerber.

"Anyone find the missing tools?" he asked the officer outside the door.

"Not yet. Still searching. There's so much shit everywhere—"

"He'd keep them clean," Andy said. "Look for a sterile area, or a sealed bag or a box somewhere. We'll cover the room."

The officer nodded and spoke to someone down the hall. Andy doubted they would find the autopsy tools. This was not Ed's working area, this was where he reminisced, where he fantasised. He'd have the tools with him.

The photographer's flash turned to the set of thin wooden shelves, held up by Y-shaped braces on the wall to the left of the bed. A few books and trinkets were arranged on it, along with a nondescript shoe box inside a clear, plastic evidence bag.

"Open the box," Jimmy said.

Hoosier obliged, trying to act important. He reached up for it while the photographer waited with his lens poised. When he lifted the lid he immediately turned his head away, screwing up his nose.

With his hand over his mouth and nose, Andy stepped forward and examined the contents.

"Jesus."

Severed toes.

Immaculately pedicured with bright red polish. Big toes. Little toes. Different sizes and shapes. Varying states of decomposition. Andy counted at least ten. And some strange, shrivelled bits of leather. No—*nipples*, two sets.

He handed the box to the photographer who snapped it from different angles. What Detective Flynn focused on next disturbed him even more. Directly across from the foot of the bed an enlarged photographic print was tacked to the otherwise bare wall. He recognised its subject immediately. It was Makedde, stunning in a short leather skirt and high heel shoes, posing for the camera.

59

Makedde's head was throbbing, her thoughts murky. She had no sense of time. Had they been driving for half an hour? Two hours? She struggled to stay awake as her body rolled on the van floor. After a blessedly smooth patch, the road became uneven again, gravel spinning under the tires. The van flew over bumps, her raw wrists protesting in pain as they tore and jerked inside the cuffs.

She spoke. "I-I don't know you. I can say that I haven't seen your—" She swallowed her words as they flew over a nasty bump, smashing the back of her head on the hard floor. She started again, trying to sound calm, to rationalise. Her throat gurgled as she spoke. "I haven't seen your face. You could walk away. I could pay you money. I have a bankcard . . ."

He wasn't listening. He didn't even acknowledge the sound of her voice.

She tried again, louder this time. "I'll give you my bankcard and the PIN number. I'll get the money for you myself if you like. You could let me go. I won't tell anyone. You could . . ." She tried to shuffle around a bit, to take the pressure off of her shoulder joints. *Do something. Anything!* What had they taught her? When one tactic doesn't work, try another. With effort, she swung her long legs up in the air above her, as if she were riding a bike upside down. Her head swam with the sudden movement. She found the door with the toes of one foot, and the wall with the toes of the other. She rocked back and smashed both feet into the door, screaming with all her might, "LET MEEEE OOOOUT!"

The door was solid and unmoving, but her captor turned his head. She had his attention.

"Shut up!" he hissed at her, his voice oddly high-pitched.

The van was still speeding across the gravel and the man jerked his head back around to face the road, but already they were skidding, the van shuddering. He wrestled the steering wheel hard to the right. A tree leapt out of the black night and crashed into the left side of the windshield, breaking it with a thunderous explosion of glass. The van lurched and Makedde's body hit the wall, a heavy toolbox sliding along the floor and slamming into her ribs. The man made a noise, a small cry, as the van turned over, the gravel now gone. Still handcuffed, Makedde was hurled against the wall again, harder, her body twisted. Then there was another, greater crash.

They'd hit water.

60

Underground sex magazines; *FETISH*, *Bound*, *S&M Hookers*. Amateur bondage pictorials. Violent portrayals of involuntary sexual acts. They were stacked in Ed Brown's closet, filed neatly in order of issue, dating back at least ten years. Ed's favourite magazine appeared to be *FETISH*, a periodical specialising in women's feet and kinky shoes. Andy searched behind the magazines. He found very little dust but he did find an unopened twenty pack of Polaroid 600 film. "Look for Polaroid photos," he announced. "Look for a Polaroid camera. Careful of prints."

Hunt and Hoosier nodded in unison.

A black sheet covered a series of odd shapes along the bottom of the closet. *What next?* Andy had the police photographer capture the arrangement on film before he slowly removed the blanket. Three jars. Big and cloudy with liquid. Containing something.

Andy's stomach churned. Each jar held an entire human foot, neatly severed just below the calf.

Christ.

The pale feet arched with lifeless elegance, toenails

again painted garish red, each in a state of perfect preservation suspended in formalin. Andy felt a familiar numbness spread through him, anaesthetising his nerves. He would be worthless to Makedde if he lost his objectivity. *No fear. No revulsion. Keep it clinical. Keep it professional.*

Flashes went off as the find was recorded.

"He gives them manicures," Andy began, "same polish, but only the feet and toes that he keeps. The ones he likes. A post mortem pedicure. Find the red polish. We want everything we can find." As an afterthought he added, "The polish is his mum's."

"We don't know he's got her," Jimmy offered, watching his partner's face closely. "He might have just fled."

"He doesn't have her? You've got to be fucking kidding me!"

"Skata! I'm sorry, mate. That's just the facts. What he will do, he will do. You are only guessing. We can't *know*." Jimmy's black hair was a mess and his olive skin looked pale. "Can I talk to you a minute?" Jimmy asked in a whisper.

Andy nodded and followed Jimmy out of Ed's bedroom into the privacy of a small bathroom. It too was clean, and was the only space not crawling with officers toting evidence bags. Andy wanted someone to search it right away but Jimmy was in his ear, speaking in low tones. "This nutter's pretty damn obsessive. I figure he's obsessed with you. He killed your wife, framed you. He's gotta have some little shrine or something. When we find it, it could help to clear you."

Andy couldn't dwell on that yet. He needed to stop Ed from killing again.

"And," Jimmy went on, "if it comes down to it, and we don't find nothin' like that . . ." He pulled a small ziplocked bag out of his pocket and gestured to it. It held a familiar gold wedding band.

Andy's eyes widened.

Hearing footsteps, Jimmy quickly pocketed the bag. Inspector Kelley walked past them and stopped.

"Inspector—" Andy had broken into a sweat.

"Flynn, I was told you were here. I took you off this case a week ago, and your wife's untimely death should be all the more reason for you to remain so." He paused. "Do you have a gun?"

"Uh, yes sir." The question surprised him. "Jimmy's .38 Smith and Wesson."

"I brought you your Glock." Kelley handed him his Model 17.

"Thank you, sir," he said, trying not to sound astounded.

"Don't assume anything. I'll talk to you about it later."

"Yes sir."

Inspector Kelley's eyes were steady. "Watch your back," he warned. "This nut case could have a thing for you. I don't think it's wise for you to hang about. We'll keep you informed."

With that, Kelley disappeared into Ed's bedroom. The Inspector was covering his arse, but he wasn't kicking him out. Andy knew he had to tread carefully.

In the putrid-smelling hall there was chatter. More officers had arrived. He overheard someone say, "Do you believe in numerology? You know what eighteen is? 6-6-6."

Then, a louder voice shouted from Ed's bedroom. "Hey, I got something!" The call came from Hunt, who was half-jammed in Ed's closet, searching the magazine collection.

Andy ran to the bedroom trying unsuccessfully to maintain a calm exterior. *Where has he taken Makedde?* Then suddenly Kelley was on him, barring his way.

"What?!" Andy exclaimed.

"You shouldn't be here, Andy." Inspector Kelley firmly gripped Andy's shoulders. Past Kelley's tall frame, Andy caught Hunt's eye for a moment. The constable was staring blankly, his face bloodless. Quickly, he broke from Andy's gaze and turned away, instinctively raising a hand to his mouth to contain his vomit.

The Redfern block of flats was lit up like a dance party with bright flashes in the night air. Photographers and television crews swarmed outside, trying desperately to get past the barricade to seize an exclusive story. A news helicopter circled overhead. Andy watched the mayhem from his car further down the street. Inspector Kelley had sent someone to fetch the Honda; another way of telling Andy to go home.

Over one hundred Polaroid photos had been slipped between the pages of Ed's *FETISH* magazine collection. Breasts. Torsos. Feet. Body parts. All in various stages of life and death. Various stages of torture. The vivid colour photos were worse than any crime-scene pictures he'd seen. They captured the final struggles of faceless bodies, twisted and tensed in the throes of live autopsies.

There was already enough evidence to put Ed Brown away forever. But this was little consolation to Andy Flynn. He sat very still in his car while a hamburger cooled on the dashboard. He had no appetite. No one who had seen those Polaroids could be eating right now. He was neither hungry nor tired, although he hadn't eaten or slept properly for a week. He'd watched Makedde for days, protecting her, and then, like a fool, he looked away.

There was something that was missing, something that would point the way. He had to think. The magazines, the photos, the shoes, the body parts; none of them were well hidden. Ed's mother would not have been able to find them, but he must have been confident that no one else was going to come looking.

61

Water crept up Makedde's thighs. She had blacked out again, and the freezing water's progress woke her. She was still inside the van. Her whole body ached. Bones were broken, she could tell. Ribs were cracked. Her collarbone? An elbow too? Her arms were practically useless, particularly on her left side. No longer forced above her, they rested weakly on her chest, elbows bent. The shackles still held her wrists together, but the chains had been yanked from the wall with the force of the crash.

No more rumbling vibrations. No more movement. Only the calming rush of water around her. The van was on a forty-five degree angle, partially submerged, and her body was bunched up against the back of the driver's seat. They should have sunk by now. Perhaps the water was shallow. It didn't smell salty. A lake? A river?

She twisted her neck upwards and looked into the cab. Empty. He was gone. The doors were closed, the driver's side window rolled down. Was it unrolled before we crashed? No, it wasn't. He must have crawled out. There were red streaks across the handle and the dashboard.

Windshield shattered. Glass everywhere. He must be injured. He had crawled away and left her.

On her back, Makedde slid herself up the floor of the van, straightening her legs. The water only came up to her knees, and it didn't seem to be rising any further. With stinging eyes she looked around and saw the mechanic's toolbox that had hit her in the crash. Everything looked different, drawers had come open, sections had come loose from the wall. The drawers in the van were full of kitchen utensils, knives and forks for camping out. No. Not kitchen knives, these were longer, thinner blades. Not forks. Different tools, gleaming and clinical.

She slid herself over to one of the drawers, her head still swimming. The drawer was clean and smelled of disinfectant. The implements it held were spotless. Scalpels. Long, thin knives. Things that looked like delicate pliers. Gadgets she knew no name for.

In a flash it came to her. *Ed Brown, the morgue attendant.* She knew him now.

He saved a lock of Catherine's hair for me.

Makedde had to arm herself. What if he came back? Wrists still bound together, she rifled through the instruments and chose a sharp, long-bladed knife. She held it in both hands. She had never cut someone before, had never sunk steel into living flesh. She knew she could do it if she had to. She would not hesitate if the man came back.

Holding the knife as tightly as she could, she slid down the van floor and leant against the back of the driver's seat. It was prickly with tiny pieces of glass, and the water around her was freezing cold. Her arms were of little assistance as she scrambled over the seatback and stuck her head through the window. She steadied herself by leaning her shoulder against the window frame. Her eyes had adjusted to the dark, and she could vaguely see a slow-moving river stretching away from the van. To her left, a muddy embankment sloped up to the road.

Count to three. One, two . . . three.

She used every bit of her fading strength to push herself through the open window. She struggled out, shackled arms outstretched, gripping her weapon, and slipped into the icy water. Her bare feet found the murky bottom and she tried to stand. Brilliant red and green stars exploded before her open eyes, her head spinning. Gradually the headrush passed, leaving a hazy residue of dizziness in its place. She held the knife in front of her pelvis and waded cautiously through the waist-deep water towards the river bank.

No sounds; just the gentle rushing of water and the wind through the branches. Twigs in the thick mud.

Snap.

Movement. There was movement in the shadows.

Makedde stopped and held her breath. Drops of water falling. Wait . . . crunching on gravel. Shadows moving. She tried to steady herself, but her head wasn't right. She held the knife out in front, tried to be ready. She knew she couldn't run, not like this. She would have to fight. She cleared her throat and tried to speak. Her voice was harsh.

"Who's there?"

No answer. More crunching. A figure forming out of the shadows. Something in its hand. Something swinging towards her fast. A hammer. *Quickly! Get out of the way!*

Sluggishly she stepped backwards but still caught a hard blow to the jaw. The muddy ground swiftly rose to meet her, stars dancing in her head. Then, like a television being switched off, the stars around her flickered and disappeared.

62

"If he hasn't taken her there, we're fucked," Andy said as they sped along.

"You might just be right," Jimmy replied. "He seemed to know too much. It has a kind of psycho logic to it. A revenge thing. You never even told me you and Cassandra had the place."

"It was Cassandra's originally, but I was going to get it," Andy explained. "It was an investment, but she never resold it. I was supposed to move in months ago."

"Let's just hope that he's the one that's decided to move in," Jimmy said.

"Think about it. He's killed at least nine women, only five of which we knew about. Where are the other four? He disposed of them well. But not these last ones. Why? He wants to get caught, that's why. Either that or he thinks he's invincible."

"Skata! If all these fuckin' psychos want to get caught, why don't they just waltz into the police station and have it over with?" Jimmy shook his head. "Nah, I'm not sold. He's just gettin' sloppy. All those sick malakas get sloppy eventually."

63

NAKED.
   I'm naked!
   Makedde woke to find herself inside a bedroom in a lot of pain. She couldn't move. She couldn't cover herself. For a moment she wondered, *prayed*, that it was a nightmare. She'd had dreams as a child where she was walking through the halls of her high school, or walking through the busy city streets and would suddenly realise that she was exposed.
   Icy air passed over her damp skin. She was freezing, covered in goose bumps. A door was open, or a window. She was spread-eagled, secured to the bed by her wrists and ankles. Some kind of gauze was looped around her head. A floor lamp was switched on, spreading a feeble light through the room. Although she couldn't move her head, she strained her eyes and looked around her as best she could. She was alone. There were dusty shelves decorated with vases of dried flowers and framed photographs. From her position on the bed, she could see the image in one of the closer photographs; a man in a tuxedo and his bride in a beautiful white dress.

There was no mistaking the smiling faces of Andy and Cassandra Flynn. This was the place he had told her about.

She struggled to free herself but the more she moved, the harder the twine around her wrists and ankles bit in. When she tried to move her jaw, a searing white pain shot into her temples and her ears.

Sounds came from nearby. Footsteps. Creaking wood. Metal. The red-haired man had returned. He came through the bedroom door, a garish vision in a surgeon's gown and mask and latex gloves. He carried what looked like a mechanic's toolbox.

He dragged a wooden table across the room and placed it beside the bed, then with a small hand brush cleaned the top. He placed a plastic sheet over the table, setting the toolbox on top of it. Makedde struggled to speak and found that she was unable to form words. Weak groans escaped her throat. The man ignored the sounds, ignored her, intent on his preparations.

He pulled the floor lamp over to the bed. The light was bright this close, and it took her eyes a while to focus. Now she was face to face with this monster, she had to know. Why Catherine? She struggled to work her mouth around the sounds but her jaw was stiff and swollen.

Suddenly, strangely, the man laughed at her. It was a hideous sound. The cackle stopped as quickly as it had started. "No talking from the whore," he said without looking at her. He turned away and continued with his preparations. She strained her wide eyes to follow his movements. He was checking the twine that secured her to the bed and it occurred to Makedde that he was going through some sort of checklist, one by one.

When he finished he turned his face to her and for the first time looked her straight in the eyes. He spoke directly and calmly. "I have to take my time with you. You are special." He said it proudly, as if she might be flattered by the sentiment. "Have you ever witnessed an autopsy, Makedde?" he went on in his odd altar-boy voice. "I know you've seen my work elsewhere. What would you like done first? I promise I will save the fatal incisions for last. I only regret that your head wounds have dulled your senses so."

She had to try and speak. Speech was her only weapon now that she was physically helpless. *He doesn't care about your pain*, she thought, *he enjoys it*. Say something that surprises him. Don't let him see your fear. She took a deep breath, forced her lower jaw down and an indecipherable noise escaped her throat. Ed cocked his head to one side, clearly amused by her efforts.

"What did they do to you?" she asked in a weak, grating whisper. His expression changed slightly. "How did they force you to do this?" she slurred.

Something flickered in his eyes. Recognition? She imagined that they changed, became those of a child. A young boy, looking at Makedde with wide, curious eyes. Remorse? No. He turned away and grabbed something. Will he cut me loose? When she saw his eyes again, the look she thought she'd seen was gone; replaced with the cold, steady glare of the man who had brought her here to kill her.

He was holding what looked like a rubber ball with straps dangling from it. His latex-gloved hands forced her jaw open and he shoved the ball in her mouth. He fitted the straps over the gauze on her head and secured it.

"No more talking," he said as he chose another item from his toolbox.

64

As the two detectives neared the Lane Cove house, they turned the siren off. They didn't want to scare Ed Brown into a dangerous reaction or a quick getaway. *If* he was there. *If*. Andy prayed that he was right. Suddenly, an image jumped out of the thick, black night like a neon sign.

"Did you see that?" Andy said, hitting the brakes.

They skidded to a halt and Andy threw the car into reverse. He'd seen something near the trees.

The blue VW van was partly submerged on the edge of the river.

"Jesus, look at that," Jimmy said, throwing open the car door.

Andy jumped out and ran down the bank, the headlights illuminating the van like a pale ghost. He drew his gun. The van was half-submerged, the back end rising out of the water. He held his Glock high in front of him, waded over to the driver's side door and cautiously looked inside. The cab was empty, the windshield broken. He examined the driver's seat quickly—there appeared to be blood

308

streaked across the open window frame, and also across the steering wheel.

"Phone for backup!" he yelled out to Jimmy. "I need a flashlight over here. It's hard to see into the back, but I think it's empty. There's blood. The bastard may be hurt. They can't be far!"

The door was jammed. Andy squeezed through the window and slid onto the front seat. Gun poised and ready, he squinted and checked the back of the vehicle. There was no time. He struggled out the window and pushed through the water to the river's edge. Jimmy was hurrying towards him with a flashlight. Andy snatched it from him and shone it across the gravel.

There were clearly visible drag marks.

65

Ed Brown was leaning over her, his breath putrid and hot against her neck. Makedde tried to spit at him, but the rubber gag caused the spittle to drip from the corners of her mouth, down her chin. She pulled at her restraints, but only felt the twine bite unforgivingly into her flesh. She could see the man's face clearly so close to hers. The lamp light played across a deep gash on his forehead. The split was long, still oozing blood, but his eyes were alert, alive, dancing in sadistic satisfaction.

"You're drooling, Makedde." Her name sounded loathsome on his lips. He was holding something in his latex-gloved hand . . . bringing it to her throat. It was a surgical sponge, dripping with disinfectant. He was cleaning her down, removing the river's soil and smell. His hands slipped over her naked body, over the goose bumps, pausing on her raised nipples. The cloth moved over her breasts, her navel, down her stomach. She tried to close her legs, but her ankles were held too far apart.

She tried to pretend she was somewhere else.

I'm walking on the beach, walking free, not here. Not with that stinging cloth pushed between my legs. Please . . .

Ed turned from her. He was reaching for something, pulling something from his toolbox with both hands. She strained her head, saw a sharp tip. He moved down her body, towards her bound ankles, caressed her bare feet with his fingertips, and slid something around her foot. Her shoes! He had fetched her stilettos from the van and was now placing them on her feet.

"Mother . . ." he sighed.

She felt so groggy. Her breath was shallow and laboured and she was trembling. He was walking back to the toolbox, arranging implements, laying them on the plastic sheet, then wiping them clean. Makedde made out what looked like a scalpel, a knife with a long sharp blade, pliers . . .

She forced her legs back and forth violently. *Break the twine!* It bit angrily into her. The pain was overwhelming, but she had to keep on. The bed posts protested with loud creaks and strains.

Ed stood over her, lips twitching. His slim, gloved hands held the disinfected scalpel elegantly and her eyes followed the progress of the sharp tip towards her naked body, towards her naked breast, her cold raised nipple.

66

There were few houses in the area. No neighbours close by. That's why Cassandra had liked it. The privacy.

The drag marks led to the house. They had to be there.

Andy sprinted up the gravel road, vaguely aware of Jimmy's presence a few feet behind him. His wet pant legs pulled against his knees, trying to slow him down, but he ran with all his might. Nearing the house now, just beyond those trees. A light—a dim light—the bedroom window. Andy raced across the grass, a flitting shadow. He ran for the front door, gun extended.

67

The scalpel blade pressed on her breast, ready to pierce. She wanted to scream. She wanted to fight back. She prayed it would end soon.

His eyes were so close to hers and yet they were so distant, part of another world she could not comprehend.

"Are you ready, Mother?"

Mother?

Those words, so terrible, spitting from those mean lips. *Are you ready . . . Mother?* Her father about to push her down the slide, those gentle hands holding her. *Are you ready?* Her mother, unveiling her sculpture, a clay figure.

She would die now . . . *she was ready to die.* Wait. She pulled herself back. That was it! She would pretend. It could stall him. Anything. Try anything.

She rolled her eyes back in her head and shook violently on the bed, convulsing and groaning. The scalpel pricked her as she moved, tearing her skin, but then moved away. She choked on the gag, as convincingly as she could manage. The movement hurt, her ribs screaming out, everything immersed in pain, but the scalpel had pulled away.

He was speaking to her now. What was he saying?

"You forget my expertise. You're not dying until I say so. Mother's going to be cured right. No fooling."

She tried to speak, to demand he release her, but the sounds coming from her throat were inhuman, her jaw too swollen.

"I told you there was to be no talking. And yet you refuse to desist." He shook his head slowly, then smiled and bent over her, placing his hands around her skull. She felt the straps around her head tighten painfully for an instant and then release. He pulled the rubber ball from her broken jaw, strings of blood and saliva hanging from her mouth. She tried to speak. He cocked his head to listen. He was playing with her now, teasing her.

He answered her chokes and moans. "No, I won't let you go. No. But you have such beautiful toes. Lovely toes. Would you like to taste them? Suck them for me?"

She nodded, gurgling a bit as she tried to speak. She looked down to the twine biting through her ankles.

"Remove the twine? No, no. I don't think you're that flexible. No, I'll bring the toes to you. Shove them in your mouth. You can bite down on those pretty polished toenails."

The scalpel moved down her naked skin, down her legs, down to her right foot. He muttered something, "The right foot, because it's *right* . . ." He slipped the shoe off and dropped it on the wooden floor.

Makedde closed her eyes, felt the scalpel sink in, the pain hot and unbearable as it sliced through. She screamed, the sound blending with everything. Noises everywhere, sounds filling her ears, colour danced before her eyes, red, green, swirling, such pain, she was falling away . . .

A loud blast. He'd shot her, he'd stopped cutting and he'd shot her. She opened her eyes, tears flowing down her face, everything blurry. Something wasn't right, she was still alive. Another blast. Wait—something on her—heavy. Someone . . . him. The man. He was on top of her. Red in the air, floating—now falling. *Blood?* Blood everywhere.

His face was close to hers, tongue protruding, those shocked eyes staring at her. His jerking body crushed against her . . . a heavy sack of twitching blood and flesh lying across her.

Words . . . words in her ears. "It's all over now, Makedde." Her name sweet again, no venom in the sound. "You'll be fine. I'm here, Makedde, I'm here. Quiet. It's all right. Don't try to speak. You're safe now."

Andy. The voice was *Andy*.

A weight being lifted off her, that convulsing mass taken away. The staring eyes no longer watching. She felt light. Her ankles suddenly free, the twine cut away. Her wrists now.

Softly—softly, something falling on her, cloth, a blanket covering her. She turned on her side and swept the cloth into her, tears filling her eyes, sobbing with joy and relief, pulling her arms and legs into her, holding herself, holding her pain.

Curled up in a tight ball, they carried her to the ambulance.

68

Andy Flynn strode down the corridor, his partner at his heels.

"After all that, she still won't believe her son did it," Jimmy said, shaking his head.

Andy didn't respond. It was taking shape now. Serial killers were never made overnight. He had to figure out the Stiletto Killer. He thought about Ed's polite and unobtrusive presence at the morgue.

"Hello . . . Earth to Flynn, do you read?"

"Yes, Jimmy. I hear you. That woman's a lost cause. She'll never come around. Eileen Brown was a prostitute, Jimmy. Different men every night, dolled up in stilettos and miniskirts with her young son looking on. Drugged out and angry, blaming her kid for being born. Little Ed snapped."

"To say the least . . ."

"The homicidal triad. You were right. The house was torched when Ed was ten. He did it, Jimmy. He tried to kill her when he was *ten*."

"Yeah. But he didn't kill her, he crippled her."

"Exactly. But he's been symbolically killing her ever since."

"So if all these malakas are really wanting to kill their parents, why don't they just do it?"

"You'd have to ask a psychologist about that one. Guilt? Displaced anger? Edmund Kemper killed his mum and practically gave himself up, but only after killing hoards of innocent women. And our Ed Brown took his time in the end, even though he knew we were onto him. Maybe in some way he was giving himself up, too." Andy was rambling again. "All he had was his mum. He waited on her hand and foot for decades after the fire. Her clients would have left after she lost her legs. Her son was the only one she had to take care of her. And I guess she was the only one Ed had, too."

"Ed Kemper, Ed Gein, Ed Brown. What is it about all these psychos named Ed?" Jimmy asked.

Andy laughed. If only offender identity were as simple as a common first name.

A doctor emerged from Makedde's room and walked up the hall in their direction. "How is she?" Andy asked.

"Improving. Getting a lot of sleep. She's healing well. We successfully drained the subdural haematoma—"

Jimmy stopped her. "Oi, English please."

She paused. "We drained her brain haemorrhage. If she had gone untreated for much longer, she would have had serious trouble. But she's a fighter. Strong as an ox. We can't say for sure, but at this stage we're optimistic there will be no residual effects on the brain."

Andy smiled. "What about her big toe?"

"The microsurgery appears to have been successful. Time will tell. She won't have much feeling in it, but she'll walk fine."

The doctor excused herself and they continued towards

317

room 312. Sitting in a chair outside her room, a young blonde in a short skirt was reading a magazine. When Jimmy noticed her, he nudged Andy's side. Andy ignored it.

Before they reached the door, Jimmy pulled him close and asked in a whisper, "Does she know about Ed?"

Andy shook his head. Makedde had not been told. She didn't need to know that Ed was temporarily in another wing of the same hospital. He was well guarded, and as soon as he was treated for a concussion and his shoulder and chest wounds, he would be transferred to Long Bay to await a committal hearing.

They approached a tall, grey-haired man who stood in the doorway. He was conservatively dressed, probably in his mid-fifties. Andy introduced himself. "Hello, I'm Detective Flynn and this is Detective Cassimatis. You are . . . ?"

"Leslie Vanderwall." The accent was Canadian. He offered a hand shake. Makedde's father had deep blue eyes like his daughter. His face was tired and worn, though still handsome. His clothes were wrinkled.

"Mr. Vanderwall, I'm so pleased you could make it down—"

"I should have flown in weeks ago and taken her home," he replied sharply.

"I'm so sorry. She's been through more than anyone should have to," Andy offered.

"When's the committal?"

"I'm afraid it could take some time to get the brief together. I'll see to it that her travel is taken care of when we need her to return for the hearing and the trial."

Mr. Vanderwall nodded. His voice softened. "I was glad to hear you'd been cleared over your wife's murder. My condolences." Andy nodded his head. "You saved my girl's life," Leslie went on. "I could never thank you enough."

Jimmy interrupted them. "She's waking."

Makedde stirred in her bed, her face swollen and multi-coloured, jaw wired shut. A large raised bruise covered her face on the left side. A section of her head was shaved.

The blonde woman was in the doorway now, looking in. "Hi. I'm Loulou," she said. She was wearing heavy make-up and looked a bit like Cyndi Lauper in her heyday. Andy thought there was something odd about her eyebrows. He and Jimmy introduced themselves.

Mr. Vanderwall had gone to his daughter's side, and the rest of them stayed near the doorway to give the father and daughter space. Mak blinked away her sleep and opened her puffy eyes, joy enveloping her face at the sight of her father. She nodded silent hellos at her three other visitors, suddenly awake and alert.

"You'll be fine, honey," her father reassured her. "You're healing well. You'll be back to normal in no time."

Andy wanted to make her laugh. "Oh, Miss Money Penny, you're a sight for sore eyes," he said.

Leslie Vanderwall looked up, puzzled, and through her wired jaw, Makedde began to laugh. It was wonderful. It was the sound of a survivor.

69

Brilliant white clouds stretched out, an endless Arctic landscape suspended in the air, soft pillows of mist cradling them as they flew steadily over the Pacific. Flying never bothered Makedde, but the white-knuckled grip on the armrest of her companion didn't go unnoticed.

"You all right, Dad?" she mumbled through an uncooperative jaw.

He turned, his face pale and startled. "You're awake."

"Yes. Wouldn't miss this view for the world."

"I knew you'd like the window seat," he said, attempting to sound composed.

"I knew *you* wouldn't like it. I still can't believe you flew all the way across the planet to get me."

He looked at her wearily. "I kind of liked it better when you couldn't talk."

Makedde still couldn't speak very well, but over the weeks she had gradually improved. She could go home for a while, but it wasn't over yet. There would be a committal hearing, and almost certainly a long trial to follow. There was indisputable evidence that Ed Brown was a killer, but as with so many victims, it could take the police months to assemble a case. She didn't know when she would have to go back.

Makedde had learnt the man who abducted and attacked her intended to try for the McNaghten defence, claiming diminished responsibility due to mental illness. There was already one forensic psychiatrist who believed that Ed Brown's psychosexual disorder was somehow interwoven with a homicidal impulse to kill women who wore stilettos. For Ed, any woman in stilettos was a whore, and all whores needed to be killed to be cured of their promiscuity.

In light of his unhealthy relationship with his mother, this defence had some value. The basis for legal insanity was delusion, and that type of delusion, if genuine, would qualify. However, Ed's sadism, precise methods and sexual interference with his victims suggested a very different side; someone purposely killing for sexual satisfaction, not seeking some delusional "cure" for perceived sins. He wasn't a textbook psychopath, but on the other hand, did he really qualify as insane? It remained to be seen how the jurors would view it.

Put him away, Makedde, put him out of your mind.

The flight home was comfortable, with ample leg room and plenty to read. The *Sydney Morning Herald* and the *Telegraph* both sat on her lap. Every day there had been an article about the Stiletto Murders, but it no longer made the front page. Mak was more interested in an article about the once powerful heir to the Tiney and Lea surgical supply empire who was now being divorced by his wife and sued for everything he was worth. Poor James Tiney Jr. He had been demoted too. It seemed that his father, who was a board member of the AMA and had been a top-notch surgeon at one stage, was ultra-conservative. He didn't take the news of his son's adultery well.

"Tiney Junior. No wonder he had a Napoleon complex."

"What?"

"Nothing, Dad."

An impeccably coifed stewardess moved through the first-class cabin offering treats.

"You've never flown first class, have you, Dad?"

"No," he replied, staring with determination at the sick bag in the seat pocket in front of him.

"See the things I do for us? If it wasn't for all this we'd be jammed up against those lavatories in the back, hearing a flush every thirty seconds. And maybe we wouldn't even be arriving home in time for the birth."

"Yes. Pushing you around in a wheelchair with that precious toe of yours and those fluttering eyelashes is an effective combination. Not to mention that thing around your neck."

"It's a collar and cuff, Dad." She had to wear it until her collarbone healed. It had been artfully decorated with a few choice messages from Andy, Loulou and even Charles, scrawled in felt pen. She remembered Andy's message, *Please keep in touch. Love, Andy.* We'll see, she thought to herself. We'll see.

"I'm going to be a grandfather," her father said.

She grinned. "And I'll be Auntie Mak."

She thought about her family. And Ed's. She had been shocked to see the old photo of Eileen Brown. Mak looked so much like Ed's mother when she was young. A copy of the photo of her and Cat had been found in Ed's wallet, too. Andy must have been relieved to know that Ed was obsessed with Makedde *before* Andy became involved with her. She sensed he still couldn't forgive himself for not finding her sooner though. And she couldn't forgive herself for not believing him. Regardless of his temper and his motive, when the search of Ed's bedroom turned up Cassandra Flynn's gold wedding ring, there could be no doubt of his innocence.

Andy cared about her, and she cared for him, but there were a lot of problems between them, and now there was distance, too.

No more fear. Never. Fear is worse than death itself.

"Nothing freaks me out now," she said. "Nothing. From now on, anyone messes with me, they're toast."

"Toast, eh?"

"Custard fried French toast. Besides, do I have psycho-magnet written on my forehead, or what? Between Stanley and Ed, I have four lifetimes of bad karma out of the way. I should be so lucky now that miracles spring from my fingertips—"

An unexpected jolt stopped her mid-sentence.

The plane dropped, free-falling for a second or two. Mak's stomach seemed to hit the ceiling and fall back down. Instantly she grabbed for her father's hand, holding it tight.

The plane quickly levelled out and a seatbelt sign flashed above their heads. The tension around them broke, chatter resuming nervously up and down the aisles. Father and daughter held hands tightly as the sound of seatbelts fastening clicked around them.

In that moment she knew the answer.

Makedde, no longer a psycho-magnet?

Don't bet on it. You're in for a bumpy ride.

EPILOGUE

"Makedde!"

That woman's name was called out again, a familiar sound reverberating through the corridors of Long Bay jail.

"Makeddeeee!"

Wilson shook his head with irritation and walked towards the sound, keys jangling on his belt. His polished, steel-toed boots echoed through the halls. The inmates on his wing couldn't mix with the other prisoners. He found that some of them got strange in their isolation, if they hadn't been crazy to begin with. He had a couple of psychotics, several paedophiles, and a couple of fellas who had been convicted of drug dealing but had squealed on the wrong people. Those types weren't safe in the general prison population. But this one, the one who took to chanting that girl's name at ungodly hours, was allegedly a serial killer awaiting trial.

Word was, the other prisoners wanted to be protected from *him*.

He was famous, but Wilson didn't read the papers, so he didn't much care. To him, Brown was just the chanting

324

pain in the arse with the stitches across his forehead, who kept smearing his own shit into his wounds to keep himself going back to the infirmary. He was definitely weird, but Wilson had seen his type before; once the trial was over, they usually stopped playing nutty.

"Makedde—Makedde—Makedde!"

"Go to sleep, Brown," Wilson said, and banged his riot stick on the cell door.

But he didn't stop. "Makedde—Makedde—Makedde!"

"Shut the fuck up!" Wilson banged his stick again, harder this time.

The chant continued, starting in a low but powerful voice, then building higher and higher until it morphed into a howling wail, the words running together. "Makedde—Makedde—Makedd—Maked—NAKED—Naked—Na—Ma—Mama—Mama—Mother . . . MOTHER!"

"Save it for the judge," Wilson scoffed, and the chanting abruptly stopped. With the peace of his area restored, he walked back to his station. He had a crossword to finish, and *Celebrity Home Shopping* was still on.

Ed Brown sat on the cot in his cell, as alert as a caged, nocturnal animal. This was but a temporary setback.

He had a plan.

Put your stilettos on, Makedde.

I'm coming for you.

THE PEGASUS SECRET

GREGG LOOMIS

What started as a suspicious explosion in a picturesque Parisian neighborhood could end in revelations that would shatter the beliefs of millions. American lawyer Lang Reilly is determined to find the real cause of the blast that killed his sister. But his investigation will lead him into the darkest corners of history and religion. And it may cost him his life.

Lang's search for the truth begins with a painting his sister bought just before she died. Could there be something about the painting itself that made someone want to kill her? Every mysterious step of the way, Lang unearths still more questions, more hidden secrets and more danger, until finally he arrives at the heart of a centuries-old secret order that will stop at nothing to protect what is theirs.
